Tripping Over Christmas

A Military Sweet Cowboy Romance in Big Sky County, Book 5

Jenna Hendricks

Contents

Books by Jenna Hendricks (Clean & Wholesome Romance)   VII

1. Prologue   1

2. Chapter 1   9

3. Chapter 2   15

4. Chapter 3   21

5. Chapter 4   33

6. Chapter 5   43

7. Chapter 6   53

8. Chapter 7   65

9. Chapter 8   77

10. Chapter 9   95

11. Chapter 10   105

12. Chapter 11   111

13. Chapter 12   125

14. Chapter 13   135

15. Chapter 14   155

16. Chapter 15   173

17. Chapter 16   187

18. Chapter 17   195

19. Chapter 18   211

20. Chapter 19   223

21. Chapter 20   235

22. Chapter 21   247

23. Chapter 22   257

24. Chapter 23   269

25. Chapter 24   277

26. Chapter 25   289

27. Chapter 26   299

28. Chapter 27   315

29. Chapter 28   327

30. Chapter 29   335

31. Chapter 30   345

32. Chapter 31   353

33. Chapter 32   367

34. Chapter 33 377

35. Chapter 34 387

Character Sheet 393

Author Notes 397

Yule Log Recipe 399

Contact Me 403

Newsletter Sign-up 405

Books by Jenna Hendricks (Clean & Wholesome Romance)

<u>Triple J Ranch</u> –

Book 0 - Finding Love in Montana (Join my newsletter to get this book for free)

Book 1 - Second Chance Ranch

Book 2 – Cowboy Ranch

Book 3 – Runaway Cowgirl Bride

Book 4 – Faith of a Cowboy

Book 5 – Cowboy Blessings

Book 6 – The Cowboy's Game

<u>Big Sky Christmas</u> –

Book 1 – Her Montana Christmas Cowboy

Book 2 – Her Christmas Rodeo Cowboy

Book 3 – Her Mistletoe Cowboy

Book 4 – Her Sleigh Ride Christmas Cowboy
<u>Crooked Arrow Ranch</u> –
Book 0 - Wounded Hearts Ranch (join my newsletter to get this free)
Book 1 – A Broken Heart Mended
Book 2 – Hope's Healing Love
Book 3 - Love's Healing Balm
Book 4 – A Crooked Arrow Christmas
Book 5 – Tripping Over Christmas
<u>Standalone Novels</u> –

Christmas Crazy in July

Rebel Hearts Anthology
See these titles and more: https://JennaHendricks.com

Prologue

Marty Winters looked outside and could do nothing but watch as the trees danced while the wind howled its displeasure. Only the day before the trees looked so inviting with their snowcapped branches. The news reporter said this storm was supposed to be monstrous, but he didn't realize it was going to cause so much damage in the middle of nowhere.

He should have.

Branches that had once been peaceful with snow clinging to them now lay strown about the white landscape providing a stark contrast now that the snow had been wrenched free of them.

The sound of a tree cracking caused him to tighten up and wince. Watching the scene play out, his mind took him back to the sandstorms in the pit. When he had joined the Air Force, he had no idea that he'd end up in the hottest and most desolate place on Earth. And be out there for days, sometimes weeks, at a time. So when he was given the chance to head out to a ranch in Montana that promised snow, he jumped at the chance.

Well, not literally, but close enough. The injury to his leg still hurt at times so he generally took it easy. But when Mother Nature tore the tree out and threw it on the roof of the barn, Marty didn't even think, he just ran.

As he ran to the barn, he prayed that those inside would be alright. He'd seen enough death and destruction to last five lifetimes. This was supposed to be a safe place, a place to rest and recover.

When he passed the other newbie, he almost grinned. Since arriving he'd noticed that she never let go of her cane. But now? Now, she was running as best she could without it. Good for her, he thought.

With his injury, he'd needed to use a walker, then a cane, while he was adjusting to his new way of walking. Now, he was good to go. Running wasn't something he enjoyed doing anymore since the pounding put too much pressure on his bad leg, but his pain was nothing compared to what he expected to see inside of the barn.

He yanked the door to the side the moment he reached the barn. "Anyone hurt?" Marty looked around and saw a tiny herd of cows all looking as though they were bulls in Pamplona and about to chase anyone around, red cape, or not. Thankfully, none of them had horns. He moved to the side and didn't notice that Marnie Gallagher had entered and headed straight toward trouble.

He'd always had a good sense of danger, and when his senses pricked, he listened. So the moment the hair on the back of his neck stood on end, he moved. Without even thinking about it, he stepped right in the path of a one-ton pressure cooker.

Marty may not have been one of those Regency period gentlemen who would do anything to protect a lady, but his dad had drilled into him from a young age to always protect women. Not because they were the fairer sex, but because women were the ones who held the future of humanity in their bodies. No matter how many surgeries a man had, he couldn't get pregnant and give birth to babies. Only women could do that. And for that miracle alone, they deserved to be protected and cherished.

When the hit came, he was prepared for it. He tightened his body and wrapped his arms around the woman in front of him. Thankfully, he'd been able to throw her, and him, to the side and they landed in a pile of hay.

"Oomph." Pain instantly shot down his leg and up through his back and chest. Marty wasn't sure, but thought he heard a cracking sound coming either from him, or below him. He prayed he didn't hurt Marnie, the girl he threw to the ground. The woman who cushioned his own fall.

The ringing in his ears was so loud, he didn't think he'd ever hear again. Then, a soft sound made its way through before a louder, gruffer voice hit his ears.

"Marty? Marty!" The woman screamed his name so loud, his entire body felt as though it had gone through the wringer and come out broken.

When soft hands felt along his back, he winced. "Ow, that hurts." Marty wasn't afraid to open his eyes, he just couldn't at that moment. But he knew Marnie was running her hands down his back. Most likely she was trying to ascertain if he'd been gored by the hornless cow.

He wasn't gored, but he sure was smashed.

Not wanting anyone to push him, or touch his back anymore, he rolled off of Marnie and regretted it the instant the lightning bolt shot through his chest and torso. He hissed through his teeth and flashed back just for a moment to when he was in Iraq and felt the shrapnel from the bomb tear his leg apart.

"What happened?" Marnie's eyes darted around them both as she lay on the ground taking in deep breaths.

"Bertha was charging for you, but I knew you were too focused on the other cow in front of you. So I ran interference. Only, Bertha didn't like it so she hit me from behind." Marty took a few deep breaths and then sat up, wincing as he did so.

"Here, let me help you get up." Marnie stood and offered her hands to help him.

"Thanks, do you see anyone else in here?" Marty asked once he had dusted off the hay from his clothes.

Marnie wobbled on her feet and put her arms out to stabilize herself. "Whoa."

"Where's your cane?" Jerod asked when he walked over. "And what happened to you two?"

In unison, Marnie and Marty both said, "Bertha."

"Ah, yeah. You gotta watch out for that one. She's fine until the storms hit." Jerod looked over to the cow in question and shook his head. "Shame on you. Attacking the newbies like that. You know better."

Bertha mooed and began chewing the hay she had pilfered. The rest of the cows were right next to her eating away.

"Well, I guess we don't need to worry about feeding the cows tonight." Marty started to laugh, then stopped and leaned over. His eyes closed and lines crossed all over his otherwise smooth face. "Ow. I think Bertha might have done some damage."

"Come on, let's get back inside. The rest of the guys can get the animals away from the part of the barn that's damaged." Jerod put a hand out to help Marty, then he looked at Marnie and quirked a brow. He said nothing, just looked at her as though he knew something was different.

Marty leaned on Jerod's outstretched arm and hobbled back to the house, hissing the entire way back inside.

The moment he entered the house, all of the women surrounded him and he wished he would have lost consciousness. Having one woman fuss over him wasn't something he really enjoyed, but having four? It was torture.

Megan shooed everyone away except for Jerod. "Help me get him into my office."

Marty almost sighed the moment the door shut and all of the sounds of worry and concern over him diminished.

"Here, sit down." Jerod ordered, then helped him into the overstuffed chair.

The next few hours went by in a blur, especially after Megan gave him something for the pain. When he had gone through the in-processing meeting, he had been told that no one was allowed to use pain meds since injured veterans were more prone to addiction. He never thought that Megan might have something in a safe for emergency use.

He'd never abused the drugs they gave him in the hospital. In fact, he'd hated them. They made him sick. So the moment he was able to stop, he did. He would still take some ibuprofen or Tylenol when the pain was too much, but other than that he stayed clear of narcotics. He'd seen firsthand what can happen when someone gets addicted to meds. It wasn't pretty.

"Marty? Can you hear me?" A soft, feminine voice was close to his ear.

"Mmm?" His mind knew he needed to say more, but his lips just refused to move.

"Are you in any pain?" She asked.

"Mmm, mope." Marty's hand moved to his mouth, even to his drug addled brain something didn't sound right. He sounded like he did after he'd had a cavity filled one time. He felt his lips, but they weren't numb, or swollen.

He tried to move his head, but found it hurt when he did so.

"Don't move. You're going to be fine. The doctor thinks you might have a couple of cracked ribs, but nothing seems to be broken, thankfully. I gave you something to help you sleep all night. You'll need lots of bed rest for the next few days." Megan patted his hand. "Weather permitting, a doctor will come and evaluate you in person tomorrow. Probably bring a mobile xray machine with him."

"M'kay." Marty smacked his tongue on the roof of his mouth and moved his lips a little bit more than before. But he still felt as though something was holding his lips together so he couldn't talk. It didn't matter anyway, blissful sleep called to him and he heeded the call.

Chapter 1

"What?" Eloise Sullivan exploded when she read the report about a returning veteran who was injured in a barn accident, of all things. "Why in the world would an injured vet be recouping at a ranch in Montana?" She slapped the paper down on her counter.

Instinctively, her hand reached for her cane, and she paced back and forth in her Houston, Texas living room. Eloise was an ADA Coordinator for a company who contracted with the VA. It was her job to ensure that any agency, person, company, and in this case, ranch, who received government grants to help the injured veterans, complied with Federal Accessibility laws and legislation.

Eloise lived on the sixth floor of a condominium in the middle of the sprawling metropolis.

As she paced, the vision outside of her floor to ceiling windows caught her attention. It still amazed her that she was able to find a decent condo next to a park. Looking out on the trees and rolling green grass, when it wasn't brown, helped to calm her down any time her job became too much for her.

She inhaled and then slowly exhaled as her yoga instructor had commanded many times over the years. Her eyes shuttered and she thought of the way the ocean lapped up on the shores of her favorite beach. The sounds of the water whooshing and receding along with the seagulls called to her. This image was always what she went to when life became overwhelming, or her anger simmered too close to the surface.

It also helped whenever she had to go inside those tiny tubes for an MRI. It wasn't that she was claustrophobic, it was that it was just too tight. What if something happened while she was inside that tube? How would she get out? It wasn't like there was a pully system that she could use to pull herself out of the long, tight tube. No, she'd be stuck until someone came to help her out. That thought always sent her screaming to get out.

Which was why she had to envision herself on the beach. A totally open space with plenty of room to move around, and no chance of getting stuck inside a place with no windows, and no way out on her own.

Eloise learned a long time ago that she was the only one who could help herself out of a tight spot. Any jam that she got into, she was the one who got herself out. Even though she lived in a city full of gentleman cowboys, she'd never once seen a white knight come to her aid, or anyone else's for that matter.

Okay, so maybe she did have a bit of a claustrophobic reaction at times. But she didn't care. Living in a condo with a view of a large park outside of her window did wonders for her mental health. And whenever she got the chance, she would drive to the coast and spend a few days at the beach, lapping up not only the sunshine, but also the great expanse of freedom.

Which brought her back to her current assignment – The Crooked Arrow Ranch in Frenchtown, Montana. It was one of those ranches that catered to injured veterans. She had heard about them, and even seen one in Texas. But the one in Texas wasn't really a fully working ranch, it was more like a bed and breakfast that catered to the injured war veterans. They had campfires, hugged cows, camped out under the stars, and once in a while rode horses.

Even though it was a ranch in Texas, most of the area around the house and in front of the barn, was concrete. There were even handrails to help those who needed a little extra help getting around.

In this day and age, she just couldn't understand why some places did a great job of providing the necessary equipment to assist anyone with a disability to get around safely, while others did not. The ranch in Texas had passed their ADA inspection with flying colors. Eloise wished that other ranches around the country were required to come and visit the Circle S Ranch just outside of Amarillo and see how ADA compliant a ranch could be.

Although Circle S wasn't a real working ranch, and they had a lot of concrete, she did understand that most ranches were covered in dirt and not designed for wheelchairs or canes. Still, the Circle S proved that a lot could be done to make a ranch safer for those who are injured and need extra help.

Which was why she didn't understand why the VA would have sanctioned the use of a working ranch to help returning and injured veterans to reintegrate back into civilian life. It made no sense whatsoever. How could a horse, or a cow, help someone with PTSD? How could it help someone who had lost a limb? Or learn how to live with their new reality?

Once she had calmed down, she took the folder and headed over to her desk. She had an old-fashioned oak rolltop desk. Her grandfather had used it in his business, and when she was a kid, she loved to sit at it and color in her coloring book. She lifted the roll top and ran a hand over the well-worn writing desk. A small smile played at the corner of her lips. "Grandpa, you'd understand if you were still here, wouldn't you." It was a statement, not a question. Eloise knew without a shadow of a doubt that her grandpa would be on her side in this argument.

Although, to be fair, he almost always backed her up. She sat at her desk and began reading through the file again, doing her best not to blow a gasket. "Oh, my stars and stripes." She shook her head and sighed. This was going to be a tough assignment.

Instead of letting her emotions get the best of her, she pulled her cell phone out of her pocket and dialed the number her VA contact had given her.

"Hi, this is Eloise Sullivan. Is Marty Winters available?" There, she sounded like a friend of Marty's instead of someone who was about to ruin their Thanksgiving dinner. Even though heading out would ruin her Thanksgiving plans, she decided to be professional and courteous. It wouldn't do to upset the apple cart before she even left town.

The timing was awful, and she knew it. Heading out for an inspection during the holiday season was not something she wanted to do, but someone had to look out for Marty, and those like him. If the owners of the Crooked Arrow Ranch weren't going to ensure the safety of their patients, then she would have to travel.

Most of her work kept her within her own state, but sometimes she travelled outside of Texas to conduct physical inspections. With her own limitations, she wasn't a big fan of travel. However, this was one trip she was definitely going to embark on.

Chapter 2

Marty Winters regretted rolling over before he had even made it on his side. "Ouch. Ugh" The distinct taste in his mouth almost made him puke; it tasted like he'd drank something that should never enter one's mouth. He chalked that up to the pain meds Megan had given him. He needed to get up and wash his mouth out before getting some coffee. At least the coffee in this place was better than decent. Shoot, it was better than most coffee shops.

That was probably thanks to the fact that Dana Stevens, the wife of the man who owned the Crooked Arrow Ranch, also worked part-time for the local coffee shop. And that coffee shop roasted their own beans. It was like heaven every time he stepped inside Frenchtown Roasting Company and inhaled all of the coffee and pastry scents.

Using his left arm as a support for his stomach, Marty finished his roll and sat up with his legs on the side of the bed. He needed a few extra breaths before he could stomach standing up all by himself. Bracing himself for the pain he remembered from the day before, he stood. Then he blinked. "Huh. Not so bad."

It wasn't that Marty didn't feel the pain, because he did. It was that it wasn't as bad as he figured it would be. Since his injury in Iraq his tolerance for pain had increased dramatically.

Once he was showered, he got dressed. Then he debated whether or not to sit and put on his boots, or do it like he normally did – standing. When he looked at the clock, he realized how late it was and decided he needed to hurry it up.

Of course, it was a mistake.

Marty knew his center of gravity was off but he didn't realize how much until he fell flat on his face. He hissed in pain, "Ow." Then someone was on the ground next to him.

"Marty, are you alright?" Dana knelt on the ground and had her hands near him but didn't seem to know where she could touch him.

"Argh, sometimes I really hate my feet." Marty lay on the ground holding his midsection and trying to breathe normally. While he didn't need an assistive device for his Air Force injury, he did still battle with balance issues. Having only one real foot was a pain he sometimes chose to ignore. His prosthetic was good, but balancing on his left foot wasn't really recommended.

"Here, let me help you up. You have a caller waiting for you." Dana put her hand out and braced herself for the tall man who was over six feet to use her as leverage to get back up.

"Someone came here to visit me, in this weather?" Marty took her outstretched hand with his left one and put his right hand on the edge of his bed to get enough leverage to get back up. Normally, he could have done it all alone. He no longer had many issues with his balance, since losing his left foot to an IED. But since he had been rammed down by a mad cow, he wasn't exactly up to par.

Dana giggled. "No, someone called the house line for you. Didn't they try your cell phone?"

His head turned to the side table where he had his phone charging. "I don't think so. But I suppose I had my phone on silent and missed it?" Once he was up on his feet, he picked up the cell phone and looked at his history. "Nope, no missed calls."

"Well, there's a woman on the phone asking for you." Dana turned to leave the room and let him finish putting on his shoes in privacy.

"Wait, what woman?" Marty couldn't think of anyone he'd given the ranch number to. His family called his cell when they wanted to talk. His VA doctor was a man, not a woman. But he supposed it could have been a scheduler calling to set up an appointment or something. Although, it was strange they used the ranch line and not his cell.

However, stranger things had happened.

"She said her name was Eloise Sullivan." Dana left and headed back to the kitchen where the phone sat on a tiny wooden table in the corner by the refrigerator. There wasn't a chair there, only a small drawer that held paper and a few pens used for note taking. She moved a chair next to the phone stand so Marty would have a comfortable place to sit while talking.

This time, Marty sat on his bed and put his boots on the way he knew he should have to begin with. "A woman caller, huh?" He grinned and hoped it was someone calling to inform him he'd won a million dollars, or something just as sweet.

However, when he got to the phone, he realized it was probably more like a Nigerian Princess leaving him money, but needed his bank account info in order to send him the money first.

Okay, so maybe not a scam, but it wasn't a sweet call.

Chapter 3

"This is Marty." He sat down on the padded chair and winced. Then decided it might be better to stand. At least he could breathe easier while standing.

"Mr. Marty Winters? US Air Force Veteran?" The woman's voice on the other end was pleasant but laced with tension. He'd heard that emotion many times since coming home from the sandpit.

"Who's asking?" This time when Marty spoke, he put on an air of superiority. Usually, these types of people wanted something from him.

"I'm Eloise Sullivan. The government contracts me to ensure that rehabilitation centers are ADA Compliant. Usually, after an incident I'm called to come in and assess the situation."

He ran a hand down his face. This wasn't good. He knew about these government contractors, they always caused problems for the little guy who only wanted to help. From what Marty had seen since arriving, this ranch was one of the best places any vet could go to. He was lucky, or blessed, to get a spot here. "I don't think that will be necessary. It wasn't any fault of anyone but myself. You can't anticipate the effect a storm will have on barnyard animals."

"Be that as it may, I still have to come out and assess the situation. I'll need some time with you, as well as the owners and the counselor at the ranch. It's required after an injury. I'll need to investigate the situation and ensure that the ranch has done all it could to become compliant with federal regulations." Eloise sounded more like a recording than a human with any emotion.

If Marty understood her hidden meaning, she was coming to see if she could shut the place down. And right before Christmas, too. He wasn't going to let that happen. "Ma'am, everything here is wonderful. I was injured because I stepped in front of a raging cow in the middle of a massive storm. The cow was angry and scared, it only acted out of fear." He almost told her that he jumped in front of another resident in an effort to save her, but he doubted that would be any better.

After a tense moment of silence, Eloise responded, "I will reserve judgement until I see the place. The owners of the ranch agreed to these sorts of inspections when they signed the contract with the VA. Given that this is the first time the VA has sent anyone since they opened, I'm sure all will be fine."

While Eloise said the right things, Marty wasn't sure what her tone implied. But it didn't sound as though she was holding judgement. It sounds more like she had already tried and convicted the ranch of incompetence, at the very least. He didn't like this. And he figured Jerod wouldn't either. "Have you spoken to Jerod yet? Does he know you're coming?"

"I have left him a message on his cell phone. If he is available now, I'd be glad to speak with him." The woman on the other line didn't sound like she wanted that confrontation, but it didn't matter.

"I'm sorry, but Jerod isn't inside right now. I'll speak with him and make sure he calls you back."

They discussed her travel plans and then Marty hung up, unsure what to think about the woman. He set the phone down and ran his hand down his face. He sighed. "Well, that wasn't good."

Marty had forgotten he wasn't alone in the room so when Marnie asked him if he was alright, he almost jumped.

Before he turned, he tried to control his emotions. "It seems our little issue with Bertha the cow made its way to Texas." He screwed up his lips. "A woman who specializes in ADA compliance is coming here, to the ranch, to make sure that Jerod and Dana are looking out for us properly."

"What?" Marnie exclaimed.

Dana, who was right behind her, asked, "What's going on? Why is an ADA specialist coming here? And when?"

Marty hadn't heard the owner's wife walk into the room but he wasn't too surprised since she had been in and out helping with the meal preparations. He took a moment to get his thoughts in line. "It seems that whomever Megan spoke with about my injury didn't like what they heard. They called someone to come and inspect the ranch."

Right after the injury, Marty had been in a lot of pain and didn't pay much attention to the doctor on the Zoom call with Megan, the counselor who was also their makeshift medic when the need arose. And since the weather was so harsh when he was hit by the cow, Megan had to phone in the injury and work with a doctor over the Internet, which thankfully held out long enough to ascertain his injuries weren't life threatening. Then, of course, they lost the connection.

But, Megan had done an admirable job patching him up. Yes, he was still in pain, but that wasn't any fault of hers. He'd be in pain for at least another week while he healed. Thankfully, it was the sort of pain that he could handle with only something from over the counter. As long as he followed instructions and rested.

That would be the key – following orders. While he had always done an admirable job following orders while in the Air Force, he wasn't good at lying low and resting. Marty was the sort who always had to be doing something.

With his injury, he knew that was a bad combination. And for today, at least, he was willing to follow the doctor's orders. But he knew that it wouldn't take long and he'd be restless.

During his time in the Middle East, he'd taken up whittling to help pass the time when he had to sit still while out on patrol. His unit had long stretches of time where they had to lay low and out of sight. It was easy to carry along a small piece of wood and a knife.

After he finished a piece, he'd give it to a local kid. They were always trying to make friends with the local children, especially the boys. One never knew if a little boy was part of the terrorist network, or just a kid needing a little bit of attention. Usually, his pieces of wood would put a smile on a boy's face and the boy would start to warm up to his team.

One boy even showed them where a cash of weapons was stored. Ever since then, he'd never been without a small chunk of wood to work with. And when he was back at base, he'd continued to work with wood and stored a few pieces in his BDU's every time he went back out into the sandpit.

Even the other men in his unit recognized the importance of making friends with the little boys. It didn't always work in their favor. But it worked enough to make it worth it for them all.

Marty hadn't realized he'd been off in his own little world until Dana touched his shoulder. "Marty? Are you alright? Do you need help getting back to bed?"

He shook his head and was glad for the distraction. The last thing he needed was to start going down memory lane. While some were good memories, others weren't. It was those other memories that always caused him problems. "No, I'm fine. Did you ask me something?"

Dana tilted her head and smiled warmly. "Do you know if that woman has spoken to Jerod yet?"

He shook his head. "No, she left him a message but hasn't spoken with him yet. I suppose I should find him and let him know."

"Why don't you sit down and have some coffee and I'll go find him." Dana led him to a chair at the kitchen table and Marnie placed a cup of coffee in front of him.

While Marty wanted to argue and be the man who went searching for Jerod, he also recognized the need to sit for a while. Although, he found sitting in a wooden chair not quite as comfortable as lying in his bed. So, when the coffee was done, he made his excuses and went to the living room where a comfortable overstuffed chair sat begging him to join it.

With a wince and then a sigh, Marty took the seat and closed his eyes.

He wasn't sure how long he sat in the reclining chair before he heard a voice. It jarred him out of a restful sleep. "Hm? Yes. I'm awake." Marty pushed his booted feet down on the footrest of the recliner and sat up straight. When the pain shot through his chest, he changed his mind and reclined it once again.

"I'm sorry to intrude on your rest." Jerod paused and looked closer at Marty. "Do you need some pain meds? Are you in a lot of pain?"

Marty realized that from the turn of phrase used, Jerod knew he was in pain, just not how much pain he was in at that moment. It wasn't so much an ongoing pain, more of a shooting pain as he tried to sit up straight. Once he reclined, the pain began to recede. "No, I'll be fine." As with most men, Marty hated it when someone saw his weakness.

Jerod chuckled. "Typical grunt."

"I'm not a grunt. I'm a TACP. You know we're very different." While Marty couldn't say much about what he did while in service, he could say some. And besides, Jerod would understand better than most. The owner of the Crooked Arrow Ranch had himself served with special forces and knew that not all military men could talk about what they did, even a year later.

While Marty's unit was most likely home and doing something different these days, it was still something best kept confidential. One never knew who might be listening. He of all people, knew how wise that was.

Jerod chuckled. "Says all grunts I've ever met." He grinned and his smile widened when Marty tried to smile.

The friendly banter between Army and Air Force was something they both enjoyed. While Marty had served, he was embedded with an Army Special Forces unit. And they had teased him all the time about serving the laziest of the military services.

It was common knowledge at the ranch that Jerod had access to everyone's military and medical records. What Marty didn't know was how much access Jerod really had.

Most of the men at the ranch held regular jobs like truck drivers, electricians, grunts, and he guessed even a sniper was in their midst, somewhere. But he and Marnie Gallagher were the only Air Force personnel, so far. And from the little bits he'd overheard he would bet Marnie had been in a military intelligence unit herself.

Most MI's couldn't talk about what they did. Some outright lied. Others just played it off or said, "I'd have to kill you if I told you." That was one of his favorite lines. He didn't use it, he just said he was a TACP and let people think what they wanted.

Most TACP's, or Tactical Air Control Party personnel, served in a plane and just flew over areas the Air Force needed intelligence from. Some served in the field, like him. And others spent their entire time working from a military base providing air assistance in one form or another.

He missed his team. He rubbed the scrub that was on his face. Since arriving at the ranch, he'd decided he would let himself grow out his beard. It was nice since the weather was so cold. The added insulation would make it easier when he went back outside.

"So, have you heard the news?" While Marty knew he hadn't napped long, he figured that Dana had found Jerod and told him what she knew already. And maybe he'd even listened to his voice mail.

Jerod nodded. "A little bit. I haven't returned Miss Sullivan's call yet. I wanted to speak with you first, and see what you thought."

Marty had no problems sharing his conversation with Jerod. In actuality, he was glad that the man had come searching for him. "I don't think there was anything wrong with what happened. I chose to jump in front of that cow, nothing more than that."

The scratching sound of the whiskers on Jerod's own face caught Marty's ear. He turned and saw how worried Jerod looked and realized that the cowboy in front of him had a much better beard growing out than he did. Then he chastised himself for thinking of something so vain. The impending visit of the ADA Coordinator was so much more important than who had the best beard. Although, if Marty tried, he knew his would grow out nicer than Jerod's.

Chapter 4

The time had come for Eloise to arrive. Jerod himself had driven to the airport to pick her up, along with his wife, Dana. The local airport was less than an hour away in Missoula.

Over the past couple of days, Marty had seen a marked improvement in his healing. He still hurt, but with Tylenol, it was totally manageable. He was even able to help with a little bit of work. However, Jerod had only allowed him to help with brushing the horses down. He wasn't allowed to carry anything heavier than a brush. It irked him to no end, but when he tried to lift a small bucket of grain, he realized why Jerod had been so insistent.

Since that incident, he'd followed the rules. Only carry the horse brush. And he only brushed the parts of the horses that he could easily, and painlessly reach. Someone else finished brushing the areas of the horse he shouldn't reach for. Although, he did sneak a couple of apples in to give the horses some treats. Since an apple didn't weigh more than a brush, he figured no one would care.

And no one minded one bit.

So far, he hadn't found a horse that took an instant liking to him. But he figured with the smuggled in contraband, one of the horses would be happy to see him. And he had been right, after two days.

The ranch didn't have a lot of horses, but they sure did have their fair share of dogs. Something which had irked Marty at first. But there was one horse that seemed happy to see him when he put the apple on his open palm. Jackson was a white gelding with brown spots who almost resembled a giant leopard.

The horse whinnied and nodded his head the moment he saw Marty enter the barn. With a grin only an animal could coax out of a man in pain, Marty headed toward Jackson and held out his hand with the apple. His other hand ran down the horse's mane.

There was something soothing, almost healing, about petting a horse. Back in the Middle East, Marty had been attached to an Army squad that had a K-9. Rocky was the best dog he'd ever met. But when Marty woke up from the explosion that took part of his leg, he knew Rocky's outcome before anyone said a thing. And since that day, he'd decided no more dogs for him. It was too painful to lose such a trusted companion.

However, in the past few days, Marty had started to wonder if having a horse might be just as wonderful as having a dog. Other than the size of the animals, they had a lot in common. Granted, Jackson wouldn't be able to sit in his lap and lick his face like Rocky did once in a while. But the horse could take treats from his hand and let him brush his mane and scratch his forelock.

Marty learned right away that horses liked it when you scratched their head and rubbed their forelock. Probably because the horse couldn't reach those spots on their own. Sure, they could rub up against something if they had an itch, or a fly was buggin them, but having a human hand rub their head, or scratch it, really made a big difference. One of which was that they couldn't get a splinter that way.

Jerod had told him that it was important to keep the wood around the horses smooth so that when they did rub against it, they wouldn't get splinters in their skin.

"Hey, there boy. Are you happy to see me? Or the apples?" Marty cooed.

A tiny whiny told Marty the horse was happy to see him. Especially when the horse raised his head enough to look him straight in the face. The Air Force veteran couldn't hold back his genuine smile. Warmth spread throughout his body and he felt himself visibly relax.

"I see someone has made a new friend." Declan Walden, a local sheep and alpaca farmer greeted him. The man had been spending a lot of time at the Crooked Arrow recently. Jerod told him that they were going to buy some of Declan's sheep and alpaca so they could learn how to shear sheep and one day make wool themselves.

Jerod was big on self-reliance. But Marty also suspected that some of the work on the ranch was created so that those who were patients there, or residents as Megan the counselor called them, could find ways to earn a living.

Most of the jobs in the Army, Marines, and even Navy, weren't all that transferable in the civilian world. Most of the Air Force personnel could easily get jobs outside of the military, or even other branches of the government. Aviation was huge, and those doing the hiring always preferred Air Force personnel to regular civilians. Especially those with flight experience. Which Marty had.

Although, he wasn't currently flight qualified. His leg wouldn't be an issue, but he still couldn't pass the mental exam. Which was what brought him to the Crooked Arrow.

"Declan, good to see you again." Marty nodded at the man. "Yeah, Jackson here has a sweet tooth. He'll eat whatever is given to him, but apples seem to be his Achilles heel."

Declan chuckled. "I see. And how are you feeling today?" The farmer looked him up and down with a narrow eye. It was almost like he was examining the injured veteran to see if his injuries were worse than the day before.

"Knock it off. I'm fine." Marty turned his attention back to the horse and the irritation fled the instant his hand felt the coarse texture of the horse's mane. "A doctor came out here with an Xray machine and it's just what they thought, bruising around my ribcage, nothing was broken. They will heal."

Jackson must have sensed his human friend's irritation because he rubbed his head against Marty's shoulder.

Marty winced and Jackson pulled back a little, just enough to keep from hurting the human any more.

"Thanks, buddy. You're the best." Marty moved his hand to rub the horse's back.

"Sorry, I just feel bad that I couldn't have been there to help." Declan toed the dirty hay on the ground in front of him while his head and shoulders drooped.

"It wasn't your fault the cows went crazy. You weren't even here at that point." Marty turned around. "It was no one's fault. This is a working ranch with one-ton animals. Someone is bound to get hurt, eventually." He shrugged one shoulder and then winced. "This is just life on a ranch."

"True. I can't even remember all of the injuries I've sustained from the animals." Declan paused for a moment. "But, since changing from cattle to sheep and alpaca, I can say that I've less injuries than before." He tilted his head. "Well, maybe not less. But the injuries I do receive aren't nearly as bad as when we ran cattle. Today, most of the issues are alpaca biting me, spitting at me, or sheep running over my feet." Declan chuckled.

"So, there really isn't any way to get away from some sort of injury on a ranch or farm?" Marty was really curious about this. When Eloise Sullivan arrived he wanted to be able to let her know that injuries were just part and parcel of life on a ranch. Disabled veterans weren't any more likely to be hurt on a ranch than someone who didn't have a prior injury. It was all about learning how to mitigate the possible injuries.

Yes, the Crooked Arrow had cattle, but not a lot. And they were looking at making some changes to include animals that wouldn't cause quite so much harm to humans. Meaning that Marty felt there wasn't any need for the ADA Coordinator to visit.

Even though he'd had several days to adjust to the fact of her visit, it still irked him to no end to know that she was coming to inspect, and possibly shut down, the ranch due to his stupidity. He didn't think he was stupid to save Marnie from the hit, but the way he went about it could have been done differently.

Declan looked as though he was giving careful consideration to Marty's question. "I think that with experience comes knowledge on how to avoid certain mishaps. No one can always avoid injury from a stampeding animal. But there are ways to keep animals from stampeding, or if they do, to calm them down without getting in the middle of the herd."

It was exactly as Marty had been just thinking, mitigation. Knowledge was power, but it couldn't always stop an animal acting on instinct, or in this case – fear. But, if the human knew more about the situation, and the animals, then the human could mitigate some disaster.

It was no different in war. Intelligence was usually the thing that made or broke a military unit. When the US military engaged, they generally planned for all contingencies and did their utmost to gather all of the intelligence they could. It was part of Marty's job on the ground to gather intelligence and call it in to his unit command team.

The reason he had been embedded with an Army Ranger unit was so that he could call in the correct information to the Air Force when a strike was needed, or change the direction if a sortie was in play. It was all about intelligence, also known as information.

He nodded to acknowledge Declan's statement. While Marty didn't have a lot of ranch knowledge, he knew that Jerod and the others who had been here for a while did. Not to mention all of the help the local farmers and ranchers provided to the Crooked Arrow on a regular basis, as evidenced by the fact that Declan was present so much lately.

Although, he had seen the way Declan looked at Marnie. Even though Declan did need to be there sometimes, Marty figured that the man had a crush on Marnie Gallagher and spent more time at the Crooked Arrow then needed. The left side of his mouth quirked up.

Jerod had made a joke recently about this being the Lucky Hearts Ranch. Marty could see why he had said that. So far, there were at least half a dozen couples who had come together thanks to this ranch. For just a split second he wondered if he would eventually be counted in that group. He shook his head to get that thought out of his mind. He was in no shape to court a woman.

And not because of his left leg, either. There were plenty of women who wouldn't have an issue with him have a partial prosthetic leg. A lot of women also wouldn't have a problem with his PTSD. Or so his VA counselor had told him.

No, he was the one who wasn't sure if a woman could handle his night terrors. The nightmares came and went as they pleased, and he could be quite violent in his sleep. Never in a million years would he put a woman through that horror. That was what had brought him to the ranch, not the need to learn how to walk or balance on his new foot.

His night terrors even frightened him.

Chapter 5

Eloise Sullivan grew up in Texas. She'd seen her fair share of ranches. And she'd even seen one that was outfitted for the physically impaired. So when they drove up to the Crooked Arrow, she almost gasped. The house was a large single story ranch house. While it wasn't as large or as beautiful as the homes owned by the oil magnets, it was nice.

She could tell that Jerod Stevens and his wife had taken decent care of the place. And if she wasn't mistaken, the outside had been painted sometime within the past few years. It wasn't falling down, nor was it in need of huge and costly repairs. It was only now that was there that she admitted to thinking the ranch had to be ramshackle and the owners squandered the money they received from the various grants.

At least not that she could tell from the outside. She still was going to hold her judgement on the suitability of the place. Although, she wasn't as willing to think ill of the place as she had been before. She would give them a chance to prove they were honest and the ranch was in good shape.

No, what startled her was all of the snow. She had seen pictures of snow-capped mountains and ski resorts, but she didn't realize that ranches could get so much snow. That was probably naïve of her, but she was still surprised to see snow drifts that were almost as tall as the house itself. "How do you manage to clear the snow? It looks like it would take forever to get the driveway shoveled. I highly doubt the city sends their snowplows out here to plow driveways."

Dana chuckled. "You'd be right about that. We have a plow attachment that goes onto the front of one of our work trucks. Most ranchers and farmers in the area have their own. We all plow our own property and even sometimes need to plow the highway out in front of our land."

Taking her time to absorb the information, Eloise turned around slowly in a circle and took in all she could see. The white fluffy snow all around her was almost pristine, except for the sides of the drive where it was evident that a snowplow had been through recently. The dirty, churned snow packed against the side of the road wasn't very appealing.

But what was appealing was the front lawn where the snow didn't even have footprints in it. No one had come out front and made a snowman here. Not that she would, either. But she thought that it might have tempted at least one person at the ranch. Maybe there were more injuries here than the VA knew about. She caught her thoughts and reined them in before she got ahead of herself.

"Thank you, again, for picking me up and letting me stay at your ranch. I understand you usually have a full house." Eloise was glad that they had made room for her. She could have done her job while staying in town at a local motel or bed & breakfast, but she found it more convenient, as well as informative, if she stayed on property.

While Jerod was the owner on record, and the man in charge, it was Dana who tended to do most of the talking since Eloise met them both at the airport. "It's our pleasure. If you need anything at all, please let me know. I want to make sure you see everything we have for the vets, and get a chance to speak with everyone as well. I think you'll be pleasantly surprised by how well everyone is doing. And how much help Jerod has been to the residents who have come through here."

From the moment she got the call, until she landed in Missoula, Eloise had been studying up on the ranch, and the residents. She knew that several were still in the area and those were the men she most hoped to speak with, besides Marty.

She found it highly odd that these skilled military men would have chosen to stay in a backwater town and work hard on ranches and farms. The US Army had trained them all so well. Now that they had been rehabilitated, they should have been able to go on to other government work. Of course, none of them would be able to pass the physical exam for the police academy, or any other type of military group, but they could easily work for corporations and make good money, if they didn't want to work as an analyst for the FBI.

Eloise doubted any of them made a good salary. One of the residents trained dogs, and he wasn't even the owner of the company, he was just an assistant. Another milked cows for Pete's sake. Surely that job didn't even pay past minimum wage.

"I look forward to meeting everyone, including those still in the area who have graduated. How many of your residents have been paired with service dogs?" Eloise knew the importance of a good service dog. The program here for pairing a vet with a service dog was probably the only thing they had in their favor, as far as she knew.

"So far, we have three who have paired with a service dog." This time it was Jerod who answered.

Eloise figured if something specific was asked, then he would probably answer. Dana seemed like the consummate hostess, which was good. Eloise hoped that the woman provided healthy meals for the men, and women, who came here to recuperate. A healthy diet was so important to healing the body and mind. She knew that from her own experience.

While she hadn't served in the Armed Forces, she had been injured. Thanks to a drunk driver and a long stretch of dark, country road, she would forever need to use a cane. Even after some of the best physical therapists had treated her, she didn't have full mobility. That was when she changed gears and decided to advocate for those who were like her. People that the current landscape of the planet wasn't built for.

The past three years had been spent advocating for those who had voices that most ignored. Or turned their backs on. Helping the disabled had become her passion, her entire life. And for good reason, too – hardly anyone understood what it was like for a person who had at one time been in great shape and then due to circumstances out of their control, no longer be considered complete. They were now damaged for life.

She never believed someone with a disability was "damaged goods", but she had come across plenty of people who believed that. Quite a few of them were the disabled people themselves. And usually because society told them that.

Now, she worked hard to ensure the Americans with Disabilities Act was adhered to. There was also some changes Eloise would like to see, but until she had enough political clout to be heard, she would work for the government and help veterans to be seen and represented. Not only in DC, but in their hometowns.

It was crazy how many small towns still didn't come up to code when it came to ensuring that the disabled were able to get around town safely. So it really didn't come as much of a surprise how small Frenchtown was when they drove through it on their way to the Crooked Arrow Ranch.

"I think service dogs are so important for returning veterans. But I'm surprised to hear that you have already placed three dogs with your residents." Eloise looked closely at the house and then turned her attention back on Jerod who was pulling her suitcase out of the back of the truck. "Isn't it difficult to get a service dog through the VA?"

Dana nodded but stayed quiet.

Jerod pulled the handle up on the purple suitcase and then looked at Eloise. "We have a local trainer whose sole mission is to pair her dogs up with our residents who need the extra help. Not all of our residents need a service dog, but when they do, they get one."

"Very admirable." Eloise hadn't known that about the ranch. She just thought that Jerod had some sort of connection within the VA itself. She guessed he did in that a trainer was here, in Frenchtown, who only paired her dogs up with the Crooked Arrow residents. That was a huge plus for the ranch.

The VA wanted to pair up disabled veterans with service dogs. Eloise knew this for a fact because she had seen a study the VA had done about the health benefits of service dogs. The only problem was supply couldn't keep up with demand. There were only so many trainers who could provide the services needed to get a service dog ready to do its job. She knew this firsthand. After her accident she had looked into the possibility of being paired with a dog.

That was when she began to see how much the disabled really needed representation and an advocate with a loud voice.

Since then, she had come a long way with therapy. While having a dog would be nice, it wasn't completely needed. Therefore, she relied on her cane and a series of apps on her smartphone to help her remember everything she needed.

Eloise was lucky, in as much as someone with a bum foot could be called lucky. She healed enough to be able to get out and about without the help of a dog. She had recently come across a young woman who needed a service dog desperately to help her take her medication. The woman suffered from seizures but if she took her meds, then they were very rare. Only a handful of trainers were good enough to train a dog to detect if a person had taken certain medication or not on a daily basis.

The woman was eventually paired with a little dog who licked her arm every morning and night. If the requisite amount of medication wasn't on the woman's arm, the dog barked and scratched to notify her that she had missed her meds. Meds that would save her life.

"Nelly is the local trainer, and she's now married to Sam Marley. He's a recent graduate of our program and was the first to get a service dog. He now helps her with the business. It seems he has a knack for training dogs. You'll get to meet them both this week." Dana grinned.

If Eloise wasn't mistaken, Dana was doing her best to show off for her. She wondered what the woman was worried about. In Eloise's experience, only those guilty over something tried so hard. It only made her want to find out the real story behind the snowy façade of the ranch.

Dinner that night was...interesting. Eloise had been to plenty of ranch dinners in her time in Texas. But she'd never been to such a large table where everyone bowed their heads in anticipation of prayer. Not that Eloise had anything against God, she'd grown up in church herself.

But ever since she was in high school, she didn't have much need for the Man Upstairs. He'd never really done much for her, so why should she bother with him? That was her philosophy. Most people in this day and age recognized there was a God, but not too many actually worshiped him anymore. At least, not too many in her circle.

However, her momma raised her to be polite so when everyone else bowed their heads, she joined them. It was just easier to bow her head than it was to object to praying to a deity she wasn't close to. She reminded herself that prayer didn't hurt anyone, it just never helped her when she needed it.

Once dinner was over, she had hoped she would get a chance to speak with Marty, alone. That never happened so she made an appointment to meet him the next morning.

Chapter 6

The day dawned cold and cloudy, but Marty smiled anyway. He was already starting to feel much better. Even putting his boots on didn't cause nearly as much pain. He still hurt, but it was manageable. Especially when he took some ibuprofen with his breakfast.

"So, how'd you sleep last night?" Jerod asked when he sat down with his cup of coffee.

"Much better than the previous night." Since the injury, Marty had been sleeping in an easy chair that was moved to his room. The doctor suggested he not lay down flat as that could make his ribcage hurt more. So, he had lots of fluffy pillows surrounding his body in the overstuffed chair and reclined it to help him sleep better.

Marty took a drink of his coffee and sighed. "I don't think I've ever had such good coffee before. I'm going to miss the Frenchtown Roasting Company coffee when I leave."

Dana chuckled, then added more eggs to Marty's plate. "You can always order coffee when you leave. Lottie has started an online store and now ships two-pound bags of coffee to anyone who orders online."

"I just might have to do that. Thanks for the tip." Marty took another sip before devouring his second helping of scrambled eggs. His appetite had mostly left him when he was first injured, but this morning everything seemed so much brighter, even if snow clouds were developing outside.

"What tip was that?" Eloise asked when she entered the breakfast nook.

"Ah, good morning, Miss Sullivan." Marty lifted his mug of hot java and grinned. "Coffee?"

She returned his smile. "Yes, please. And please, call me Eloise." She looked around at everyone. "Everyone, please don't be so formal with me. I'm just here to see how Marty's doing, that's all."

He noticed the careful smile and narrowed eyes of the woman and wondered if there was more to it. She seemed polite and nice, but he still had a feeling she wasn't going to like the ranch. The woman seemed too...boushie. Like one of those women on social media who constantly posted about make-up.

Dana set a cup of hot Joe in front of Eloise. "Do you prefer black, or...?"

Eloise picked up the mug and shook her head. The white mug had a picture of a cowgirl and the words "Cowgirls Get 'er Done" on it in red. The side of her lips turned up in an almost smile. "I like cream and sugar, if you have it."

Dana chuckled before heading to the fridge. "We have just about any type of creamer and sugar or sugar substitute one could wish for."

Jerod piped up, "My wife works part-time for the local coffee shop and she knows all of the best ingredients." He took a long drink from his mug before getting up from the table. "Sorry, but I must get back outside and finish the repairs to the barn."

"Repairs?" Eloise furrowed her brows and looked at the big Army veteran turned cowboy.

"Yes, that storm did more than hurt Marty." Without saying any more, Jerod took the offered thermos from Dana and kissed her cheek before heading back outside.

Dana picked up Jerod's dirty dishes and set them in the sink. "So, Eloise, what are your plans for today?"

Megan entered the breakfast nook attached to the kitchen and poured herself a cup of coffee before sitting at the table.

"Marty and I have a meeting, but I'd love a tour of the ranch, if anyone has the time." The ADA Coordinator looked around at the faces around the table. There weren't many people there, just Marty, Dana, Megan, and a quiet Marnie.

Before anyone could offer to show Eloise around, Marnie stood up. "Thank you, Dana, for the wonderful breakfast, as always. I need to get back outside myself and help."

Marty noticed the way Eloise watched Marnie get up and use her cane to help her walk. Marnie attempted to pick up her own dishes before Dana stepped over.

"Why don't you go on ahead. I can take care of these for you." Dana smiled and picked up the dirty dishes.

Marty knew from his own time needing a cane, that it wasn't always easy to clean one's mess up when using an assistive device. Marnie needed to use her cane to walk around which left her with only one hand to pick up her dishes and take them to the sink. When he was first learning to walk with his new prosthetic, he had to make several trips each time.

Usually, Marnie was stubborn and didn't like it when someone helped without her asking for it, but this time, she seemed grateful to get away as quickly as possible. "Thanks, Dana. I'll come back in later and help you prepare dinner."

"Sounds good. Tell Declan I said Hi." Dana turned away and headed to the sink with the dirty dishes. Then she turned around and called out, "also tell Declan I've got a fresh pot of coffee on if he's interested."

Out of the corner of his eye, Marty noticed how Eloise watched the interaction closely. When Dana mentioned Declan, it seemed like Eloise was going through a mental checklist looking to see if she knew the name.

"Declan is a local sheep farmer who is helping us out." While Marty wanted to be helpful, he didn't think he needed to give Eloise too much information.

"Thanks. I heard the ranch was looking at getting into sheep and alpaca ranching, in addition to all of the other things you already do." The area between her eyes crinkled before she picked up her mug and took another sip of her coffee.

"Yes, Jerod is really working hard to ensure that there are plenty of opportunities for everyone here at the ranch. We can all learn a viable trade, if we want, as well as use the animals to help the residents with various aspects of their rehabilitation." Megan, the ranch counselor, looked at Eloise with an expression that Marty wasn't sure about.

The therapist who worked closely with Jerod on developing new methods of treatment, was watching Eloise very closely. It seemed Marty wasn't the only one unsure of Eloise's motivations for being here.

Eloise continued to sip her coffee. When she put it down, she turned her gaze on Megan. "Why are there so many different programs here?"

Megan eased back in her chair and a look of satisfaction crossed her face. "Recovery isn't a one size fits all program. That's why the VA isn't always successful. They treat their patients more like a production line instead of hand-crafted and priceless artifacts."

Eloise raised her brows. "Talking as though people are nothing more than items isn't making you look good."

Megan leaned forward and rested her arms on the table. "Eloise, as someone who has sustained an injury, did you find that the first thing the doctors tried just worked for you?"

The visitor's nostrils flared, and she shook her head. "No, it took a lot of effort on my part to make sure a variety of treatments were attempted before I found what got me where I am now."

"Exactly. The VA has worked with our residents for a long time before they come here. We offer alternative therapy. Things the VA isn't able, or willing, to try in their hospitals." The counselor leaned back and picked up her coffee mug and held it in her hands.

"It sounds as though you don't think very highly of the Veteran's Administration," Eloise accused.

"Quite the opposite." Megan shook her head and then took a sip of her coffee. "I've learned that treatment plans are too varied for the VA, or any medical group, to be able to provide. Like I said, it's not a one-size fits all kind of program. Sure, a large portion of the veteran's population will be healed through the more traditional treatment options the VA can offer in mass quantities. But not all patients heal the same."

Eloise lowered her head and looked at the coffee mug in her hand. "Kinda like an ice cream shop. I see your point."

Marty's mind was swirling with their back and forth. He pinched the ridge between his eyes and sighed. "I'm not following."

With a nod, Megan said, "not everyone enjoys chocolate ice cream. And not everyone likes vanilla. Some like strawberry, and others prefer bubble gum. There are so many flavors available because tastes vary so greatly. It's the same with treatment options. One patient might be just fine with the counseling options the VA offers. Another might not see any help from counseling until medication is included. And don't even get me started on all of the different types of medication available." She shook her head.

Marty nodded. "I see what you mean. Just because a treatment program works for one person, doesn't mean it's going to work for everyone else. Which is why only a small portion of veterans are sent to ranches like this one."

"I've heard of mountain-top retreats and yoga camps that help." Eloise sat back in her chair and looked at Marty. "You're not a yoga type of man, are you?"

Marty laughed out right. "No. Not at all. I'm an action sort of guy. Sitting around and humming, or whatever it is they do, isn't my cup of tea."

Nodding, Eloise continued, "but you do like to be doing something physical, not just adventurous." It was a statement, not a question. As though Eloise had taken in his character and finally realized what would speak to him.

Marty looked into his mug and nodded. "Yes, but I've still got issues to deal with. I know that. I think I focused on what I could see, my new foot, and worked hard to fix that issue. And in the process, I ignored other issues."

The sounds of water running and dishes clanking all of a sudden stopped. Eloise lifted her head and noticed Dana trying to leave without saying a word. It was strange that she would leave them alone at the table.

Megan noticed where Eloise was looking. "Dana is very discrete, but she doesn't believe it's her job to listen in to serious conversations, or even when a resident is opening up to me, or anyone else."

While Marty didn't say more, he did squirm in his seat.

Eloise turned her attention back to the man she was there to advocate for. "If you aren't here to help you learn how to adjust to your new foot, then what did bring you here? If you don't mind me asking."

This time it was Marty's turn to have his nostrils flare. In that very moment he was glad for Dana's sense of discretion. If only Eloise had the same sense. "I'd rather not discuss this with you, if you don't mind."

The blood left Eloise's face and her hands came up as if in defense. "I'm sorry. That wasn't appropriate." She sighed. "I have the need to protect anyone I come across who has been injured." She wiped a hand over her face.

Marty took pity on her. "Don't worry about it. Unless you've served, you can't understand why veterans don't want to talk to strangers about their issues."

Megan put a hand on Eloise's arm. "This is another reason why we have such a variety of options to help those who want help. They can choose how they work on their issues, even if they don't want to talk about it."

Marty stood and picked up his dishes. "I'm going out to see if I can help Jerod and the rest of the residents fix the damage from the storm." He took his dirty dishes and set them on the counter next to the sink. He noticed that Dana hadn't finished her cleaning but wasn't sure if the soapy water still in the sink was for him to use or not. He decided not to mess with her set up and walked out.

"Nosy women." Marty put his outer gear on and fumed at the audacity of that woman. She wasn't here to work with him, she was here to work against the ranch. Why did she need to know what he was dealing with? She didn't. Marty figured she was just a nosy busybody, like the town gossips he'd heard so much about.

When Marty opened the door, he almost turned around and went back inside. However, the scene in front of him, while daunting, was more appealing than what he just left.

Chapter 7

The cold, biting wind whipped against Marty's face and he bent his head in order to keep walking straight toward the barn. It wasn't as bad as when the storm came through, but it was strong enough to chill him to the bone. He was grateful that the inside of the barn wasn't as cold, or windy, as outside. Even with the hole in the roof.

"Hey, done so soon?" Jerod handed Marty a cup of hot coffee.

"Thanks, I thought it would be better if I helped out here right now." Marty took the cup and wrapped his gloved hands around the warmth and drank.

The heat of the liquid permeated every inch of his body. When Marty had drank the entire cup, he sighed and reached for another cup. "Sorry, it's cold out here."

Jerod chuckled. "Yeah, it took me two winters to get used to the cold. Back in the Middle East we all got used to the heat and sand, but coming here was such a shock to my system."

"But you got used to it?" Marty eyed the tall man dressed in black snow boots, thick jeans, and a large black Gore-Tex jacket. He also sported a wool beanie under his cowboy hat.

Tony Sullivan, another resident of the ranch who had been recovering from his latest round of skin grafts, was still wrapped up in a jacket and several scarves. "The cold and snow is so much better than finding sand in all of the un-mentionable parts of my body." He chuckled.

The rest of the guys laughed along with him.

Dixon, another resident of the ranch who was usually quiet and hung out in the background, chuckled. "Just be glad we don't have those gi-ant monster scorpions here."

All of the men quieted and shivered.

Marnie scrunched her nose and said, "Eww. I heard of those. Are they really as large as the pictures on the Internet show?"

All of the men looked gravely at her and nod-ded.

Jerod jumped and screamed, "Scorpion!"

Marnie's eyes widened and she jumped up on the side of the stall she had been standing next to. "Where? Where?"

Dixon flinched, but didn't hide like he had been doing earlier in the year. "He's only joking. Those scorpions aren't found here at all. Don't worry." He glared at Jerod.

Jerod put a hand in the air when he realized what he'd done. "Sorry, man. I shouldn't have done that."

Marty eyed them and was about to ask when it dawned on him, Dixon was suffering from PTSD. The screaming probably was difficult for him to deal with. While Marty knew he himself was trying to recover from PTSD, he knew his case wasn't anywhere near as bad as Dixon's. Not that he knew much other than the fact that Dixon had been there since the beginning of the ranch, which was coming up on two years.

Everyone handled PTSD differently. And all of the treatment plans were different as well. If Dixon still wasn't ready to go out into the world after two years, how long would it take? Would he ever be able to heal from his own demons?

Whoever said war was hell hadn't underestimated the effect it had on everyone who fought, or even served, in a war zone. The amount of destruction was one thing, but the utter loss of life, and humanity, that accompanied the battles was something Marty hadn't expected.

History books were full of the battles and lengthy descriptions, but no one had been able to accurately describe how a person felt after fighting, and doing things they'd never thought they would have to do in order to survive. Even Marty knew that he might have to kill people when he signed up to join the Air Force. But he chose the Air Force in an effort to keep from having to be in the middle of such destruction. Even if he had been a drone pilot and dropped bombs on targets, it wouldn't have been the same.

Some of his buddies had said it wasn't much worse than playing a video game. Most of his friends who had gone on to work with drones conditioned themselves to think of it as a video game. They said it was easier that way. Even though they knew deep down it was much more than that.

However, Marty knew his role wasn't a video game, or even a simulation. He had been in the thick of things. He had seen firsthand the amount of evil that permeated the Middle East. If he hadn't been a believer in God before joining, his time in the sandpit would have made him one. Because how can there be so much evil if there wasn't also a God? The Bible must have been the truth. All through the Bible the authors described Satan and his demons and how much evil they brought. The more light that God and his followers shined, the less evil could thrive. But when God wasn't shining his light and was instead hiding it under a bushel, then evil thrived.

He even warned us early on that the descendants of Isaac would always be battling the descendants of Ishmael. His time in the Middle East proved that beyond a shadow of a doubt.

Before Marty could think any more about the warnings God had given to all mankind in the Bible, he heard a loud noise. One that sent him flying for cover. "Insurgents, get down!" He screamed out.

All of a sudden, Marty was back in the desert, and he scrambled to find his pack. "Where is it?" He hissed. He looked all around him for his pack so he could call in for reinforcements. This was exactly what his job had been, he communicated with the Air Force and called in airstrikes on certain missions.

The sand was scorching hot, and his mouth was dry. He'd lost his chapstick some time ago and his lips were already dry, almost cracking. He still had water, but he didn't want to drink it all before they could refill their canteens.

His squad was on its way to a rendezvous point for resupply. A package was due to drop in only three hours. They'd make it as long as they weren't ambushed. He could make it just a little bit longer before he needed water. But these terrorists were standing in their way. If he and his team didn't get past them, and soon, they could miss their drop altogether. Which would mean they'd be out of water, food, and possibly even ammunition.

Then a sharp pain hit his ribs, if felt as though he had been pierced through by a bullet, or some other projectile.

The pain that jarred him out of his memory was so sharp, he thought for a moment that he really had been shot. But when his hand touched his ribcage and came back clean, he blinked his eyes a few times. Everything was blurry. The images refused to take shape. Then another sharp pain hit him in his chest. When he looked around again his surroundings began to take shape, at least more than the globs of grey and black he had just witnessed.

"Marty, are you with us, man?" A deep voice asked from a distance.

While Marty was no longer back in the sand-pit, he felt as though he was in a cloud of fog. He could see shapes and heard people talking, but he wasn't sure where he was. "What?"

"Marty, it's Jerod. You're at the Crooked Arrow Ranch in Montana. You're safe. We're all safe. Just breathe and lay back."

Jerod helped Marty lie on his back, on the ground. Someone had put something soft under his head and he focused on breathing. "I'm safe. I'm safe. I'm safe." Marty kept repeating the two words until his breathing evened out and he no longer heard his heart beating erratically in his head.

"What happened?" Marty asked after he had come to his senses and remembered where he was.

"The wind threw another tree limb at the barn. But this time it didn't do much damage." Jerod helped Marty to his feet. "Did you go back?"

Marty knew exactly what Jerod was asking. He wanted to know if Marty had gone back in time to a situation where he was in intense danger. They all did it. Marty knew that from their group sessions. Everyone who suffered from PTSD had flashbacks at some point. Others had them more often than he did. Some not as much. Surviving these situations and moving past them was all part of the healing process.

When he was back in the VA hospital, his counselor warned him that he'd have to remember some of the bad times. He had also said that there would be times when he'd lose himself to a memory. But getting through and processing the memories was what would heal him. Those who tried to suppress the memories only made their situations worse.

Too many who survived the atrocities of war came home only to commit suicide because they couldn't process what had happened. He wasn't going to allow that to happen to him. Marty knew he had a road to travel down, but with help he could do it. And he would arrive at his intended destination stronger than ever.

"Yeah, it was bad, but not the worst." Marty shook his head and stood up. Then he took in his surroundings. None of the men there looked at him with pity. They all knew the drill, except for Declan, but he'd been around the ranch long enough to know how to react.

What surprised Marty was how Marnie was handling it. She'd not seen battle, but she did serve in the Air Force. She was a ranch resident thanks to a training accident in Germany that blew off all five toes on her left foot. While she understood the problems with having to relearn how to walk once she received her prosthetic toes, Marty wasn't sure if she suffered from PTSD. Most likely she didn't.

But the woman wasn't looking at her with pity, she was curious. He noted how her head tilted to the side and she was looking him up and down.

"How do you manage to keep your balance? Especially after a trigger episode?" Of all people, a woman was asking him in a no-nonsense voice how he was able to walk?

He shook his head and would have chuckled if his ribcage didn't hurt so badly. "Balance is no longer an issue for me. I don't even have to concentrate when I walk on my prosthetic foot."

"Hm. I wonder when that will happen for me." She shrugged and moved away. Then she turned back. "Do you want some more coffee?" Her reaction was more like someone who had witnessed a friend suffer from nothing more than a cut, or tripping over a loose rock while hiking.

Marty grinned. She was exactly what he needed in a friend. She didn't push him to talk about his feelings, and she didn't show any pity. "Yes, please. That would be great." Her question about his ability to balance so well was completely normal since it was the one thing she was having difficulty with herself. He made a mental note to talk to her more about it later, when no one else was listening.

Everyone got back to what they were doing, which was fixing the gaping hole in the roof of the barn. The earlier storm had sent a tree into it and now they had to practically rebuild one side and part of the roof before the storm tore any more of the building away. Thankfully, the animals had another place to stay dry and safe while the residents of the ranch, along with Declan's help, fixed the hole.

Every now and then Marty looked at Marnie and wondered how she was able to just accept the loud sounds and the jarring winds. Since the incident with the flying tree limb, he'd caught himself flinching several times already.

Even with the limit to Marty's actions imposed by Jerod, he still managed to help move a few things around and hold ladders while others climbed them. By the time they were done for the day, his body ached like he'd been hit by that tree limb instead of just having the tar scared out of him.

He figured that by tackling Marnie in an effort to save her from the non-existent terrorist, he probably set back the healing to his bruised ribcage by a few days. But he could deal with that.

If only he could get past the triggers that caused him to do stupid things, like tackle a woman and lay on top of her in order to keep her safe.

One day. One day he would no longer worry about bombs going off around him, or rapid fire into his little squad. However, the rest of it would most likely stay with him forever.

Chapter 8

Thankfully, no one said a thing to Eloise about the trigger event and she had no idea that Marty had freaked out in the barn. Knowing what he did about her, Marty figured she'd have the ranch shut down before Thanksgiving if she had heard about it.

His mental state was none of her concern. She wasn't a licensed therapist, only an ADA Consultant – meaning she was responsible for ensuring that businesses had to put in place things to help those who needed assistance, like the yellow rubber bumps at each dip in a sidewalk, or the pathway out of the stores. The things that caused carts to jump all over the place and drinks to spill.

Before his accident Marty hated those things. He still did. But now he understood why they were needed. The visually impaired needed something to help them note that there was a change in elevation on the sidewalk. The bumps meant different things depending on the size and placement. But the gist of it was to inform someone who couldn't see that there was a drop off in front of them.

However, that wasn't exactly something that would work on a ranch. They had very little concrete or asphalt, if any. Mostly, they dealt with dirt and rocks and the ground was never even anywhere on a ranch. There was of course grass and fields full of a variety of plant life, which would never work with those bump pads, either. So Marty had no clue what Eloise could do to help the ranch become more ADA compliant.

The scent of strong coffee and baking bread interrupted his thoughts when Marty got close to the kitchen. He'd slept well the night before, thankfully, and now he was starving for a good breakfast. If he hadn't been so hungry and in need of a dose of caffeine to get his day started, he might have turned around when he stepped in the kitchen and noticed who was staring at him.

"Marty, I heard you were working in the barn yesterday." Eloise tilted her head to the side and looked him up and down. "I thought you weren't supposed to do anything but rest?"

After a slight hesitation in his step, Marty headed toward the coffee maker. "Good morning, Eloise. How'd you sleep?" The insufferable woman had no clue how to interact with humans in the morning. She might be cute, but she wasn't good with people.

Even though Marty tried to ignore her jabbing question, she didn't give up. "Good morning to you, too. How are you feeling today?"

He sighed. And when he tried to take a deep breath, the pain that shot through his chest caused him to wince. Thankfully, he was facing away from her and was able to hide his facial expressions. "Better than yesterday. Thank you." He said nothing more but instead focused on making his coffee.

Dana walked into the kitchen, and it was the three of them. She paused and looked between Marty and Eloise. "Marty, good morning. What can I get you for breakfast today? I've got any type of egg you want, or I can whip up some pancakes. And I was able to save you some of the bacon and sausage."

A sigh released from Marty, and he turned around with a tiny smile on his lips. Dana always seemed to know how to make everyone feel better and diffuse a tight situation in the process. He was about to leave the kitchen, so he didn't have to be alone with Eloise and her pesky, intrusive questions, but changed his mind when his stomach gurgled. "How about an omelet? Just use whatever you have available and leave one or two pieces of meat to the side?" Marty lifted his brow in question.

"That's easy. You sure you don't want any pancakes?" Dana held up the package of bisquick to show how easy it would be to make it.

He chuckled, then winced. Marty really needed to remember to keep his movements smooth, and not jerky. Laughing was not allowed at the moment. "Thanks, but I think an omelet will be perfect today. And maybe some toast? Or a bagel?"

Dana pointed to the oversized bread box next to the toaster. "Go ahead and choose whatever you want."

Loving the idea of waiting a bit longer before he had to sit at the breakfast table with the nosey woman, Marty moved to the toaster and loaves of bread. He chose the sourdough loaf and put two pieces into the toaster. While he waited for the bread to brown, he went to the refrigerator and pulled out the margarine and a large bottle of huckleberry jam. "I gotta say, this is the best jam I've ever had. Where do you get it?"

"Hm?" Dana looked over her shoulder at the man and grinned. "There's this place up near Glacier National Park that sells the best Huckleberry anything." She shook her head and laughed. "I order from them online and get large quantities every few months. I can get you the information for when you leave if you like. They ship anywhere."

"I'd love that." Marty took a sip of his coffee and thought about what she had said. "Is Glacier very far from here?"

Dana shook her head. "Nope, it's not far. We sometimes take day trips up there with the residents. Although, during the winter, we usually just play it by ear since you never know if a day is going to be good for driving up into the mountains or not."

"Well, if I'm still here come spring, I'd love to take a trip up there and check it all out for myself." The sound of toast popping up grabbed his attention and he turned back around to fix his toast. It was done early, but he didn't care. He could get started on the toast before his omelet was ready.

Once his breakfast was done, Dana put a large plate down in front of Marty. He smiled and thanked the chef. Marty feared she would leave him all alone with Eloise, who had been strangely quiet as his breakfast was prepared.

So when the owner's wife sat down at the table with a fresh mug of coffee, he was pleasantly surprised.

"Mm, this looks awesome. Thank you, Chef Dana." Marty started to grin with a mouthful of bacon, sausage, cheese, and mushroom omelet but felt it would have been too rude. So instead, he chewed his food and enjoyed the tangy taste of the sharp cheddar cheese mixed with all of the other flavors.

"I'm glad you like it. So, what's on your agenda for today?" Dana asked.

Instead of Marty responding, it was Eloise. "I need to spend some time with Marty today and discuss the accident." She didn't bother looking to the man in question, instead she kept her gaze on Dana. "I also need a thorough tour of the property. I need to know where the incident took place, who all was involved, and where the residents are allowed to go on the ranch."

Dana's coffee mug paused midway to her mouth. She sighed and set it back on the tabletop. "Have you ever been to a ranch designed to help recovering veterans?"

Eloise nodded. "I have. And I realize that a ranch is very different from a city office. But there are still some safety precautions that must be taken. To protect not only the veteran, but you and your husband."

"Inside the house, we do have quite a few places where handicap accessories have been installed, like the bathrooms. Those are all up to code for the State of Montana. We were inspected before the doors were opened." Dana's back stiffened and her eyes narrowed when she looked at Eloise.

Marty wondered if there was going to be a chick fight. On the one hand, it would be fun to watch. Dana would kick Eloise's butt, easily. But on the other hand, he knew that Dana was too much of a lady to resort to fisticuffs, even if her husband's ranch was threatened. Instead, he slouched in his seat and hurriedly finished the bite in his mouth so he could interrupt their glaring competition. "Ladies, I think it's getting a bit chilly in here, don't you? Why don't I take Eloise around on a tour?" He wiped his mouth with his napkin and smiled in an effort to try and diffuse the situation. While he wasn't a bomb expert, he knew that subtlety was needed when taking a bomb apart. And this situation was starting to feel as though it might get explosive.

Dana took a deep breath. "I think that will be a good idea." She stood up and took her mug to the counter to top it off. "Be careful out there, it's very cold and the wind is still whipping about." She looked at Eloise. "I don't want to see any more accidents."

For just a second, Marty thought that was a threat, but then he relaxed and realized Dana was being literal. She didn't want to see anyone get hurt, not even Eloise who might be here to shut the ranch down. "Got it. We'll be extra careful."

Instead of finishing off the last few bites of omelet, Marty downed his coffee and stood up. He took his dirty dishes to the sink and pecked Dana on the cheek. "Thanks."

Dana blinked up at him and then chuckled. Then she swatted him back with her dish towel. "Get going, but don't go too far. I'd rather you wait to show Eloise the fields when the winds have died down and Jerod can inspect the land, to ensure that it's safe."

"Understood." Marty threw out before heading out of the kitchen with Eloise in tow.

They were both in the entryway where their cold weather gear had been stored.

While Eloise put on her snow boots, she kept looking at Marty.

The man felt the lady's eyes on him the entire time. Once his boots were on, he stood up from the seat he used and grabbed his jacket from the coat closet. "Something you want to say?"

"Actually," Eloise started to say, before she stood up. "I'm curious why everyone is so warm to each other but cold to me. Is it because I'm not military?" She stopped when he handed her a white puffer jacket.

Marty turned around and rubbed his chin. "Are you here to shut us down?"

Eloise practically jumped back and scoffed. "What?"

"Since you first called, we've had nothing but coldness from you." Marty tilted his head and looked Eloise up and down. "You are putting off an air of superiority and quite frankly, rudeness."

Eloise's eyes practically bulged out of their sockets, and she put a hand over her chest. "Me? Rude? I don't think so. You all have been the rude ones."

Marty rolled his eyes and was about to speak, then stopped himself. He stood up tall and thought about her and everything that had been said so far. He wasn't sure how to coax it out of her, but if he was going to get back on solid footing with this woman, he needed to know her intentions. "Are you here to shut down the ranch, or not?"

Long, black lashes fluttered up and down. Eloise's lips pursed and then she let loose a long sigh. "I'm not here to shut this place down, exactly."

He put his fist on his waste and glared. "And what does that mean, exactly?"

She sighed. "My first priority is to ensure your safety. The safety of all of the wounded veterans. I know there are unscrupulous groups out there who get money from government, and private, grants only to skimp on the necessary precautions. I'm an advocate for those who can't advocate for themselves, or don't know how to do so."

Marty tisked and shook his head. "You think that Jerod and Dana are taking advantage of us? Really?"

Eloise began to squirm under his intense stare. She looked anywhere but at the handsome man who was challenging her assumptions. "I don't know. That's what I'm here to find out. To be honest, I don't know that an actual working ranch is a good place for injured veterans to go to heal when the VA has done all they can to help."

Marty crossed his arms over his chest and glared at the little woman in front of him. "If you've already made up your mind, why did you even bother to come here? You're going to miss out on Thanksgiving with your family and friends. So why even bother? Why not just send in a report with your," he uncrossed his arms and did air quotes, "findings."

Eloise arched a brow when she noticed what he had done. "I never send in fake reports. I always go out and examine the properties before filing my report."

"But, you think that this ranch isn't doing what it says its doing? And you're here to prove it, right?" He crossed his arms over his chest again.

"I'm here to find out what happened when you were run down by a cow. You were inside a barn, for Pete's sake. How does that happen?" Eloise threw her arms in the air and let out a huff.

"You obviously haven't been on too many ranches before. Especially during a winter storm." Marty uncrossed his arms and put his jacket on. Then he zipped it up before putting on his thick, leather gloves. Once they were both bundled up warmly, he led her outside.

They began in the front of the house. "We don't spend much time out here in the snow, but I wanted you to get an idea of how large this property is." He eyed her and her cane. "You might want to find a wooden cane instead of the metal one you have. Wood will stand up better to the elements."

"Thank you for your concern, but my current cane is just fine." Eloise bristled at his comment.

"Suit yourself." He shrugged, not too worried about her. As long as they didn't have to walk through icy mud or water, he figured she'd be fine. But her hand was going to be very cold holding the metal handle. Especially since her leather gloves didn't look to be rated for below freezing temperatures.

He pointed out that the front of the yard went all the way to the road. Then the land went to the left for as far as they could see. The right, where their closest neighbor lived, was only about a quarter of a mile. The same distance as one lap around a high school track. "The largest part of the land is out back. It goes back pretty far. They have almost one hundred acres of land." Marty motioned for Eloise to follow him around the side of the house.

While the front had been covered with snow, and quite plain, the back had a lot more to see. It was all still covered in snow, thanks to the snowstorm that had just come through, but there were several outbuildings and lots more trees scattered around the paddock.

"Have you seen all of the land yet?" Eloise asked as she looked around. She wasn't snarling, but she wasn't smiling either.

Marty wasn't sure what she thought of the winter wonderland in front of them. He thought the land was beautiful and wanted to spend more time out here once the temperatures rose a little bit. "No, not yet. I've only been here for a couple of weeks. Before we can ride off on the back of a horse, we have to go through some classes. Jerod wants to make sure we are all trained before he lets us ride. Even if we have prior experience."

Eloise stopped in her tracks. "Really? He has horseback riding classes? Does everyone do it?"

Marty shrugged. "I don't know about the guys who have already graduated, but those who have been here for a while have done it. Marnie and I were scheduled to do the class this week, but the snowstorm kinda squashed those plans."

"So, tell me. What caused your injury, really?" Eloise gave him the side-eye before she began walking again.

"Like I said over the phone, the cows were upset from the snowstorm and the tree falling into the barn. They were riled up and I just got in the way of one. I realize now that I shouldn't have tried to get in the middle of a herd of cows, but..." Marty shrugged. There was no way he was going to change what happened, he'd much rather he was injured than Marnie. If he had it to do all over again, he would. But Eloise didn't need to know the details.

"And what about Marnie? She was in the barn, too, wasn't she?" Eloise kept moving forward and didn't notice how his brows shot up to his hairline.

He realized that someone had sent in a report about the incident without telling him what they said. He'd never said anything about Marnie being in there with him, did he? He didn't think so. "Yes, she was in there, but she didn't get hit by a cow." He didn't share that she was hit by him, in an effort to get her out of the way of the charging cow.

They both stopped when they were in front of the barn. Eloise looked at the barn door and then opened it. When she stepped inside, her nose scrunched at the scent of barn animals and manure. "And you like being here? In this?" She motioned with one hand around the inside of the barn.

Marty grinned. "Yeah, I do." He looked at the cows that were in their stalls being milked. Then he looked over at the horses. They were eating hay and swishing their tails back and forth. It reminded him of the dogs when they were happy and wagged their tails. A sense of peace and welcome filled his chest. Even though he had been injured not that long ago, he still believed he was right where he needed to be.

Eloise looked over her shoulder at him and pursed her lips.

He caught her look and nodded. Instead of turning away, he continued to look at the woman. Sure, she was a city girl through and through, but he had spent most of his life in the city, as well. He didn't realize he was the cowboy type until he arrived at the ranch. Before he was hurt, getting up early and tending to the animals before breakfast was something he enjoyed. Although, not being able to do much since his injury wasn't nearly as fulfilling, he still liked it here. Much better than the sandpit, that was for sure.

"Okay, show me what you do here on a daily basis." Eloise had one hand on her cane while the other was at her side, but her eyes were focused on the cows. It was as though she was keeping an eye on them to make sure that they didn't get out of their pens and charge her.

"Well, someone milks the cows twice a day. Normally, they aren't difficult. They are quite docile, actually. We don't have many milking cows so it goes pretty quickly. There are cattle that's raised for beef." He pointed toward the back of the barn. On the other side of the back wall was the lot where the cattle were currently kept for ease of feeding.

"I hear that there are some cows for cuddling. What's the deal with those? And which ones are they?" Eloise arched a brow.

Marty chuckled. "Don't worry, the Jersey cows aren't the cuddling ones."

"Jersey cows? Are those the milking cows?" Eloise asked.

He nodded. "Yes. They are. And I don't think anyone really cuddles with the cows we currently have. At least, I haven't seen it yet." Marty took his hat off and scratched under the wool beanie had on under his cowboy hat.

Dixon walked up and shook hands with Marty. Then he turned his smile toward Eloise. "We do have a couple of cows that can be cuddled, but they're out back right now so I wouldn't recommend it."

Eloise tilted her head to the left. "Why not? Are they aggressive?"

Dixon laughed. "No, not at all. It's just that it's too cold outside right now to sit in the snow and cuddle with them. If you want, I can arrange to bring one inside later on."

"Oh, no that's fine." She raised one hand and shook her head.

Marty noticed the fear in her eyes and stifled a laugh. He'd have to see about bringing her back when one of the cuddling cows are inside. He'd love to see her freak out over watching him cuddle one. Or maybe he'd get Dixon to cuddle one? He wasn't sure if he could sit on the ground with a cow at this point in time. Not that he feared a cow, it was that it sounded very uncomfortable, and possibly painful for his healing ribs. He rubbed a hand over his midsection and winced.

Eloise must have noticed because she stopped mid-sentence and turned to Marty. "Are you alright? Did something happen? Do you need to sit down?"

Her rather quick change in demeanor almost caused Marty to laugh, something he still wasn't ready to do yet. "No, it's just when I move wrong, I get a bit of a twinge. That's all." He did everything he could to stop wincing from the pain in his ribs.

"Are you sure? I don't want to cause you any more pain." She glared at Dixon. "Do something to help him." Eloise pointed at Marty.

Chapter 9

The one thing Marty hated most, was people fussing over him. He shook his head and put a hand in the air. "No, it's not needed. I'm fine. Really."

Dixon raised a brow but stayed quiet.

Eloise, on the other hand, started in with more questions.

"Actually, I think I could use a cup of coffee about now. It's pretty cold out here. Why don't we go back inside?" Marty moved to leave, but Dixon stopped him.

"We have a pot on here in the barn. If you need something hot, there are some insulated to go cups in the office next to the coffee pot." Dixon moved to get Marty a cup of coffee.

"Thanks, I'll go and get it myself. Maybe you can show Eloise the horses?" Marty didn't wait for an answer, he took the chance to flee the overbearing woman and her strange behavior.

One moment she was cold as ice, the next she was acting like a mother hen. If she didn't stop this back and forth he'd end up with whiplash. But, he'd never been good at understanding women and their actions. The one thing he hated almost as much as being fussed over was the games women played. Why couldn't they just say what they wanted? He was a straight-forward kinda man and he appreciated it when a woman said she was interested in him. He did not appreciate it when they played games, like being mean only to grab his attention. Or ignoring him when what they really wanted was for him to praise them, or something.

Marty took his time fixing his coffee in one of the to-go cups they kept outside. They were supposed to only be used by visitors. Each resi-dent had a reusable insulated coffee mug to use outside, but he'd not taken one with him today. He'd have to remember to do that next time.

After a few minutes, he began to feel like a coward. Sure, he'd run away from the crazy lady the first chance he got, but she was his re-sponsibility. After taking a few bracing drinks of the strong coffee, he turned around and headed back out to where she was getting a tour from Dixon.

Marty paused in the doorway as he watched Dixon's face light up as he spoke about the horses and cows. The man was normally quiet, and Marty hadn't seen him show any interest in anything before. Could it be that he was interested in Eloise? Something in his gut churned and he scratched his head. He wasn't bothered by the attention Dixon was showing the pretty gal, was he? He didn't think he was the jealous type. And he certainly had no plans for Eloise himself, so why did it bother him that Dixon appeared to be flirting with her?

He cleared his throat and put on a happy face and walked back into the part of the barn that housed the horses. "Dixon, has everyone taken the horseback riding class?" Marty found he really was interested in knowing who all was able to ride the horses.

Dixon nodded. "Yup, and everyone has really enjoyed riding horses, too. Jackson is a favorite amongst all of the residents. He's a calm gelding but strong and never seems to act up."

Eloise perked up. "Are there horses here who do act up?"

Dixon's face flushed and he stuttered. "Ah...Um...No. Sorry. The horses here are all older and calm. I was just thinking about some of the horses I'd seen in town over the past two years. Some of them are pigheaded and can act up. But we don't have any of those."

Marty wanted to laugh but bit his tongue instead. The pain from his teeth was much better than the pain that would shoot through his chest if he tried to laugh. "Kinda like those cowboy movies Jerod likes to watch on Monday nights?"

The entire house usually sat in the TV room and watched the old black and white westerns. John Wayne was everyone's favorite cowboy. He had actually been surprised to know that some of the more recent actors he liked had played cowboys too, like Val Kilmer and Kirk Douglas.

But the one that really surprised him the most was Tom Selleck. He had never known that actor had played so many cowboys. Before moving here if asked, he would have only been able to mention Quigly Down Under as a western that Tom Selleck starred in. Now? He'd seen at least three and knew about a couple more. Of course, those were all in color, which he preferred.

"Exactly." Dixon pointed to Marty. "Excuse me, but I need to start taking the horses out for some exercise." Dixon walked away as quickly as he could without looking like he was running away from Eloise.

A snort escaped him before he could stop it, and Marty winced when his chest ached. Would he ever heal? If he didn't stop laughing, or snorting, he doubted he would.

"Alright, ummm, let's head over to the area where the cows were stampeding. But you have to be very careful, the roof is mostly fixed, but not completely. So there could be more debris or nails on the ground." Marty hadn't been allowed to help fix the roof when everyone else had worked on it. He was allowed to help with a few minor things, but mostly stuck in the house, or off to the side. But he did know that they still had a few minor things to fix, like painting and sealing the wood. But that would have to wait for a dry day.

Eloise stayed quiet while they walked across the barn.

In front of them was a yellow caution tape sealing off the area. Even though the roof had been replaced and the debris swept up, Jerod had kept the area closed off.

Eloise reached out to take the yellow tape down, but before she could a loud voice interrupted her.

"Don't. We have to keep that area clear for now and it's not safe for anyone to venture into." Jerod walked up and joined the two, causing Marty to sigh with relief.

Eloise turned and looked at Jerod. "Aren't you done fixing the roof yet?"

Jerod put his thumbs through the hoops on his jeans and grinned. "For the most part, but we still have some finish work to do, like painting. And I need to clean the area again to ensure that there are no nails, or anything else, that might cause issues. You want me to ensure that our residents are safe, don't you?"

It was all Marty could to keep from laughing out loud, which would have hurt, so he turned around and hid his huge grin. While Eloise did seem like she really did have the safety of the veterans in mind, she wasn't going about it very nicely. And if she tried to close the ranch down, Marty would be the first in line to kick her to the curb.

The woman hung her head. "Thank you. You're right. I do have the welfare of the servicemen and women at heart." Eloise looked up and took a deep breath. "And in that spirit, I would like a tour of the grounds once it's safe to do so. I understand you have several docile horses. I'm an experienced rider and would enjoy a ride through the fields when you can manage it."

"I'd like to wait until some of the snow has melted or blown away. I need to ride through the fields myself before I allow anyone, experienced or otherwise, to accompany me. It's a safety precaution. I don't want any of the horses to get injured." Jerod started to move toward the horses, then stopped when Eloise began speaking again.

"But, how are you going to ride through the land if you don't want the horses to get hurt?" When Eloise tilted her head and looked thoroughly confused, something inside of Marty's chest loosened and looked more closely at the woman.

She was pretty, he'd noticed that before, but her blue eyes sparkled like the sky on a bright winter's day. So far, he'd only noticed her steely blue eyes, but now they held a sense of wonder, or maybe curiosity, that Marty wanted to know more about.

With a short chortle, Jerod waved for them to follow him to an outbuilding. "I have more than horses here. When I'm not sure about the terrain I can take out one of our four-wheelers. We usually only need them for when we're fixing fence lines, or hauling food out to the back pastures. I prefer riding horses to riding machines."

Jerod opened the door to the outbuilding that was about the size of a two-car garage. When he stepped inside and turned on the light, Marty whistled low and long. He hadn't been inside this building yet. And he wished it was something he'd had a chance to experience before his injury. "That's once sharp Gator." He pointed to the four-wheeler painted red and black.

The ranch owner walked over to the vehicle and put a hand on top of it. "It wasn't in working order when a neighbor donated it to us last year. A couple of us spent several weeks working on it and finally got it working. Then Sam painted it for me before he moved out." Jerod grinned from ear to ear.

Marty could tell that the man cherished the vehicle. The red was more like a cherry red fire engine and the black lines were sleek and stood out in just the right spots to give the Gator the look of a sports car. He ran his fingers along the side and without even realizing it, he opened the driver's door. "Do you mind?"

Jerod cleared his throat and looked at Eloise before turning back to Marty. "I think you might want to wait until you get the all clear from the doctor. Riding a Gator isn't like being in a car. It will most likely hurt when you go over the first bump or rock."

After Marty sat in the driver's seat, his head fell forward. "I know. I've driven these before and I remember how rocky they ride." Then his head lifted and he gave his companions a small smile. "But, it is a lot of fun."

"That it is," Jerod replied. "As soon as you can, I'll take you out."

With a grim nod, Marty exited the vehicle and closed the door. "Eloise, when Jerod takes you out, be sure to use goggles and wear your seat belt."

While the men had been chatting, Eloise had also been admiring the sleek vehicle. "Can we go now?" Her head popped up and the shine of her face told both men she was happier than they had seen her so far.

Jerod's brows arched. "You enjoy four-wheeling?"

"Enjoy?" Eloise scoffed. "I love it. I think you boys forget that I'm from the great state of Texas. I might live in the city, but that doesn't mean I don't know how to play out in the country."

"Well, alright then. If the weather holds, we can go out tomorrow morning after the chores." Jerod's eyes narrowed. "Wait, tomorrow is Thanksgiving. How about Friday? Will that work?"

"Yes," Eloise nodded. "I think Friday will be perfect. Thanks."

When Eloise left the smaller outbuilding, smiling to herself, Marty prayed she wasn't up to no good.

Chapter 10

To say that Eloise Sullivan was close to her family would be overstating things. But to say she wasn't close, wasn't correct, either. She and her family usually got together for the holidays, but there had been years when some had to work. So, this year, when she told her mother she would be out of town on an assignment, she had been surprised that her mother wasn't happy. It wasn't as though she was planning on missing Christmas with her family, just Thanksgiving.

So it was that when she called her parents to wish them a Happy Thanksgiving, she realized why her mother was so upset. Eloise frowned into her phone, knowing that her mother couldn't see her face.

Her brother had brought a single friend to meet her. It was a good thing they weren't talking over Zoom or Skype as her frown was so pronounced, she would have bet that she'd have permanent frown lines etched into her face the rest of the day. Not that she really cared, but she didn't want to look older than she really was.

Having recently turned thirty-three years old meant that wrinkles were something she needed to be concerned about. In fact, she expected that her mother would have already started giving her anti-wrinkle cream if they lived close to each other. Eloise didn't think she'd get through Christmas without at least one gift of wrinkle cream. She sighed and knew what was coming. It was the same old story, *when are you going to settle down and get married? I want to have grandchildren while I'm still young enough to enjoy them.*

Eloise tired of the machinations of her mother, and it seemed now her brother.

"Mother, I've told you before I don't like being set up. It never works out. They take one look at my cane and either they bend over backwards to appear as though my disability doesn't bother them, or they ignore me." Eloise wasn't sure which response was worse. At least on this ranch, no one cared about her cane, or her physical limitations.

They weren't exactly bending over backward to be her friend, but that was to be expected. This was a business trip, not a vacation. She never made friends on these inspections. Almost half of them ended up with the company either having to spend a ton of money to get up to code, or they closed their doors. A few were even tried and convicted of fraud. Word to the wise, never try to scam the Federal government. It never ended well for those who were caught.

"But honey, this man is different. He knows all about your accident." Her mother paused, then whispered, "he's in a wheelchair. It's a perfect match."

"What?" Eloise practically screeched over the phone. Then she looked around when she realized how loud she'd been. In a softer voice she said, "Mother, just because two people have a disability doesn't mean they will make the perfect couple. Physical attributes aren't nearly as important as temperament, and how well two people can get along. Does he have the same interests as I do? Or will we never have anything in common to do? Please..." She couldn't go on. Instead, she shook her head and wished her mother a Happy Thanksgiving and hung up.

Eloise almost jumped when she heard a cough behind her. She turned to see that Marty was standing in the door of the small sitting room she had used for her phone call. Since his face was tinged pink, she realized he had heard part of her conversation. "Mothers." She held up the cell phone in her hand and shrugged.

"Sorry, I didn't mean to overhear, but when you yelled out, I came to see if you were alright." Marty quirked his lips and looked down. "We had a mouse issue the other day, out in the barn, so I just wanted to make sure you were alright."

It was exactly what Eloise needed and she laughed. "Do you get many mice inside the house? Isn't that what a good mouser is for?"

When Marty looked up, he was smiling and all signs of embarrassment were gone. "We do have a mouser, Zipper. But with the weather one never knows if something will get past the cat. I take it your mother thinks you're going to find a husband here?"

Eloise blinked, then chuckled nervously. "No, no. That's not it." She sighed. "My mother had set me up for a blind dinner date today. Since this assignment came out of the blue, she didn't cancel. He's there with my family."

"I don't understand. What was that about him being disabled?" Marty asked.

She waved her right hand in the air and then sat down. "Don't worry about it. Does your mother ever try to set you up?"

"Uh, that would be a hard no." Marty shook his head and sat down on the chair across from Eloise. "I've been in the Air Force and away from home for over nine years now. She does, although, ask when I'm going to get married." He grinned.

"They're all the same, aren't they?" Eloise fidgeted with the phone in her lap. This was the nicest Marty had been since they met. She wondered if she should open up with this line of questioning for all of her clients. Then realized that wouldn't be any better. It would probably be worse. No one liked to be asked about their marital prospects.

Marty stood up and cleared his throat. "Sorry, I was coming to find you anyway. Jerod asked me to let you know that dinner was ready." He smiled and held out a hand to help her up.

"Thanks." Eloise took his hand and felt a shock go straight through her fingers all the way to her toes. Her eyes widened when she looked at him and noticed that he felt it, too. She prayed it was just static electricity from the carpet but didn't think that was it. Neither spoke as they made their way to the formal dining room where the largest dinner table she'd seen outside of a restaurant was full of people and food.

The noise of the dinner guests caught her attention, and she didn't think about that shock for the rest of the night. Instead, she wondered what it would be like to live at the ranch all the time and have such lively dinner companions each and every night.

While everyone laughed, ate, and joked with each other, after stating what they were thankful for, Eloise watched. She didn't speak unless directly spoken to. Instead, she watched as the past residents and the new ones all seemed to share in something she'd never seen at any of the residential places she'd inspected before.

Not even the other ranch in Texas had such warmth amongst them all. That ranch was a bit different as it wasn't really a working ranch, more like a therapy ranch or spa. There were activities for the residents, but they didn't learn how to milk cows, care for chickens, and certainly didn't herd sheep or alpacas. They didn't even have a cow to cuddle.

Here, it seemed they all worked the land together, as well as spent time volunteering for the local community events. She hadn't thought she'd care to see what they did at the Christmas Tree Farm everyone had spoken about, but maybe she did want to see it after all.

Chapter 11

When Eloise got up on Friday morning, she expected to see lots of people in the house, or at least around the house working the land. But she was surprised to hear that some of the residents had left to go Black Friday shopping. She almost blurted out, "Where does one shop around here?" But held her tongue. Instead, she asked, "So, what's everyone's plans for today?"

Jerod was sitting at the breakfast table sipping his warm coffee.

Eloise noted, not for the first time, that coffee seemed to be a big part of life here on the ranch. "Is coffee the lifeblood of a rancher?" She smiled and almost laughed, but thought it might sound condescending if she laughed about it.

Dana shrugged. "It probably doesn't hurt that I've worked at the local coffee shop since before I met Jerod. It's only a part-time job for me, but we get a good discount on freshly roasted coffee. And everyone does seem to enjoy it."

"Plus," added Jerod. "It's cold outside during the winter. Coffee helps to warm the bones." He lifted his mug in Eloise's direction and then nodded toward the coffee maker on the counter. "You might want to grab an insulated mug and take it with you when we go out today."

Eloise grinned and headed to the coffee maker before making her customary toast and butter for breakfast. "The coffee is really good, I'll grant you that. Better than my favorite corner coffee shop."

"That's because we roast the beans ourselves in the store. You can't get coffee any fresher than the Frenchtown Roasting coffee." Dana grinned and then pointed to the stove. "Would you like a hot breakfast before heading out? I can make you eggs, pancakes, bacon, anything you want."

For just a moment Eloise considered turning down Dana's kind offer, but she changed her mind and grinned. "You know, I think I'd like eggs. Is over easy alright?"

"Of course. Once you have your toast take a seat and I'll bring you the eggs. Did you want to add some bacon or sausage?" Dana asked.

Eloise shook her head. "No, thank you. I don't normally have more than toast or a bagel for breakfast so the eggs will certainly fill me up before heading out." She fixed her coffee before putting two slices of sourdough bread into the toaster.

While Eloise wished Marty could go with them, not because he's a handsome man, but because it would have given her more time to speak with him and find out how he's really doing, she understood that due to his injuries, riding in a Gator wouldn't be smart. However, the time with Jerod would be well worth it. She'd get to ask him all sorts of questions about the ranch, and how he is able to help the residents.

Accepting Jerod's suggestion of bringing a thermos of hot coffee with her, Eloise headed off to put on her outerwear once she was done with breakfast. Excitement began to creep into her heart, and she found she was all smiles by the time she met Jerod outside by the shed that housed the four-wheelers.

"I must say, I'm very impressed with your ranch so far." Eloise admitted when she sat herself in the two-person vehicle and closed the door.

Jerod looked at her and paused in putting on his seatbelt. "Thank you. I really appreciate that." When he heard the satisfying snick of the seatbelt latching, he grinned. "Are you ready for some fun?"

The excitement Eloise had felt began to turn to something else, and her stomach turned. She put a hand on her stomach and then checked that her seatbelt was firmly latched. "I think so."

Jerod's laugh filled the little space in the shed and echoed around the room. "Hold on, it can get a bit rough once we get out into the fields. After a big storm like what we just had, I never know what to expect."

Eloise gripped the padded bar above her head and said, "Alright let's get going."

Jerod took it nice and slow as he pulled out of the shed and then headed toward the back fields. Eloise had offered to get out and open the gates and close them, but he said she was a guest and it was his job to take care of the gates.

Once they had cleared two different fields, he opened the throttle just a bit and she felt her body pushed into the seat. "Woo hoo!" She didn't realize it, but she was having fun. Eloise couldn't remember the last time she'd been four-wheeling. Probably not since before her accident. She realized with a pang that she hadn't done much but work since her recovery. She rarely even went out with friends anymore.

Was that what she was seeing here at the ranch - friendship? The sounds of the engine made it difficult to talk, so as they rode around the land, zigging and zagging to miss trees, fallen branches and unknown lumps of snow, she thought back to her friends in Texas.

After her accident, they had come around quite a bit to help her and see if she needed anything. But she'd been depressed. And she didn't like her friends seeing her the way she was. Over the past five years, she'd rarely seen them. Mostly, it was birthdays and holiday parties.

But, as she thought about it. She realized that they had invited her to lots of different events and activities for the first couple of years. She'd almost always turned them down. The past two years she'd only received emails for the bigger events. And most of those she didn't even attend. Eloise couldn't even remember the last time she had invited any of them out to do anything. Or come over to her apartment for dinner.

The Gator began to slow and she brought herself out of her own memories and focused back on the here and now. "Is this the back of your property?" She looked around and noted the fence was taller here, and made of sturdier wood. Most of the fences they had driven around in the property were shorter metal fences. A couple of them had been the slat wood kind, but they looked really old. This back fence appeared to have been only a few years old.

Jerod pointed to the left. "Over there, see that?"

Eloise looked and nodded. Her heart fell when she realized what had happened.

"That tree is going to have to be cut up, but we can use it for firewood. And I'm going to have to get the guys to help me fix the fence line before we can use this back lot for grazing. Thankfully, we won't need to worry about it for a few months. We never use the back lots for grazing in the winter. I prefer to keep the stock closer to the house so it's easier to feed them and keep an eye on them."

"That's smart. So, will you fix this fence soon? Or will it be fine to wait for the spring?" Eloise asked. She hated to see that a tree had fallen on his back fence and at least thirty feet of it would have to be replaced. The tree had been a large one, too. It had probably been here on this spot for a hundred years, or more.

Jerod sighed. "I'll need to clear it as soon as I can, but the fence will have to be stabilized until we can fix it. I won't wait for the spring, but will wait until some of the snow melts away. I'm just bummed that the tree fell. That's one of the state's 'Big Trees.' It's always hard when one falls to a storm."

"Big Trees? What does that mean?" Eloise could see the tree had been big. She figured it was a Western Larch only because that was a typical tree for the region. But she didn't know what Jerod had meant other than to say it was a big tree, which was obvious.

"The State of Montana keeps a registry of their tallest trees. Some are actually the tallest of their species in North America. There's a Western Larch Tree named Gus near Seeley Lake that's currently the largest in the US, and maybe even the world. Montana is proud of all of its trees and people come from all over the world to see them. Our tree isn't on the registry, but it's well over a hundred years old, possibly close to one hundred and fifty years old. It's sad when a Big Tree falls." Jerod turned off the vehicle and undid his seat belt.

He stepped out into the snow, which went up past his calves. "It's really deep here, so be careful if you want to get out."

Eloise looked around and decided she'd stay in the Gator. "I'll wait here, unless you need me to get out?"

He shook his head. "Nope. I'm just going to take some pictures with my phone and then put a red flag here to note that I've seen the issue." He walked around the back of the Gator and opened a toolbox.

Eloise couldn't see what he was doing until he stepped away from the vehicle. She noted he had a red piece of fabric. It wasn't shaped like a flag, but more like it was just a scrap piece of red fabric. It couldn't have been any larger than one foot by one foot, but once he tied a piece of rope through a hole in the end and then tied it to the top of a fence post, it stood out like a beacon. She doubted anyone would miss it if they were within a hundred feet. Especially since almost everything around them was either white from the snow, or brown from the wood.

Once Jerod was back inside the Gator, Eloise turned to him. "Does this happen often?"

"The storm? Or the fallen tree?" He asked.

She tilted her head to the right and thought about his question. "Well, all of it. The storm was rather large from what I understand. And there is still a lot of snow on the ground. Then the tree," she pointed to the fallen beast, "that can't happen very often or else you would never have Big Trees in Montana."

"True. It's all pretty rare. Especially this time of year. We weren't expecting a storm of that magnitude here before Thanksgiving." He turned to take one last look at the fallen tree. "And the tree. Well, I'm just glad I didn't grow up here knowing that generations of my family looked upon that tree. Some maybe even took fallen branches to use as kindling, or even firewood, in the past." His nostrils flared as he turned the vehicle around and headed back toward the house.

"Yeah, I guess there's a lot of history here for the locals, isn't there." Eloise really wasn't asking a question, she was more agreeing with Jerod. "So what makes this ranch so different from the one I visited in Texas?"

Jerod didn't say anything for a while, and Eloise didn't push him, since the sound of the motor was louder than she would have liked. But when they slowed and approached a locked gate, he stopped the Gator.

"I don't know anything about that other ranch you keep mentioning, but here in Montana, it isn't just a place to live. We live off the land and support each other. All of us here are disabled veterans. Sure, we have different issues, but we all understand better than anyone else can what it's like to lose the life you dreamed of and have to start all over again." Jerod ran a gloved hand across his mouth before he stepped out of the Gator to unlock the gate.

When he got in and moved the vehicle through, Eloise stayed quiet and considered what he said. It wasn't until he had closed the gate, and got back inside the Gator that she responded. "So, a tough life living off the land combined with a shared past is what has helped everyone here become so close?"

Before he moved the vehicle again, Jerod thought about Eloise's question. Then he replied, "It's much more than that. God is at the heart of everything here. While we don't require the residents to attend church, they all do. And with that comes a sense of community that has led us to volunteer so many hours a week for the town as well as the local events."

"Wait, you're getting federal funds and you include God in the program? Doesn't that go against the rules behind the federal funding?" While Eloise had grown up in church, she wasn't exactly excited about attending church on Sunday with everyone. She hadn't stepped foot inside a church, not even for a wedding, since before her accident. She wasn't about to start now.

Jerod shook his head and smiled. "Nope. We don't require attendance. And as far as I know, the Constitution still protects Freedom of Religion. Everyone attends on their own accord. I drive a van and offer a ride into town for church on Sundays and for various church events throughout the year. If residents want to attend then they do."

"I noticed you pray at the dinners. Do you require everyone to join in?" She wasn't sure if prayer before a meal at a Montana ranch went against the typical rules surrounding prayer in schools, this wasn't exactly a school, after all. But she wasn't sure the Treasury Department would appreciate funding a religious organization, either. Unless they forced their beliefs on anyone, she doubted she'd report this information.

"Nope. I do the prayers, unless someone says they want to say a prayer. And no one is forced to say anything. If they don't want to join in by bowing their heads and folding their hands, or joining hands with their neighbors, they don't have to. I just ask that they respect the beliefs that everyone else holds and wait until the prayer is done before eating." Jerod put the Gator in gear and slowly headed toward the next locked gate.

"I see." Eloise figured that was fair. It wasn't that she wanted to stop anyone from worshiping God, she just didn't want him foisted down her throat. Or anyone else's for that matter.

"Does this mean that you won't be attending Sunday services with us this weekend?" Jerod didn't look at her, but Eloise could tell he was watching her reaction out of the corner of his eye.

"I don't know. I wasn't planning on going to church while here. I didn't even bring a dress." Eloise knew that a dress wasn't required, but some of the more traditional churches preferred women to wear dresses.

Jerod laughed. "No worries there. We're mostly a cowboy church."

"What's that mean?" Eloise arched her brow and watched Jerod's smile.

"It means that everyone wears jeans, cowboy boots, and cowboy hats. In the summer you'll see women wearing sundresses with their boots, but since most of us live on ranches and farms, dresses aren't really common. Besides, in weather like this, almost everyone is layering a lot of clothing to keep warm." He made his point about the cold when the wind whipped up and he shivered.

Eloise understood how he felt in that moment, as she too, was freezing cold. She picked up the thermos of coffee she had brought with her and opened it up. "Want some coffee? It's not piping hot, but it's warmer than what's outside right now."

"Yes, please." Jerod pulled over and they enjoyed the rest of the coffee and he even pulled out a bag of pastries that his wife had packed for them in case they needed a snack. "The cold weather always makes me hungrier."

"I know, right?" Eloise grinned and picked out a chocolate croissant from the offerings.

Once their coffee break was over, they didn't speak much as they finished up the short drive back to the house. Eloise considered all she had learned, while she watched the beauty of the scenery pass her by. This place was definitely more beautiful than the ranch in Texas. While that ranch was nice, it was full of concrete. This ranch had very little concrete. It was all green trees, brown dirt, and white snow.

The sun was out and shining down on the glistening snow that hadn't been touched by humans until they drove through it. Eloise realized that the ranch in Montana was pure beauty. As she watched some of the snow melt and fall out of tree branches, her heart began to melt as well.

She was starting to warm up to the ranch and its workers, as well as its residents. They had something here she'd never seen before. At least not while out inspecting facilities that assisted with the disabled. There was hope and peace here. And while the natural beauty of the landscape certainly added to the wonderful feelings and sensations, she couldn't help but wonder if the Crooked Arrow had something that no one else did.

Chapter 12

Marty couldn't believe the smile on Eloise's face when she and Jerod walked inside after their ride around the property. It was lunchtime and not everyone was back from the various activities they had committed themselves to on this Black Friday. For him, laying around the ranch and being practically alone was rare. After breakfast, Dana had gone into town to work at the coffee shop. Which left him all alone in the house for a while.

He had said he'd set out the sandwich fixings and make sure the bags of chips and containers of premade salads were all out and ready for anyone who came in to eat. It was the least he could do since he wasn't allowed to go out and help with anything. He did try to help feed the animals earlier, but was told in no uncertain terms to get back inside.

He'd have to ask Megan to tell everyone to stop babying him, he hated this sort of treatment. Even as a kid he always had something to do, even if it was just sports. After his surgery where he lost his foot, he still kept himself busy with physical therapy. Which was probably why he didn't have such an issue with his balance or need to use a cane anymore. Come to think of it, he did recover in that area rather quickly.

Marty recalled one of his doctors commenting on his rate of recovery, but his therapist wasn't nearly as happy with his mental condition. Which was why he had been sent to the Crooked Arrow Ranch. Diving for cover and searching for a weapon when his PTSD kicked in meant that he couldn't be out in the world by himself, or even with his folks.

The doctors had worried he'd hurt himself, or worse – hurt someone else. That was the last thing he wanted. So he'd agreed to come to the ranch. Since he'd been here he'd only had one bad instance. He's suffered through a couple of night terrors, but that didn't hurt anyone but himself. Although, it didn't help matters that he'd injured himself. Thankfully, he would recover. Nothing was broken, just severe bruising and lots of sore muscles. Even his bruised ego had already started healing.

Now, if he could just convince Eloise that the ranch was perfect as it was, everything would be great. He'd enjoy his time there and maybe even find a way to put the PTSD behind him. Or at least find ways to safely deal with the stress of his time overseas.

When Marty realized the time, he headed into the kitchen to begin setting out the lunch fixings. While he was thinking about his journey so far, he'd not heard Jerod and Eloise enter the house. It wasn't until he heard a crashing sound that he realized he wasn't alone. At first, he started to turn around, but then an explosion went off in his mind and all he could see were stars. Not the kind in the night sky, but the kind one saw when blinded by a bomb exploding nearby. He dove for cover and reached behind him for the radio to call in the attack, then felt extreme pain shoot through his chest all the way through his back.

He gritted his teeth and did his best to keep from yelling in pain. His hand went over his chest expecting to see either a knife or a bullet wound, but he found nothing.

"Marty, man are you alright?" Jerod called out in an even tone.

"What?" Marty shook his head. Then he felt a soft hand on his and he almost jerked back, until he realized it was the soft hand of a woman. No woman in the Middle East would reach out and touch him. Unless she was in the military. And he didn't have a woman in his squad. He blinked away the stars and then the clouds until he could see clearly the face of an angel. "Eloise?"

Before she could respond, Marty felt a wet tongue on his face. He blinked back some of the clouds and realized a dog was licking his face. "Rocky?" He shook his head and hissed back pain. It wasn't Rocky. Rocky was the K-9 dog from his unit back in the sandpit. He was a Belgian Malinois and looked like a German Shepherd. The dog he was staring at, and who stared back at him, was totally different.

"Hey boy, who are you?" Without moving, Marty spoke to the dog.

Razzle only did a light woof and then turned around and headed back out of the kitchen.

"Eloise? What's going on?" Marty turned his confused eyes on the woman who had crouched near him.

"Yes, I'm here. You're in Montana and everything is fine. Do you remember what happened?" Her voice was so soft and almost silent that he had to strain to hear her.

"I heard...an explosion? No, a crash?" Marty put his hand to his head, and only then did he realize that his hand was bleeding.

A soft smile covered Eloise's face and she took his hand away from his face. "You're hurt. Looks like glass. Let me help you." She stood and helped him to his feet.

"But, that dog?" Marty asked again.

Eloise looked back at the door leading out of the kitchen, then shook her head. "I don't know who that dog is."

"Don't move. I need to sweep away the glass from the pickle jar that broke," Jerod commanded before he turned to the broom closet. "And I think that's one of the new dogs Nelly just received this week. They must be here for the afternoon to do more training."

"Pickles?" Marty's mind was still a bit foggy, but it started to come back to him. "I heard a crash before the dog came in."

Eloise winced. "I'm so sorry. That was me. I dropped my metal cane on the wood floor in the mud room and it hit the edge of the freezer back there. You did warn me about needing a wooden cane. I think I might have to see about that this weekend."

"Don't worry. I shouldn't have reacted that way. If I'd been paying more attention, I would have heard you enter and not been surprised."

Marty wanted to wipe his hands along his pants but thought better of it when he noticed the glass shards digging into his palm. He hissed when Eloise took a larger piece out of his hand.

"Sorry, this is probably going to hurt but I need to get the glass out of your hand. Once Jerod cleans the glass from around our feet, I'll need you to head to the sink so we can clean off the blood and I can see if there are any more shards of glass in your hand." She kept her eyes on his hands and didn't look him in the eyes.

"Doesn't that bother you?" Marty watched as Eloise's fingers moved around along his bloody palm and she picked at the larger shards and put them on the table next to her.

"No, not at all." She looked up and directly into his eyes.

Marty noted the various shades of blue in her eyes. They were like paint strokes and the harder the artist pushed down on the brush, the darker the blue was. But where the artist barely touched her eye, the blue was as light as a spring afternoon with billowy clouds all around. He sucked in a breath and refused to break eye contact.

Their eyes were glued together until Jerod hit Marty's leg with the broom. "Hey, man. I need you to move your foot so I can get all of the glass up. Why don't you two head over to the sink and clean your hand up. You're bleeding all over Dana's floor. She's gonna have a heart attack if she comes home to see this mess.

The lighthearted banter broke the connection Marty had begun with Eloise, and he chuckled. "Heaven forbid I do anything to upset Dana."

"And don't you forget it." Jerod joked back and the kitchen got cleaned up rather quickly while Eloise tended to Marty's hand.

"I don't think you'll need stitches, but if you want a doctor to look at it, I can drive you into town." Eloise wrapped his hand with a bandage that Jerod had pulled from the rather large first aid kit he kept in the house.

Marty had been watching Eloise work and stayed quiet so she could concentrate. As she worked, he began to feel awkward. His reaction wasn't normal. A cane dropping on the ground shouldn't have sent him into a spiral like that. He looked at his watch and wondered when Megan would return. They didn't have a session scheduled again until Monday, but he knew he could talk to her anytime he needed to.

"Is it safe to come in?" A voice Marty recognized sounded from the doorway. He turned to see Nelly standing in the door holding the collar on the dog he'd seen. The dog who helped to bring him back to reality just a few minutes earlier.

"Nelly, come on in. Did your dog get any glass in his feet? We had a spill." Jerod pointed to the liquid still on the floor, waiting to get mopped up.

"Is that what that sound was?" Nelly knelt down and inspected the dog's paws. She smelled them and grinned. "Pickle juice, huh? Thankfully, I don't see any glass but I'll keep an eye on him to make sure nothing worked its way inside his pads."

Marty looked over and noticed the dog was looking directly at him. "Nice dog. What's his name?"

Nelly grinned. "This is Razzle. He's new, but almost fully trained. I just got him and another dog, Tyco, earlier this week from another trainer who closed his business down." She frowned when she mentioned the other trainer.

"Really?" Jerod asked. He headed to a closet in the back of the kitchen, near the mud room, and pulled out a Swiffer mop. "Why did he go out of business? There aren't nearly enough trainers these days. Surely, he had enough business to keep going."

A sad look overcame Nelly and she sighed. "He had health issues. For a while, at least, he won't be able to work. Working with the dogs can be very physical, and he's going to be bedridden for a while. Heart attack."

"I'm so sorry to hear this." Marty looked at Nelly, then down at Razzle. "But that is one fine looking dog. I doubt you'll have trouble finishing up his training." Marty wanted to pet the dog, but with his hand bandaged and the open wound, he decided against it. While he wasn't the K-9 handler on his squad, they all had loved Rocky. A twinge of regret filtered through Marty, and he turned away.

Razzle pulled at Nelly's grip on him. "Fuss." She ordered him to heel. And he sat after he tried once more to get away and go to Marty. "Braver Hund!"

"Huh, you use the German commands to train your dogs? We had a K-9 in my unit and his handler used German, too." Marty's eyes took on a faraway look and then he shook the memories aside. He told himself it wouldn't do to dwell on the past.

"Of course, it seems to be the best language to use. Dogs are so much smarter than humans give them credit for. I've learned that the service dogs seem to know the difference between English words and German. They've associated the German commands with work, and English with play." Nelly patted Razzle's head.

Razzle wore a black collar, with a matching black leash. But he also wore a red service dog vest. Emblazed on the vest were the words – *Service Dog in Training. Don't pet.*

The service dog in training vest was much smaller, and most likely lighter, than what Rocky wore. In the Army, K-9's had their own bullet proof vest and also had a few pockets with various items that his handler might need in a pinch. All of his food was carried in the handler's pack. And the squad also helped by carrying some treats and other items that the K-9 might need. Even though the K-9 was the responsibility of the handler, the entire squad helped with taking care of the dog. And the dog in return, took care of them. He really did miss that dog.

Chapter 13

Friday afternoon was spent lounging around and watching football on the television. Most of the house had vacated once the excitement of his newest injury had died down. While watching commercials, Marty took a quick look at his bandaged hand and realized it really wasn't that bad at all. He could probably take the bandage off, but seeing as how he was on a ranch, he figured he should keep the bandage on the rest of the day. Then take it off before going to bed. If it scabbed over nicely, and didn't open during the night, then he'd not worry about covering it up.

It wasn't like he was going to be outside all day long on Saturday working. He sat up quickly and thought about the weekend plans. Maybe he could be outside working after all. The team was heading to the Christmas Tree Farm on Saturday for the town Thanksgiving dinner. And they were also going to have try-outs for the Live Nativity. Maybe if he worded it right, he could help out somehow.

Anything would be better than another day lazing about. Plus, this would give him the perfect opportunity to show Eloise what they do for the community. And how much it helps them all.

It was late when Megan showed up. He wished he had called her to talk about what happened earlier, but he didn't want to interrupt her day off. So, when Megan came home and looked at Marty, she frowned.

"What happened to your hands?" Megan pointed with her right hand to his bandaged hand.

"Ah. Yes." Marty cleared his throat and realized he really should have at least texted her. "I wanted to talk to you about this. Are you up for it?"

Megan had her coat, purse, and the rest of her winter weather gear in her hands. She motioned with her head to join him. "Follow me." When she headed to her office, Marty got up and joined her.

Once the door was closed behind them, and before she had all of her gear stowed, she asked him, "What happened?"

Marty sat down in the chair across from Megan. "There was a crash, and I had another episode." He paused for a moment to collect his thoughts. All that day he had ignored what happened, even tried to forget about it. But it was hard to forget about his bandaged hand. "I was in the kitchen earlier and someone dropped something in the mud room making a loud crashing sound." He proceeded to explain to Megan what happened, but stressed that he was fine. No one else was injured.

"So, you dropped a jar of pickles and in the process cut your hand?" Little lines formed between Megan's worried eyes.

After Marty rubbed his arm over his mouth, he looked at Megan and wondered what she was thinking. "How do I handle sudden loud sounds?"

Megan took a moment, then tilted her head. "It's not that easy. Until your subconscious can process everything, you're going to have to be more careful. This isn't something that you can just choose to change in the blink of an eye. It's a process. For some it's easier than for others. But, if you really want to work on it, then you will get better."

Not sure what to make of that statement, Marty sat back in his chair. "What's that supposed to mean?"

Megan leaned forward in her chair and put her arms on the desk in front of her. "It means that this might not be your last injury. I hope you don't hurt yourself anymore, but you will need to pay more attention to your surroundings for now."

"But...Oh, stars and stripes. This is going to be much harder than learning how to operate with my new foot, isn't it?" Marty hadn't thought it would be this difficult to get past his PTSD. Or at least, he didn't think his episodes would continue on once he arrived here.

With a quick shake of her head, Megan sat back in her chair. "I don't know. As I've said in the past, everyone recovers, or heals, at a different rate. We will just have to take it one day at a time. Did you see a doctor?"

"Eloise was really sweet and cleaned my hand up right away." Marty shook his head. "It seems to be healing just fine. And none of us thought stitches would be needed so we didn't go see a doctor."

"I'm sure she did." Megan did all she could to keep from smiling.

"Hold up." Marty put a hand in the air. "I think you need to give her the benefit of the doubt.

And maybe even spend some time getting to know her. I'm starting to think she's not here to just shut this place down."

"Lucky Hearts Ranch strikes again." Megan chuckled.

"What?" Marty asked.

Megan waved a hand in front of her face. "Oh, nothing. Something Jerod once said. Maybe you're right. But enough about her, tell me about your flashback."

Once Marty had gotten it all off his chest, he felt much better. A bit raw at times, but he knew that real healing wasn't going to be easy. Instead of watching more TV he headed off to bed once he and Megan were done discussing the day. He even spent a minute praying to God and thanking Him for sending him to the ranch. While Marty knew he still had a long way to go, he also knew that he was in the right place to get the help he needed.

When Marty awoke Saturday morning, he felt more refreshed than he had in a while. Even his ribcage didn't hurt as much as it had. He took a closer look at his hand and it looked as though it was healing nicely. The scab that had developed overnight seemed as though it was going to hold. As he dressed for the day, he realized that he didn't have any night terrors, or even nightmares, last night. Which was rather refreshing.

As he entered the kitchen, he still had a smile on his face and he wished everyone a good morning.

"Good morning, to you, too." Eloise returned his smile and then continued eating her breakfast of a bagel with jam.

Once Marty had his coffee made, he looked over Dana's shoulder. "Watcha making today?"

Dana picked up the last slice of cooked bacon and handed it to Marty. "Here, sorry but I was only able to save you one slice. You slept in later than usual today. And I've gotta run but I'm scrambling some eggs for you."

"That was very nice of you. But you do know that I can make my own breakfast, right?" Most days Marty had been up early enough to get a hot cooked breakfast from Dana before she had to either head into town for her part-time job at the coffee shop, or head off to some appointment or other. He knew she was working a lot this weekend, it was a holiday weekend and he knew from his own experiences over the years that holiday weekends were always busier in a coffee shop. Even in small towns.

"I know, I know. But I hate that I can't provide a home cooked breakfast for anyone in the house. Especially those who want one." Dana nodded to Eloise, who usually just had toast and coffee for breakfast.

"Here, let me finish making my own breakfast and you head on out for your job. I don't want you to be late on my account." Marty took the spatula from Dana and gave her a light tap with his hips to get her to move.

"Someone sure is in a good mood today." Dana put her hands in the air and backed away. "I like it."

Marty grinned at Dana and then took a large bite of the bacon. Then he focused on his eggs and moved them around until they were the perfect consistency for his liking. Before he kicked Dana out of the kitchen, he had put two slices of bread in the toaster, and it popped just as he was pouring the scrambled eggs onto a plate.

After Marty took a seat across from Eloise, he asked her, "So, what's on your agenda for today?"

Eloise had been reading something on her iPad and when Marty spoke to her, she lifted her head. "I was thinking that I'd head over to the tree farm and see what everyone is doing. I also thought I'd see if there was something I could do to help out."

"Mind if I join you?" Marty dug into his eggs with gusto after dousing them with hot sauce.

"Okay, but have you been cleared to work today?" Eloise was hesitant with her acceptance of his offer, but she didn't seem to be upset by it.

Which only gave Marty hope that no one else would try to stop him. If Eloise, who thought he was so badly injured, didn't try to stop him, why would anyone else bother? Marty grinned. "I'm not going to do anything too physical. I just want to head over and see where I can be of some use."

Her eyes sparkled when she realized what he wanted. "You're one of those guys. The type that can't sit still." Eloise didn't pose it as a question, she had figured him out and was letting him know it.

Marty swallowed his last bite of eggs and put a hand up. "Guilty, as charged. I've sat around long enough and I feel rather good today. I'm not saying I want to haul trees over to people's car or anything like that. But I do think that I could help pick out trees, put the tags on them, or something like that." He shrugged and he didn't wince when he did so.

Eloise paused the conversation while she sipped her coffee. When she tilted her head, Marty could see she'd made up her mind.

"Alright, let's do this. After we clean up our breakfast dishes." Eloise stood up and took her dishes to the sink and washed them by hand. She didn't bother with putting anything in the dishwasher.

Marty, however, only rinsed his dishes and added them to the almost full dishwasher. He stood back and put his hands on his hips. "Do you think I should run the dishwasher?"?

Eloise bent down and looked at the contents of the machine and nodded. "Dana would probably appreciate the help. Is there a little sign to show that the dishes are clean?"

"Yup." Marty pointed to a circle magnet that showed a dirty cow face up and a clean cow facing down. He turned the magnet so the clean cow was face up after he put the soap in the dishwasher and started the cycle.

Eloise grabbed her winter gear along with the keys to the truck that Jerod left for her to drive should she need it that day. Jerod had left before Marty had gotten up for the day and he took the ranch van along with most of the residents. They were all volunteering for the day at the tree farm, except for Dana who had to work part of the day at the Frenchtown Roasting Company.

So, it was just Eloise and Marty in the truck when they pulled out of the driveway and headed off to the Makinaw Christmas Tree Farm. Eloise thought about the veteran sitting next to her on the bench seat of the old Ford pickup truck. He was looking out the window watching the bare fields pass by. Here and there horses or cattle dotted the scenery.

Some of the snow had melted, but the fields still looked like a bag of cotton balls. The snow was thick and billowy everywhere she looked. Thankfully, the roads had been fully cleared since the last storm, and a nice layer of salt covered the roadway. It wasn't that Eloise didn't know how to drive in extreme weather, it was more that it reminded her of her accident. And she hated the reminder.

If she wasn't driving, she would have thought the sight beautiful. But she was driving. Other than a quick look at the man beside her, she kept her eyes on the road. And her hands gripped the steering wheel at the ten and two positions. Occasionally, she glanced in her rearview mirror, but she was more worried about the oncoming traffic, what there was of it. Even though it was Saturday of a holiday weekend, she didn't see too many vehicles out there. And those that were on the road, stuck to their lane.

Not thinking about it, she reached out and clicked the radio button on. It was too quiet, and she didn't like where her mind was taking her. It was dangerous to go back and relive that day. A half smile slowly spread over her face when she heard the trumpets blare signaling the start of a Faith Hill Christmas song. She loved the entire album and had it in her iTunes account.

Santa Claus is Coming to Town is one of Eloise's favorite Christmas songs. If anyone looked at her list of digital songs, they'd probably find ten different versions in there.

Before she even realized it, her shoulders relaxed, and she leaned back against the seat. It was another minute or two before her right forefinger began to tap on the top of the steering wheel in tune with the song.

"I still can't get over the fact that Christmas music covers the entire radio up here so early." Marty turned his attention to Eloise. "Back home, I had Satellite Radio, and the Christmas stations would come on early, but the regular music stations never played Christmas songs until after Thanksgiving. And even then, it wasn't twenty-four-seven."

Eloise chuckled. "I know. I think in small towns Christmas is a bigger deal than larger cities like Houston, or Miami."

"Oh, no. In Miami Christmas is huge. Especially for the tourists. But the radio stations I listened to seemed to enjoy just a sprinkle of the Christmas tunes spread out through the day." Marty looked straight ahead. "But, I do like Faith Hill. She has a wonderful voice."

"Yes, she does." The song ended and the next one, while it was a country Christmas song, didn't warrant any more comments. "So, have you had a chance to see all of the tree farm yet?"

Marty shook his head. "Nope, not yet. Part of the reason I wanted to come out today was to see the place. I've never been to a real Christmas Tree farm. You know, the kind where you chop down your own tree. I've always wanted to, but Florida doesn't exactly have a lot of Christmas trees growing over the state."

"We have a good amount in Texas. But I've never chopped my own tree down, either." Eloise bit her lower lip, trying to decide if she should share what she normally did for Christmas. "I don't even have a real tree."

"I like the fake trees. My mom has one of those ten-foot-tall pre-lit trees. She stuffs it full of Christmas decorations and when the whole family is there, you can't even see the bottom of the tree through all of the presents." Marty sighed and put one arm on the back of the bench seat.

Eloise grimaced. "Yeah, my mom has a six-foot fake tree. It's pretty."

Marty turned his head and looked at Eloise. "What about yours? Does the top rub against the ceiling of your place? No room for a tree topper?" He chuckled.

"Ah, not exactly." She rubbed the side of her neck and kept her face forward, not wanting to see his expression when he realized what she was saying.

"Wait," his arm fell to the seat next to him as he turned slightly to see her better. "Are you saying you only have one of those tiny tabletop trees?"

"Oh, look." Eloise pointed to a large sign in the field on Marty's side. "I like that ad for the tree farm." On the billboard was a family gathered together and grinning as they watched the dad chop the bottom of a tall Noble Fir tree.

"Don't change the subject." Marty sounded as though he was shocked.

But when Eloise looked at him out of the corner of her eye, she noticed he was holding in a laugh. "I'm not. We're heading to the tree farm. The one listed on that billboard."

"Eloise? What sort of tree do you have back home?" His tone no longer sounded like he was about to laugh.

She took a deep breath. "I actually don't have a tree up this year."

"What?" The man practically exploded with his outrage. "How can any woman not have a Christmas tree up?"

Hackles raised, Eloise had to control her anger. She didn't think it was very gentlemanly of anyone to assume that just because she was female that she went all out for Christmas. What if she was Jewish? Or some other religion that didn't celebrate the birth of Jesus? "Do you have your own tree up?"

"That's different. I don't have my own place, and you know it. Why don't you have a tree up?" The tone of Marty's voice calmed, and he sounded as though he had gotten over his shock at her admission.

"As you know, I was called here before Thanksgiving. Most people don't put a tree up until after Thanksgiving." There, she thought. That should mollify him.

He rubbed the beard growing in on his chin. It looked like he was having difficulty getting a good beard going. There were uneven spots and it just didn't look quite right on him. Not that he wasn't handsome, because he most certainly was. But Eloise thought he'd look much better with the two-day stubble that a lot of men maintained.

"You said you didn't have one this year, not that you didn't have the time to put one up yet. It also sounded as though you normally only did one of those tiny tabletop ones that no one decorated year after year. They just put it away already decorated and then pulled it out the next year and set it somewhere without really thinking too much about it." Marty watched as Eloise's cheek turned pink. "Just as I thought."

"It's not that I don't like trees, I do. It's just that I'm rarely home. And when I am home around Christmas, I normally head to my parents a week before Christmas Day. So there's no reason to mess with a big tree." Eloise used to have a fresh tree every year in her own apartment. But since her accident she hadn't really had it in her heart to do much. She wasn't even the one who had bought the tiny tree she put on her table back home the past few years.

Her best friend brought it over the year after her accident and told her it would help her to get into the spirit. It didn't.

She felt his eyes bore into her. An uncomfortable feeling crept up her spine. She wasn't used to people looking too closely at her, and this cowboy was staring intently at her. If she didn't know better, she'd think he was pulling back the layers she used to protect herself from anyone being able to read her correctly. She didn't like that feeling, not one little bit.

"Something happened to make you dislike Christmas, didn't it?" While Marty didn't seem to know much about her, he was able to devise that there was an issue with her and Christmas.

Eloise didn't like it when someone could look into her soul and discover something she didn't want them to. "My past is my past. Let's forget this topic and look to today." She squirmed in her seat and almost missed the turn-off for the tree farm. "Look, we're here." She turned into the parking lot, which held a lot more cars and trucks than she expected.

"Huh, I wouldn't have expected this to be a big weekend for picking up Christmas trees. Do you think that cutting down your own tree means it will last a lot longer than one that was bought in a tree lot?" Marty leaned forward in his seat to get a better look at all of the commotion outside.

That thought almost had Eloise laughing. "Are you kidding? Of course, a truly fresh tree will last longer. Most of the trees you see in tree lots down south were cut before Thanksgiving. It's amazing that they last as long as they do."

"Well, when I was a kid my mom swore that by putting in an aspirin with fresh water each week, the tree would last through the new year.

She checked the water level every day and filled up the tree stand, but every week she also added another aspirin." Marty shrugged and took his seatbelt off when they parked.

"She's right. Daily watering and adding aspirin weekly will help it. There are other things that one can buy, but my mom also does the aspirin trick. She does it with flowers, too. And her flowers last almost two weeks." Eloise thought back to the years she lived with her parents and remembered all of the DIY tips her mom shared with her and was glad for those times. She may not celebrate Christmas anymore like she did, but wasn't it really a holiday for kids and old people? If she ever had kids, she'd probably celebrate it more. For the kids.

"My parents started using the fake tree after I left for the Air Force. Mom said it was easier than cleaning up after a real tree, and she could put her tree up before Thanksgiving." Marty chuckled. "My first-time home for Thanksgiving was strange. Most of the house was already decorated for Christmas and we hadn't had our Thanksgiving turkey yet. I guess it makes sense with Black Friday shopping and all that."

Eloise closed and locked the truck door after getting her cane and purse out. "I've seen houses that looked as though Santa Clause threw up Christmas all over it. I can see how those people need to decorate early. It must take weeks for some of those houses to get decorated."

"I think a lot hire the work out. I have a college buddy who put himself through school doing Christmas lights every year. Last I heard, he did big corporate Christmas decorations and was even working with the local baseball stadium to do these giant walk-thru displays where they charge an arm and a leg just to walk around the stadium." Marty shook his head.

"You mean something like that?" Eloise stopped and pointed to a tunnel of lights with a blow-up tree that stood taller than most homes she'd seen in the area.

Marty turned to see what she was pointing at and he grinned. "Well, it looks like my buddy has been here."

Eloise laughed. "Somehow, I doubt a Christmas tree light installer from Florida flew all the way up to Frenchtown, Montana and set up a few lights just for a tree farm."

Marty rubbed his chin. "I don't know. That tunnel to Santa looks a lot like something I've seen back home."

She chuckled and felt all of the tension from earlier in the truck evaporate. Even though it was daytime, lights were on all sorts of Christmas decorations. And the amount of blow-ups made it look as though she'd stepped into a magazine ad for Christmas decorations. "I didn't realize we'd been transported to the North Pole."

"I know, right? At least it's cold enough to feel like we're up at Santa's workshop." Marty grinned from ear to ear.

"Well, I heard that Santa and Mrs. Claus live in Frenchtown. I haven't seen them yet, have you?" The lighthearted question made it sound as though she wasn't all that interested, but Marty thought she might be more than even she realized.

"Ho, ho, ho. Merry Christmas!" Santa yelled out from behind the couple.

Eloise turned around quickly and couldn't hold the shock inside. "What? Who?" She shook her head.

"Well, I see we have some new visitors." Santa looked at Eloise, then to Marty, and grinned. He put his black gloved hands into the belt around his thick waist. "I think we might even have an unbeliever here."

Mrs. Claus walked up next to her husband. "Chris, that's no way to greet visitors." The smile that crossed the woman's face was nothing more than pure joy.

Eloise felt the warmth and welcome of the wife of Santa Claus. She didn't even want to keep her burgeoning grin to herself. She let herself take in the joy the woman was sharing with everyone around her. Then she took in the clothes.

"Wow," Eloise whispered.

Marty nodded, mouth wide open. "Yeah."

Chapter 14

Marty loved Christmas. He always had. And he'd seen his share of Santas and Mrs. Clauses, but he'd never seen anyone who looked like this couple did. He had to do a double take and look around them to see if there was a Hollywood camera crew close by. Surely, this couple was straight from the set of blockbuster Christmas movie.

If he were to look up on the Internet what the jolly couple looked like, he was most certain the picture would be of this couple standing before him.

Santa wore the traditional red suit with white fur trim. The black belt was a thick leather and the buckle looked like it had been spit polished as though he was in the Air Force and preparing for a full inspection.

The black boots were shining, but the signs of the snow were evident on the bottom of the shoes. His red, furry hat fit him as though it had been made specifically for his head. For that matter, the entire costume looked bespoke. It had to have cost him a fortune.

And was that jacket that Mrs. Claus wore familiar? For some reason, he thought he'd seen that same exact red cape somewhere else. It probably was a Hollywood costume. Although, he didn't see any professional camera crews around. Maybe they were on the other side of the farm and this pair of actors were on break? He wasn't sure, but if they weren't actor, then they must be the real thing.

Mrs. Claus reached out and took one of Eloise's hands in her own. "Are you just in town for the day?" She let go of Eloise's hand and stepped back. "No, you are here for a longer visit, aren't you?" She noticed the cane, but didn't comment, or even linger on the assistive device.

When she turned her bright smile on Marty, her hands flew up to her face. "Oh, you're one of the new residents at the Crooked Arrow, aren't you?" Mrs. Claus turned to her husband. "Chris, I told you we needed to get out to Jerod's ranch and welcome the newcomers."

"I'm sorry, sweetheart. You know how busy I am this time of year." Santa chuckled and his stomach moved like a bowl full of Jell-O.

"How'd you know?" Marty whispered. He couldn't believe that this pair of actors knew who he was.

When he first arrived at the ranch, the other residents who'd been there since last Christmas had told him about the resident Santa and his wife, but Marty thought they were totally over-selling the couple.

Mrs. Claus tilted her head and took her husband's arm. "I'm sorry. But I don't know your name. You just have that military look to you. And Jerod told me he was expecting a few new residents."

Santa chuckled. "She's not a mind reader, but really close to it." He kissed her cheek and looked at his wife as though he was still in love with her today just as much as he had been on their wedding day.

Marty understood that look, it was one his dad gave his mom all the time.

"Oh, please." Mrs. Claus waved a hand in front of her face. Her cheeks tinged pink and Marty could tell she was embarrassed. "It doesn't hurt that I noticed you two getting out of Jerod's truck."

A hearty laugh rolled out of Marty, and he bent over. "Oh, don't make me laugh." When he stood back up, he winced and put a hand over his chest.

"Marty? Are you alright?" Eloise put her hand on his back when she moved in close to him.

"Oh, nutcracker. I'm so sorry. I heard about your accident." Mrs. Claus moved closer, put a hand out to touch him, then pulled it back. "How can I help?"

"Don't make me laugh. At least not a hearty laugh." Marty grimaced and stood up tall.

"I heard about your dramatic rescue." Santa nodded. "I really appreciate a true hero. There will be something extra special under the tree for you this year, my boy." He put a hand on Marty's shoulder and lightly squeezed. "I think you'll heal up nicely. Just take it easy for a few more days. Bruised ribs aren't anything to mess with."

"Dramatic rescue?" Eloise narrowed her eyes and looked between Marty and the man dressed in the Santa costume. "I thought you got in the way of a charging cow?"

"Santa! There you are." Jerod jogged up to the group. He looked between Marty and Eloise, then back to the Christmas couple. "I think Cove and Daniel are looking for you. They need to ask you something about your set-up." Jerod led Santa and Mrs. Claus away.

"Ah," Eloise held up a finger but didn't get a chance to stop Jerod, or Santa. She looked at Marty. "What did he mean?"

"It was nothing. You know how local gossip can be." Marty felt his cheeks warm, and he needed to get as far away from Santa as possible. "Man, their costumes were outrageous, weren't they?"

Eloise nodded. "Yes. I think Mrs. Claus's coat is from a movie."

Megan joined them. "Actually, the movie version was a copy of Jessica's cape. I think Angela Lansbury had been through town right before she played Mrs. Claus in the 1996 movie."

"Do we have that movie at the ranch? I think I want to watch it this weekend. I know I've seen it, but it's been forever." Marty put a hand on his chin and rubbed at the beard he was attempting to grow out.

"I think we can arrange that. Somehow, the ranch has collected a rather large assortment of Christmas movies over the past two years." Megan turned and began whistling the tune to Santa Claus is Coming To Town.

Marty shook his head and followed the camp counselor with Eloise in tow. "What is going on here?" He looked around at all of the hustle and bustle and noticed the small booths where they were selling all sorts of handicrafts. He noticed the booths had a sort of German Christmas market feel to them. "Are those booths crafted after gingerbread houses?"

Eloise looked to where Marty pointed and her perfectly manicured eyebrows rose to her hairline. "What happened? Did we transport to the North Pole?"

"Does it feel like they're trying too hard?" Marty asked. Then he barked a laugh when he saw the mini snow carnival. And then he regretted it the instant the pain shot through his ribs. In a pained voice, he asked, "are those kids pretending to be elves? Or are they really elves?"

"Let's go look and see." The child-like smile that crossed Eloise's face was contagious and Marty followed her.

The carnival had the typical rides, a zipper, a small Ferris wheel, a carousel, swing ride, bumper cars, and a tilt-a-whirl. But they were all Frosty themed rides. They also had a couple of food trucks with a Frosty The Snowman theme selling the typical fair foods of corn dogs, fried pickles, hamburgers, and one even sold grilled chicken and pineapple. That one caught Marty's attention and he decided that was where he wanted to go for lunch. But for the moment, he wanted to explore more.

"How do they manage all of this chaos?" Marty stopped in front of the barn and watched as a few of the ranch residents went inside followed by others he didn't recognize.

"I honestly don't know." Eloise sounded as though she was just as lost as Marty was. "What? I mean, why are they doing all of this?"

"Ah, the newbies." A tall man with black hair under a Stetson hat stood next to Marty rubbing his gloved hands and grinning. "I heard that you two were here."

"How do you know who we are? And who are you?" Marty asked.

The man held up his hands as if in surrender. "Sorry, I should have introduced myself. I'm Cody Makinaw, owner of this tree farm." He grinned and spread his hands out wide.

"Oh, yes. I should have recognized you from the pictures on your website." Eloise put her hand out and Cody shook it. "Nice to meet you, I'm Eloise."

"Nice to meet you, too. And this gentleman," Cody motioned to Marty, "must be Marty. I hear I'm not to allow you to do anything physical right now." He arched a brow as though he knew that Marty would try to get around the limitations the doctor put on him.

"Yes, it would seem you've heard of me." Hoping to change the subject, Marty looked to where a large group of people were standing. "What's going on over there?"

Cody looked to where Marty pointed. "We are going to hold the town's Thanksgiving dinner here. Didn't you hear?"

"Yes, I did. But do you mean to tell me that the entire town is here today?" Marty had seen a lot of people, but he thought that there might be some tour groups there or something like that. When Dana and Jerod had told him about the Thanksgiving dinner, he thought that they might get one hundred people. But if he wasn't mistaken, there were several hundred people on the ranch at that moment in time.

Cody looked around. "Well, not the entire town right now. But a lot are here to help set up. We should see upwards of a thousand people pass through here today."

Marty spluttered and slowly shook his head. "You have that many people in town?"

"No," Cody shook his head and chuckled. "We have a large part of the county that will show up, not just townsfolks. Plus, it's opening week-end here at the tree farm so there will be others coming through who aren't part of the French-town community."

Eloise had been watching and listening, but she finally joined the conversation. "Do you get a lot of people buying their trees this early in the season? Won't they die out before Christmas Day?"

"Nope. Cutting your own tree and taking it home the same day it's cut, will provide up to six weeks of a beautiful tree as long as you take proper care of it. We have a postcard that we give to everyone who wants it. You can put it on your fridge and be reminded to check water daily. As well as put in a preservative that helps the tree last longer." The tree farm owner seemed to be very knowledgeable about his trees. He went on to describe in detail which trees lasted longer than the others. Firs tended to last longer and lose fewer needles. Especially the Noble Fir.

"When does the ranch typically get it's tree?" Eloise asked.

Cody rubbed the back of his neck and stomped in place a few times, probably to keep his blood pumping and stay warmer, longer. "Usually, you will get your tree during the week after Thanksgiving. I think Jerod has already picked out the main tree but he won't cut it down until one day this week when he has the time."

"Why not get it this weekend since everyone is here?" Marty asked.

"Good question. Do you know how many hours the residents put in here as part of their volunteer service time?" Cody's question caught Marty off-guard.

When he first arrived, Jerod explained to Marty about the requirement for so many hours a week. All of the residents volunteered up to thirty hours a week for various organizations around town, which included the tree farm. But with the destruction of the town hall, Jerod explained that the majority of their time this month would be spent at the tree farm. However, since Marty's injury, he wasn't sure how he was going to meet those volunteer hours. "Yes, but I guess I just thought that it would be easier to just grab a tree and bring it home today when we were all done."

Cody winced. "It's not that simple. Today is one of the busiest days for your team. Especially since Dana and Marnie are also managing the try-outs for the Nativity. I think everyone is going to be too tired to deal with a tree tonight."

"Right. I hadn't considered that." Marty matched Cody's wince. If he hadn't been injured, he could have lent a strong hand with everything going on today. "What can I do to help?"

Cody looked at Eloise and his eyes narrowed.

Eloise raised a hand. "I'd like to help, too. I may not be a resident of the ranch, but I do enjoy helping whenever possible. Even if it's at a crazy Christmas tree farm." She chuckled to show she was joking.

Marty knew her joke wasn't too far off the mark. This place looked like a chaos jack in the box exploded all over the ranch.

Just then, Marty felt a presence next to him, but when he turned his head, he didn't see anyone. Then he looked down and grinned. He recognized the dog sitting at his heels. "Well, hello Razzle." He put a hand on the dog's head and rubbed his ears.

The dog leaned against Marty's leg and his eyes closed in pure pleasure at the attention.

"Marty, Eloise. Nice to see you both here." Nelly joined them and smiled at everyone.

Marty expected the dog trainer to call her dog back to her, or to even put a leash on the dog, but she didn't.

"Nelly, it's good to see you, too. Is Sam here?" Marty asked. He hoped the former Crooked Arrow Resident, now Nelly's husband, would join them and let Razzle hang out with them some more. Marty had missed having a dog around.

While Razzle was a service dog in training, he wasn't wearing his work vest at the moment. Which meant that Marty could play with the dog until they put his vest on. Then it would be hands off. He realized that having the dog at an event with so many people would really go a long way in training him, and the other humans, to learn when to touch a service dog, and when to stay clear.

When a service dog was working, he would have a vest on that denoted he was a service dog. Razzle had one that stated he was in training and asked people to stay clear. A service dog needed to be able to focus on his job when he wore the vest. Each service dog could have a different job while on the clock, so to speak. Some just worked as a companion. Which wasn't to say their job wasn't important, because even companion dogs had an important task.

People who needed a companion dog might not be able to handle crowds very well. So the dog acted as a go-between for the human. Others acted as an extended appendage, or extra eyes. And some even helped with ensuring a human took his or her medication in a timely manner.

Back at the VA hospital, Marty had seen a service dog notify everyone around that his human was in the process of having a seizure before it was evident to the human eye. Service dogs were trained not to bark, so when they did bark, it grabbed everyone's attention. Especially when humans noticed the dog barking and wearing a service dog vest. That visual indicator told all humans something was wrong.

A service dog was different from a military K-9 dog. But even dogs who served in the Armed Forces understood when they were working and when they could play. And since Marty had been imbedded with a K-9 squad, he had learned how to care for a dog and love him. Rocky had been more than a teammate; he had been family.

Marty's throat tightened at the memory of Rocky. He'd give anything to go back and change things, but he knew that wasn't possible. He was in Montana in that very moment thanks to Rocky's quick thinking. He'd forever be grateful to man's best friend.

Nelly looked around and smiled when she spotted her new husband. "Yup, he's getting us some hot coffee. And here he comes now."

"My ears are tingling. Were you talking about me?" Sam Marley, who wasn't nearly as tall as Marty, grinned and handed his wife a mug of steaming hot coffee. Then he kissed her cheek before addressing everyone else. "Sorry, did any of you want a coffee?"

"I'm good, thanks, Sam." Marty nodded.

Sam Marley had a prosthetic left arm and like Marty, he'd learned how to use it and didn't seem to have any issues getting used to his new reality. He could hold a cup of coffee and not squash it.

Marty didn't have a prosthetic hand, but he did have what he liked to call a bionic foot. It wasn't bionic, but it made him feel more manly thinking he might be like the Six Million Dollar Man.

Eloise also declined, as did Cody.

"So, tell me, Eloise. What do you think about the tree farm?" Nelly asked. They had met at Thanksgiving Dinner and the two women seemed to hit it off fine. Nelly had even invited Eloise to come and tour her own ranch and see how the dogs were trained.

Eloise raised both hands and sighed deeply. "This is nothing like what I've seen before. It's like Walt Disney and Santa got together to create a totally new kind of theme park." She grinned. "I think I'm going to like being here."

Not for the first time, Marty wondered about the change in Eloise. He hoped she was just worried about him when she first arrived and that was why she had come off so strong, and negative toward the ranch. But the last two days he'd seen a different side of her. A softer side. One that he hoped he could be friends with.

Even though she hadn't said how long she'd be in town for, Marty had to wonder. He didn't want to come off as being rude, or hoping she'd leave soon, but he did wonder what her process was. He knew she had to speak to several more residents and check out Nelly's ranch. Other than that, he really didn't know what else she had to do. It sounded to him as though she'd only be in town for a couple more days. From his perspective, she could leave on Wednesday if everyone spoke to her right away.

Was that what he wanted? It was what he hoped for when she first arrived. But after seeing the excitement on her face, and her willingness to help out at the tree farm, he was starting to soften to her presence. Maybe it wouldn't be so bad if she stayed for a while and helped him, or rather helped them, to enjoy this holiday season.

Cody's head popped up when he heard his name. "Sorry, my job never stops here. Gotta go. But Marty, if you want, I think my wife, Sadie, could use some help in the store." He put a finger up and narrowed one eye. "But don't you dare lift any trees. Jerod will have my hide if your injury gets worse."

Like Marty hadn't heard that warning before. If he was being honest, it was starting to get a little old. He wasn't a little boy who had no clue how to limit himself to candy, or in this case, physical labor. He knew he couldn't do more than walk around and talk. Lifting a shopping bag might not be bad, as long as it wasn't full of rocks. "I know, I know." He eyed Eloise. "This one here has reminded me several times to-day."

"Hey," Eloise raised her hands. "I'm here to ensure your safety. And don't pretend as though you haven't already tried to do things you shouldn't."

Nelly laughed. "Typical male. Especially a male veteran."

"Hey, I resemble that remark." Marty chuckled in good nature. He knew they were just worried that he'd hurt himself even more. Further injury was the last thing on his mind, but he also didn't want to sit around eating bonbons and watching soap operas. That just wasn't him. He was an active sort of guy and inactivity rubbed him raw.

"Okay, where is this store located? I think I can ring up sales, too." Eloise turned her head around trying to see where the main sales office might be located.

Everywhere Marty looked, he saw registers, but he had yet to see where someone might go to pay for a tree. "I take it you want us to help ring up tree sales?"

"Oh, it's much more than tree sales." Sam laughed and shared a smile with his new wife.

"Cody, you go on ahead. I'll show them where to go." Sam waved at Cody as he walked away.

Nelly tilted her head to the side and watched Razzle stick close to Marty. "Dogs like you, don't they?"

"Yeah, and I like them. We had a K-9 in our squad." Marty looked down and ran his hand down Razzle's back. The tawny boxer rubbed against Marty's leg, letting him know to keep going. The dog enjoyed his attention.

"Were you in the Army? I thought you were in the Air Force." Nelly asked.

Marty grinned. It wasn't the first time someone assumed he was Army when they found out he worked in a K-9 unit. The only Air Force jobs that had dogs were usually MP's. The Military Police used dogs to help patrol air bases and keep them safe. It was rare for an Air Force dog had another job. It happened, but most civilians didn't understand it.

"I was attached to an Army squad. The handler in my squad was Army. And the dog outranked us all." Marty chuckled. That was something he hadn't been prepared for when he joined the Army squad in Iraq. There were other soldiers in their platoon who outranked Rocky, but in their squad Rocky was the highest ranked non-commissioned officer (NCO).

Sam chuckled. "Let me guess, if I asked you what you did, you'd have to kill me after telling me?"

Marty put his hands on his hips. "Why would you say that?"

"The only Air Force that I ever came across embedded with Army were Military Intelligence." Sam winked.

"Actually, I was the guy with the phone." It wasn't all he did, but telling people he was the radio operator generally shut them up. Anyone who had seen a war movie knew what he was talking about. Those guys never did anything too exciting, except for carrying around heavy equipment. What he did was a little bit more, but no one needed to know that.

"Hmm, a K-9 unit, an Air Force radio operator, and in Iraq. Thank you." Sam put a hand on Marty's shoulder and moved them all in the direction of the tree store.

Marty noticed how Eloise furrowed her brows and watched Sam. Was she just as confused as Marty was?

Chapter 15

Eloise had to shake her head. These veterans were talking in code and she had no clue how to decipher it. But, if she wasn't mistaken, Marty didn't really understand what Sam was saying, either.

Instead of worrying about the secret conversation, Eloise looked at the sights as they made their way to the main store. "Wow. That's a large building. Is that the house? Or the shop?"

The building she was gawking at looked more like a small house. If she wasn't mistaken, it was about fifteen hundred square feet. People were milling about outside as well as in the door.

It was built in the log cabin style and had a chimney with billowing smoke so she knew the inside would be warm. Which was nice since her toes were starting to go numb from the cold. As were her fingers. She'd already lost all feeling in her nose and cheeks. The only reason she could still feel her lips was because she'd covered her mouth with her wool scarf when they began walking this way.

She was a long way from the warmth of Texas. Even in the winter Texas was balmy compared to the Middle-Of-Nowhere, Montana.

Their little group stopped close to the wooden porch. On it were a couple of display cases showing the different trinkets and ornaments they must sell inside. It was a combination of handicrafts and store made Christmas items, like the cowboy Santa Claus who would go perfectly on a side table back at the Crooked Arrow.

Nelly put her arm out like a tour guide. "Welcome to the Makinaw Christmas Tree Farm. This building was finished earlier this year and is the Christmas store, not the house. That," she pointed behind them to a large ranch style rambler, "is the home of the Makinaw family."

Eloise's mouth opened like a fish. How did Nelly know what she was thinking? But she followed the woman's arm and noticed the house. While it wasn't something she'd seen on Dallas, there weren't any oil tycoons here. It was large enough to house a family on a ranch, or in this case, a Christmas tree farm. At any rate, it was much larger than her apartment back in

Houston. But it did look to be close in size to her family home.

The Sullivans didn't have a ranch, or a farm, but they did have a nice home on over half an acre that was almost three-thousand square feet. Her mom loved to entertain, and her father had his business associates over for a monthly dinner. When Eloise was young, they lived outside of Houston city limits. Today? The house had been swallowed up by the urban sprawl of the new Houston city limits. There was even a giant strip mall only five miles from her parents' house that had a twenty-screen cinema, several large shops, in addition to way too many smaller shops. One could spend all day walking through the area and get in more than ten thousand steps.

Before her injury, Eloise did enjoy spending a Saturday here or there walking all of the shops in the outside mall. Now? She didn't do anywhere near that amount in one walk. Shoot, Eloise was lucky to get ten thousand steps in one day. A normal day for her back home was just under eight thousand. Using a cane to walk a track wasn't exactly fun, or easy. And forget about using a treadmill, canes and electronic walking tracks just didn't mix. Although, she did find that using a bike wasn't bad. So she had one in her little apartment, instead of going to a gym.

Eloise looked off to the side and saw a sign showing the beginning of the Christmas trees. None of them were cut and just waiting for people to pick out, like what she remembered from her childhood. Although, they didn't go to a tree farm, they went to the local hardware store and picked out a tree from a roped off area in the parking lot. The hardware store trucked in trees from Northern Louisiana and Arkansas.

But this year was going to be different. While she doubted she would still be in Montana come Christmas Day, Eloise did think she'd be there for at least another week. Which would give her a chance to experience a true country Christmas season. Maybe, if she didn't have another assignment, she could stay there and write up her report on site while she enjoyed the season. That was, if Jerod didn't mind her using one of the precious few bedrooms he had available.

No one had said anything yet about more residents joining them before Christmas, but from what she'd seen, Eloise believed that if someone was ready to leave a VA hospital, this would be a much better place to be for the season. Unless, of course, they had family who could care for them until the new year.

"What do you say we go and check out the trees?" Marty suggested. He didn't seem to be keen on going inside of the store.

Eloise figured it was because of the chaos and mayhem that she saw there. If it were her choice, she'd be over with the trees, too. But the warmth of the store was calling to her, if not for all of the kids and was that a crying baby? She shivered. It wasn't that she hated babies, she just didn't have much experience with them. Who wanted to trust their precious baby to a woman who needed one hand for her cane? She had seen a baby papoose contraption once that seemed like a great way for her to carry around a baby, if she ever got married and had a family.

She shook her head. What was she thinking about that for? "Yes, I'd love to check out the trees. I've never been to a real Christmas Tree farm before. What types of trees do they grow here?" Eloise directed her question to Nelly.

"Well, I'm no expert in trees, but I think they have more than five different types. Sam would know better than me. He's actually helped out here for the past two years. I think he misses it." Nelly looked around and once she found what she was looking for, began to smile. "Sam, over here." She waved the man toward her.

Sam kissed his wife's cheek and put an arm around her waist. "Hi, miss me already?"

Nelly chuckled. "Actually, we had a question about the trees." She pointed to Marty and Eloise. "These two wanted to know more about the farm and what types of trees are grown here."

Sam put a hand to his heart. "You mean you didn't miss me?" The comical expression of pain on his face had Eloise chuckling.

She liked Sam. Not in a romantic way, but more in the way of a cool kind of guy. This was only her second time talking to him, but he seemed as though he was pretty well adjusted. Although, she did notice his dog at his side.

Eloise noticed Nelly's cheeks turn a light shade of pink. Then she leaned in closer to her husband. "I'll show you just how much I missed you, later."

Sam cleared his throat and the saucy look on his face was replaced with a look of a man who wanted to get away. His eyes darted in the direction of the parking lot and it appeared as though he was about to turn away. But Nelly stopped him. "Not now. We have work to do." She winked.

"Ah, you're killing me, woman." Sam kissed his wife's cheek again and then turned to see Marty and Eloise who both had looked away.

Eloise was checking out the dog sitting at attention next to Sam. It was a rust colored boxer with a golden honey chest. He was sitting there not moving, but it seemed to Eloise that he just rolled his eyes heavenward at Sam's quips. Could dogs do that, she wondered.

"This is Rogue, did you get a chance to meet him properly the other night?" Sam patted the dog's head.

"I did." Eloise smiled and waved at the dog. She knew better than to try and pet him while he had on his service dog vest.

Sam watched her for a moment, then grinned. "Yes, he's on duty right now. But when you come by the ranch, I'll be sure to take his vest off if you want to play with him. He loves playing with this rope we have that's got a ball at the end of it. We've gone through like three of them already, he can't ever get enough of that toy."

Nelly grinned. "All of our dogs seem to have their favorite toys or activities. It's really cute all of the different personalities they have."

"I knew a K-9 who loved to play tug-of-war with a knotted length of rope." Marty looked off into the distance and Eloise wondered if he was thinking back to the dog he worked with in Iraq.

"No balls in the field, right?" Sam, who must have known something about Marty's experience, asked.

The question must have brough Marty back to the present because his nose flared and he sucked in a deep breath. Then he nodded. "Yup."

"Well, I don't know what your plans are this week, but we have more dogs than we can work between the two of us." Nelly paused, then continued. "How would you like to come by the ranch and help us out a little bit?"

Marty shook his head. "Oh, I wasn't a handler. I don't know how to train dogs."

Nelly lifted a hand to stop him. "I don't need another trainer, just someone who likes dogs and can help us to exercise them and maybe do the feeding while Sam and I work on training."

Marty's nose scrunched. "I don't have to muck out stalls, do I?"

Sam's hearty laugh caused all around to smile. "I once asked that same question. And no, if you don't want to clean up after the dogs, you don't have to. Any help you can give would be much appreciated."

"Why do you have more dogs than you can handle?" Eloise tilted her head to one side and looked at Nelly.

"Long story short, another trainer had to quit all of a sudden and his dogs needed homes. I took two of them. You've met Razzle, he's one. And he has a friend, Tyco, who is also just about ready to be paired with a veteran." Nelly pointed to Dixon. "I think Tyco might have chosen him. But I'm not certain, yet.

Dixon lifted an arm and waved. He walked over and wiped a few droplets of sweat off his forehead. "Man, am I glad to see you. This place is mobbed. Marty, can you help me with the trees?"

Marty perked up at the request for help. "Sure, what do you need?"

Eloise opened her mouth to speak, but thought better of it and closed her lips, tightly.

"I know you can't do anything laborious, but if you can help people to find a tree and then tag it, I can work with the guys to help cut or carry the trees. Basically, you'll tag the tree and give the customer the other part of the ticket that they'll take into the store so they can pay for it." Dixon's eyes looked so hopeful, Eloise knew that Marty wouldn't say no.

Stars and stripes, Eloise wanted to help the poor guy out. She knew he didn't do well with large crowds and was very impressed that he still worked at the tree lot. Especially after seeing all of the crowds here and having to deal with the noise. She wasn't suffering from PTSD, but she wasn't too happy with it all, either.

Dixon Carter had lost a leg in Iraq and he now had a prosthetic. Like Marty, he adjusted to his new gait and didn't seem to have any issues with the new leg. His issues all stemmed from the explosion itself. The soldier suffered from severe PTSD and he had a rough time around crowds. If anyone needed a service dog, it was Dixon.

Eloise didn't understand why he hadn't been assigned one yet, but that wasn't what she was here for. She always needed to remind herself to stay focused on the job at hand. She was here to evaluate the Crooked Arrow Ranch, not Nelly's dog service. Although, she was going to get the full tour and try to spend a day or two working with the dogs, just so she had a better understanding of service dogs.

She hadn't been contracted to evaluate the service dog trainer and she needed to keep that in mind. Maybe one day she would, but not today.

"Sure, I'd love to help however I can. But..." Marty ran a hand over his mouth and looked out toward the closest grove of trees. "I don't know anything about Christmas trees. Like what is that kind there?" He pointed a grouping of trees that were shaped like the traditional tree one might see on a Christmas card.

Dixon grinned. "I'm glad you asked." He pulled a brochure out of his back pocket and handed it to Marty. "This is a nice overview of the trees Cody sells here. And a map that shows which tree is grown where."

"Really?" The boyish grin on Marty's face lit up his eyes before he looked down at the full-color brochure he held. He scanned the cover and nodded. "Yeah, I've seen a lot of the Douglas Fir tree in my day. But they aren't my favorite."

"I'm with you, bro." Dixon clapped Marty on his shoulder. "Keep looking the brochure over. Feel free to walk amongst the trees and when you're ready, come back to the Christmas Store and let Sadie know you're ready to start helping. She'll give you a tree farm apron to wear along with the ticket book."

"Apron?" Marty's eyes narrowed and he grimaced. "No one said anything about wearing a girly apron."

Dixon chuckled. "No, man. It's not girly. Think hardware store or barbecue grill master. Sadie will want you to wear a santa hat, but it's actually cool." He pointed to the one he wore.

Eloise checked Dixon out and frowned. "Where's your apron?"

"I'm heading inside to get my apron and a ticket book now. I'll let Sadie know to expect you soon." Dixon waved and walked away.

"Do you mind if Razzle and I tag along for a little bit?" Nelly asked Marty.

Marty shrugged, unsure why she'd want to hang out with him. "Are you looking for a tree for your ranch?"

"No, we've already picked ours out and will get it on Monday, when they aren't too busy." Nelly pointed to Razzle. "I was hoping to see how this guy here acted in the trees and with kids running around and coming out of nowhere. I want to make sure he doesn't spook easily."

Eloise smiled and thought that was a great idea, but she kept quiet. It was Marty's choice, not hers.

"Sure, I guess." Marty reached out to pat Razzle on his head, but pulled back at the last second when he remembered the dog was on duty. "Sorry about that."

"No problem. Once Razzle is done, I'll take his vest off and you play with him if you want." Nelly let some slack out from the dog leash and signaled for Razzle to walk next to her.

"Sam, you going to join us?" Nelly turned around when Sam didn't follow.

"I'm going to see if Jerod needs help with set up in the barn." He waved to everyone and headed in the opposite direction.

"I wish I was allowed to help with barn setup. I heard they needed a lot of help for the Thanksgiving dinner tonight." Marty ran a hand along the back of his neck and looked longingly in the direction of the barn.

Most of the strong men had gone that way to help. Eloise didn't know Marty well yet, but she knew enough of his character to realize that he wasn't happy to be sidelined when the place needed more strong backs to help with setup. She would have helped herself if she wasn't shadowing Marty that day. It was times like these that she wished she didn't need her cane.

Chapter 16

"These are the Noble Firs, right?" Eloise pointed to a line of very tall trees that had thick branches of fir needles and exuded an aura of superiority. She'd always loved the Noble Firs since they didn't loose too many needles and were perfect for holding heavier ornaments.

Marty looked at the trees, then down at his handy, dandy, guide. "Yup, this is the Noble Fir tree. And from the tag this row looks to be all over eight feet tall. Nice size." He walked down the row and stopped in front of a tree that was marked at being over nine feet tall.

He took one of his gloves off and felt the needles on one branch. "This feels as though it's had plenty of water. While the needle is soft and pliable, it's not loose." He ran his hand along the branch and not one single needle fell to the ground.

Nelly was two trees away from them and she grinned when she noticed how Razzle was watching Marty. The dog was obedient, and he stayed within arms reach of Nelly, but he was as close to Marty as he could get without disobeying her order to heel.

Marty had noticed how Razzle stuck as close to him as possible. The dog must have sensed his love of dogs in general. There was no way the dog would know that he had worked with K-9's in the military. He didn't believe that dogs were that smart. They were smart, but understanding all of the discussions that went around him? Marty knew that wasn't possible.

But a dog's intuition was something that a smart human never underestimated. He remembered several times when his unit was saved because Rocky kept them from going a certain way. One time, there was even a trip wire that they missed thanks to Rocky's insistence that they don't go down a certain alley. Staff Sergeant Anderson, nicknamed Andy, wanted to inspect the alley when Rocky was adamant about not going that way.

Once Andy and Rocky had investigated, they found the trip wire that was hooked up to an IED. Had they gone that way and tripped the wire, they would have all blown up to pieces. And that was only one of the many times that Rocky had saved their lives. The Army was smart to assign K-9's to units like his. It was too bad that not all units could have one. Marty knew that a lot more lives would be saved if there were more dogs trained to be soldiers.

"I wonder what tree the ranch is going to get." Eloise turned to look at Nelly. "Do you know what they usually get?"

Nelly grinned and shook her head. "Nope. I can't say."

Eloise narrowed her eyes and tilted her head down. "You can't say? Or don't know?"

Nelly shrugged and turned to keep walking. She didn't use any voice commands, but one little tug on the leash and Razzle was joining her.

If Marty wasn't mistaken, the dog gave him a knowing grin. That, combined with Nelly's reaction, told him she knew. And the tree was probably spectacular. He couldn't help but smile in anticipation of what was to come.

Once they had seen the different types of trees offered on the farm, Marty led the group back to the store and introduced himself to Sadie Makinaw. "Hi, I'm Marty Winters. And this is Eloise Sullivan." He motioned to the woman on his right. "Dixon told us to see you when we were ready to help out in the tree farm."

"Of course. Welcome to the farm, and thank you for your service. Not only to us, but to our country." Sadie shook hands with both of the newcomers. "Eloise, how are you finding it here in Montana? Different from Texas I'd bet."

Eloise's eyes widened and her head nodded up and down. "Oh, yes. While we have lots of ranches and farms in Texas, it's all so very different from here. We don't have nearly as much green as you do. Or the level of snow."

"I bet. Are you keeping warm? If it's too cold outside for you, you're welcome to come inside and warm up." Sadie led them to a small backroom that had a sign on the door labeled, *Employees Only*.

"Thank you, but I should be fine. I might need to come in once in a while and warm my hands but that should be about it." Eloise looked longingly over her shoulder at the wood stove in the corner, where a couple of chairs held some elderly gentleman who were drinking something hot while they chatted.

Sadie looked at where Eloise was faced and chuckled. "Yes, that's the spot where quite a few of the men come in and sit a spell while their wives and daughters shop. I'm thinking we might want to expand the area this summer so that more men can sit down and give the women more time to browse." She waggled her brows.

"You mean so that the ladies can take their time spending more money here?" Marty arched a brow but couldn't hide his smile. He didn't blame Sadie for wanting to keep people here longer, shopping and spending money. It was a business, after all.

"You do have a lot to see here. Not just inside this shop. There are all of those handicraft booths, too. I'm not a big shopper, but I know that if I end up spending time here on the farm, I'll be spending more than I planned." Eloise's eyes twinkled and she smiled from ear to ear.

Marty's heart practically stopped when she turned her million-watt smile on him. He didn't know what was happening, but found he was nodding and agreeing with whatever she said. Once Eloise had turned her attention back to Sadie, he breathed a sigh of relief and chided himself. He couldn't have his head turned by her, or anyone else. Not now. This wasn't a vacation; he was in Frenchtown to work.

Well, maybe not exactly work, but he did have an agenda. One that most certainly did not include flirting with a pretty lady or losing his heart.

"Here ya go." Sadie handed them both red aprons with the tree farm name and logo printed on them.

"Thanks. Now, how does the ticketing work?" Marty did his best to focus on the task at hand and shove aside the strange desire he had to make Eloise smile like she had, again. Even though her smile made him feel as though he was soaring through the clouds, he couldn't think about that. He did have an actual job to do right then and there, and that was to sell more Christmas trees.

After Sadie had explained how the ticketing worked, and what their part in it all would be, Marty and Eloise headed back out to the trees. They were to roam around and be available should anyone have questions, or a need to buy a tree. When customers came to the tree farm side of the property, they were given a ticket and told what to do, but not everyone knew they needed a ticket in order to claim a tree.

It was up to Marty and Eloise to either help a customer tag their tree, or to help them figure out the process and give them a ticket if they didn't already have one.

"So, do you understand how this all works?" Eloise asked Marty when they were walking through a grove of Spruce trees.

Marty put a gloved hand out and ran it along the lights that decorated the tree. "Yup. We help the customer to tag the tree they want, and then they go inside the shop and pay. Once their tree is paid for, they can chop it down, or get help from one of the ranch hands who will also wrap it in that red netting. Once that's done, then they will carry the tree to the customer's car or truck and help them to secure it for the drive home."

Eloise smiled and headed out of the Spruce tree section and began looking for the Balsam Fir section. "I've only seen this type of tree on TV, or as a fake tree in someone's living room." She giggled and picked up her pace when she noticed the dark green conical shaped tree not too far from where she was. "Come on, slow poke."

Marty grinned and picked up his pace. He began to chuckle at their lighthearted banter but winced when he felt the pain in his chest. It wasn't as bad as it had been, but it still hurt enough that he didn't want to laugh. Not yet, at any rate. "Slow down, we have time. You don't want to run over the kids, do you?"

Her laughter floated away on the wind and Marty couldn't stop grinning. He was having fun. And he couldn't remember the last time he had had this much fun. It wasn't like they had an amusement park, or even a tree farm, in the Middle East. And he'd been back and forth between a US base and the various bases in or near Iraq for too many years to count. This was exactly what he needed to heal and Marty was going to let himself enjoy this time.

"It's amazing what helping others can do for one's own mental health." Marty stated when he caught up with Eloise.

"I know what you mean. A part of me feels like I'm shirking my duty and shouldn't be having fun. But then I remind myself that I'm here doing exactly what I was asked to do. So why not let myself enjoy it?" Eloise shrugged and leaned in to smell the pine needles on the eight-foot Balsam Fir in front of her.

If Eloise wasn't careful, she might decide she liked Christmas again.

Chapter 17

It took a week, but Marty was finally feeling good enough to chuckle without more than just a twinge of pain. It was more uncomfortable than painful. But it was worth it to spend the week with Eloise. Marty couldn't believe how wonderful she had turned out to be.

"Marty, did you want to go to Nelly's ranch first, then over to the tree farm?" Eloise had found that she enjoyed playing with the dogs in the morning, before heading out to help at the tree farm almost every day since last Saturday.

Marty found he enjoyed it as well. Not since he was in Iraq did he have a chance to play with dogs. "Sure, sounds good to me."

A small smile played at the edges of Eloise's mouth before she finished the coffee in her mug. Today, she was drinking out of a mug that was red and in white letters was printed: *Know coffee, Know peace. No coffee...wait, that's impossible.* It was split up and one part was on one side of the mug and the other was on the backside.

Marty loved the eclectic collection of coffee mugs. Nothing matched. It seemed as though Dana and Jerod had collected them from thrift stores, garage sales, or item close-out deals since there were only one of each. Some of the residents had their favorite mugs and drank out of the same one every day, but he and Eloise seemed to prefer grabbing whatever was handy, and not already spoken for. He quickly finished his breakfast and put his dishes in the dishwasher. "Thank you, Dana. As always, a fantastic breakfast."

Dana turned her head and smiled at the two heading out of the kitchen. "It was my pleasure." She was pulling ingredients out of the fridge and preparing a roast to go in the slow cooker. "Dinner will be ready by five, if you come home in time."

Marty waved a hand and followed Eloise out of the kitchen. "I love her cooking. I say we plan to come back in time for dinner tonight. I think my waistline can't handle much more fair food."

Eloise lightly chuckled and nodded her agreement. "If we don't stop eating all of that junk food, I'm going to need a new wardrobe soon." She patted her belly and frowned.

The two of them settled in the truck they'd been using since they didn't drive over to the tree farm with Jerod every day. Their routine kept them out longer than the majority of the ranch, but Marty found he enjoyed being helpful, and active. Sitting around watching TV never helped him, unless it was a celebrity bake off show. Those, he could watch all day long. "Say, did you catch last night's episode of Christmas Bake Off?"

"What?" Eloise scrunched her pert little nose and glanced at Marty before turning into Nelly's ranch.

"You know, the one with all of the celebrities? They have a Christmas version and they did all sorts of cool Christmas desserts. They even had a modified version of a yule log that looked like it might almost be doable, besides being delicious. It actually won the night." Marty wasn't much of a chef, but he had spent some time with his mom growing up and baking during Christmas. One year, they tried making a yule log together and it was an absolute mess. They never tried again.

Eloise raised a hand to her mouth, probably to stifle a laugh. "Are you kidding me? Do you bake? Really?"

"Ah, not often. In fact, I haven't baked a single dessert since my first tour in Iraq. But as a kid I usually did with my mom. Although, I do enjoy watching that celebrity chef yell at the other celebrities. It's a riot when a celebrity who's noted for his bad attitude ends up in a corner trying to hide from Chef Black.

"Oh, I do like to watch Dane Black. Especially when one of my favorite actors is on his show. I love how they bring on people who aren't famous for cooking, but have them compete in the kitchen. It's hilarious when a Hollywood bad guy breaks down crying, or shaking, after being berated by Chef Black." Eloise turned the steering wheel and angled the truck so they were parked on the side of the house closest to Nelly's barn.

"Yeah, I've always wondered if the cocky celebrities that go on that show change afterwards. It would be interesting to interview their staff two months later, or something like that." It was something Marty had thought a lot about lately. Would putting a snot-nosed celebrity in their place on TV help them to be nicer? He wasn't sure, but it was something to think about. Mostly, he just liked getting baking and cooking ideas. Sadly, they were ideas he never used.

After closing the truck and walking around the side to join Marty, Eloise looked at him.

"I haven't seen the Christmas episode, I was working on my report last night. But I think I want to see that episode. I've never attempted a yule log, they take so long to make and too many ingredients for me."

"I hear ya. But the recipe from last night used a box cake for the base. It was an angel food cake, I think." Marty rubbed his chin and thought back to the list of ingredients from the show. "I think I'll go online tonight and see if I can find the recipe. Then ask Dana if I can try making it."

Eloise stopped in her tracks. "You want to try making a yule log? Here, at the Crooked Arrow Ranch?"

After a scratch of his ear, Marty turned thoughtful eyes on Eloise. "Well, yeah. Why not? Tis' the season and all that. Want to join me?" He grinned.

"Ah...maybe? I need to speak with Jerod and see how much longer he's willing to allow me to stay. I'm almost done with my report. After that, he has no reason to extend his hospitality." Eloise hadn't really named a date to leave, not yet. She never liked to commit to leaving until she had all of the information she needed.

However, she rarely typed up her report on-site. Usually, she spent about a week with the company or group, and gathered up information, took pictures, interviewed people, ect. Then she took all of her data home and compiled it there before sending her official report on to the government organization who tapped her to do the investigation to begin with.

"I think that if you keep helping out at the tree farm and here at Nelly's ranch, I don't see why Jerod wouldn't want you to stay. We have several rooms open, so it's not like you're taking up a spot that's needed." Marty didn't want to see Eloise leave, not yet. She was fun. But more importantly, he'd noticed a marked change in her since she arrived. It seemed she could have used a place like the Crooked Arrow after her injury to help her heal from the emotional scars of everything.

He just might have to speak with Jerod about letting Eloise stay longer. It might be a good case study for helping those years after their injury.

"Well, I'd love to keep helping. That's not the problem." Eloise bit her lower lip and then changed the subject. "So, five dollars says that Razzle ignores me until he's had your full attention for a few minutes." She grinned and began walking toward the barn again.

"I think you're jealous. You like Razzle but hate that he prefers me to you." Marty ducked away from Eloise's hand. Sometimes, she lightly slapped his arm when he teased her. It never hurt, but he loved to outrun her, and outwit her. The smoldering look she gave him whenever he did it warmed his chest in a way that he still couldn't understand. But he wanted to learn what it all meant.

Nelly walked in on Eloise giving Marty a five-dollar bill. "What's going on?"

As Marty pocketed the bill, he chuckled. "Eloise lost a bet with me."

"You cheated. Razzle took one look at you and then he came to say hello to me. What did you do?" Eloise put her hands on her hips and glared at the man.

With eyes wide with innocence, Marty put a hand on his chest. "Who me? I didn't cheat. Razzle came up to you first. Just proves you don't know dogs as well as you think you do." He winked and then leaned down to give the dog a good scratch. "Such a good boy."

Razzle rubbed up against Marty's leg and let the man scratch between his ears and all down the back of his head and neck. When Marty stopped, the dog gave him such a sad look, that Marty had to rub Razzle's back.

"He really seems to have taken to you, Marty. I haven't seen him like anyone as much as you. He really didn't come to you first?" Nelly tilted her head and put her fist under her chin as she watched the man and dog interact.

Marty stood up with a sheepish look on his face. He rubbed his chin and then pulled the money out of his pocket he'd accepted from Eloise. "Actually, he would have come to me first if I hadn't motioned for him to see Eloise first." He handed the five-dollar bill back to Eloise.

With a shake of her head and a chuckle, Eloise took the money back. "I knew you'd done something to win. I told you he liked you best." Once she'd put the money back in her purse, she leaned down and called Razzle over to her. "Come here, boy."

Razzle looked to Marty first, then when the man nodded his head, the dog walked over to Eloise. She still had her gloves off, so she ran her hands down the dog's head and back. "You're such a good boy, aren't you? Why do you like Marty so much? Huh?" She grinned but didn't look at Marty, just kept her attention on the dog.

Nelly chuckled. "You two make a great pair."

Marty's face heated and he turned away from Razzle and Eloise. Sure, he liked Eloise, but them as a pair? He wasn't into long distance relationships. So anything more than friendship had never crossed his mind, had it? He didn't think it had.

Nelly watched his face turn pink and she laughed. "I meant you and Razzle. Have you ever considered having a service dog?"

"Who? Me?" Marty shook his head. "I don't need a service dog. I can walk just fine."

Razzle stood beside Marty and looked from his trainer to the man he had chosen.

Nelly grinned. "Why do you think mobility is the only reason a veteran would qualify for a service dog?"

Marty shrugged. "I guess I don't know much about what qualifies a person. I can get around fine. I'm not like Sam or Tony. And I don't have MS like Dakota. Why would I need a dog to help me see, or move around?"

"Service dogs help in a variety of ways. They aren't just extra appendages or eyes. They also help when someone is experiencing issues with PTSD, and some are even smart enough to tell the human if they missed their medication that day." Nelly took a step back and put a thumb in the front pocket of her jeans.

"How do you know I suffer from PTSD?" Marty looked from Nelly to Eloise. He knew that Eloise had seen him have one episode, but he'd never told Nelly about his issues, other than the fact that he had a prosthetic foot. Anyone who watched him walk knew something was wrong, and he didn't care if people knew about his not-so bionic foot. He had received a purple heart for it, and that is public knowledge.

"I didn't know exactly. But you are on the list as someone who has been pre-qualified. Megan gives me a list of the residents who are already pre-qualified by the VA to receive a service dog. Your name was on it. Is that ok?" Nelly sucked in her lower lip and she blinked a couple of times while she waited for Marty to answer.

Eloise didn't say a thing. She stood there watching and waiting to see what might happen.

Marty wasn't sure how comfortable he was with the knowledge Nelly had. It didn't sound like she knew exactly what he was suffering from, but the fact that she had a list of qualified veterans didn't sit well with him. He wasn't sure why, though. It wasn't as though Nelly had a list of all the issues each of the residents were dealing with, it was just a list of names the VA had said they would approve to have a service dog, wasn't it? "That list, it doesn't state what's wrong with us, does it?"

She shook her head. "No, it doesn't say why you qualify. I don't need to know that until we go to pair you with a dog. I have to ensure that the dog is trained to handle whatever your needs are. If you need a right hand, then the dog needs to be one that can stick to your right-hand side and help where needed. If you need to take a certain medication, and it's imperative, then I need to know what it is and give the dog extra training for the taste of the medication on your skin."

"And if I have a different issue? One that's not easy to see?" While Marty had basically told her he had PTSD, he wasn't ready to say it out loud to a woman he didn't know very well yet.

Nelly rubbed the side of her neck and looked again at Razzle. "I think Razzle has already chosen you. So, no matter what you need help with, I think he'll be up for the needed final training." She tilted her head. "Do you want to tell me what it might be?"

His nostrils flared. He hated talking about his PTSD issues, and hated to discuss his night terrors even more. Marty's head tilted and then he looked down at Razzle when the dog began to whine. Immediately, the stress and discomfort he felt fled and he leaned down to scratch the dog's head. "Hey there, Razzle. It's alright. I'm not upset."

The dog nuzzled his head under Marty's chin, causing Marty to grin from ear to ear. "It's amazing how a dog can help change one's attitude right away. Isn't it?"

"Yes, it is," Nelly agreed. "I do need to know your situation so I can train Razzle, if you want to partner with him. It is a true partnership so he needs to understand what you need help with. You don't have to say anything now." She looked toward Eloise and winced. "But, we do need to set up an appointment for us to at least discuss your needs."

Marty's shoulders slumped and he sighed. "We can set up a meeting. I'm still not sure I'm convinced I need a dog. I'm of the belief that only those in the most dire of circumstances should accept a service dog. There are others out there who need one more than I do."

"Like I said, there are many reasons a person could be paired with a service dog. And Razzle seems to have already chosen you. If you didn't even have to say anything, you just pointed to Eloise and he understood your command, then he's already begun bonding with you. It's not the human who chooses the dog, it's the dog who chooses the human." Nelly had told Marty this before, but she repeated it anyways.

"Kinda like a cat." Eloise chuckled and put a hand over her mouth when Razzle turned his face to glare at her.

"Whoa, that seems to be fighting words." Marty pointed out the look on Razzle's face. "If I'm not mistaken, I think he just about showed you his teeth." He turned to Nelly. "Does Razzle have an issue with cats? We have barn cats at the ranch."

Nelly laughed out loud.

Razzle barked once and nodded his head.

Marty looked at the dog, then grinned when he realized what Razzle was doing. "Is he laughing at my question?"

"I think so." Nelly patted Razzle's head. "Good boy. He actually does well with cats. We have a barn cat here who seems to like Razzle. And his paperwork stated that he was cat friendly. Do you have a cat back home?"

"No, I don't." Marty shook his head. "This dog is smart, isn't he?"

Razzle bounced up and down and woofed twice in what Marty took to be an agreement.

"Wow, I've heard that dogs were really smart, but it seems to me as though Razzle completely understands our conversation." The wide eyes on Eloise's face only emphasized her astonishment.

Nelly agreed. "Let's head inside, with Razzle, and we can fill out the paperwork." Nelly motioned for Sam, who was only a few paces away, to join them. "Sam, why don't you show Eloise what you need help with today. I'll take Marty inside to do some paperwork so I can get a better idea of what he needs."

Marty's hands went up. "Whoa, hold on. I didn't agree to partner with Razzle. I'm still not convinced I need a service dog." He scratched his head wondering how things got so out of control.

"Alright, then how about you and I talk about why you're at the Crooked Arrow and I can let you know if a service dog would be beneficial for you." Nelly motioned for Marty to follow her.

"Come on, Eloise. Let's go have some fun playing with the dogs. One of them has this tennis ball on a long string that bounces from the ceiling. He loves to jump up and try to grab it. It's fun to watch a dog jump." Sam chuckled and led Eloise away.

Marty watched them walk away and he noted the dog that walked beside Sam without a leash, or any commands to do so. "Rogue and Sam seem to have a symbiotic relationship. Does the dog always just stick to Sam's side?"

Nelly had a soft look on her face as she watched her husband walk away. "Yeah, the two of them really are partners. Rogue is perfect for him. They aren't joined at the hip twenty-four-seven, but when Sam needs Rogue, the dog just knows it and shows up."

"Is that how all service dogs are?" While Marty had spent time with a K-9 in Iraq, Rocky wasn't tied to Anderson's hip. In fact, when they were back at base, the dog had his own life. He was always close to John, but the dog was able to roam around and hang out with the other dogs on base.

"Pretty much, if they're trained right and the dog chose the human. It's really important that the dog is as invested as the human. Otherwise, the dog may not be able to help as much as a dog that was properly paired with a human. Does that make sense?" Nelly held open the small door on the side of the barn, not the main door, but the one that led to the office she kept in the barn for just such conversations.

"I think so," Marty answered. "But that doesn't mean that I want a service dog."

Nelly sat behind her desk and motioned for Marty to sit in the visitor's chair opposite her. The office was small, but it was just the right size for one office desk, an executive chair, and two visitor chairs. There was also one tall four-drawer filing cabinet in the corner next to a printer stand that held a printer and several reams of paper. "Please, take a seat. Would you like some coffee or tea?"

Marty sat down in the chair that had been covered with a dark patterned brocade. There were horses and wagon wheels placed in various places on the material. The chair was stuffed with just the right amount of filling. "Thank you, but I'm good. So, what do you need from me?"

"Well, if you're comfortable telling me about what has brought you to the Crooked Arrow, I can let you know if you'd make a good match with Razzle, or not." Nelly picked up her notepad and pen and waited for Marty to begin.

Chapter 18

Marty felt as though he was sitting across from a therapist. She was telling him to open up to her and share his deepest, darkest, secrets. That was something he wasn't sure he was ready to do. But he supposed he should say something.

"Don't worry, whatever you share with me is kept in the strictest of confidence. And I don't need much in the way of details. I just need to confirm that you are struggling with PTSD, or if it's something else." The way Nelly looked at Marty was though she was a counselor who oozed compassion.

It wasn't pity, or anything else. Marty had seen plenty of emotions in the past two years, he knew what they meant when directed at him. No, this was most definitely compassion mixed with something else. He couldn't be sure, but he got the impression that she also felt hope when looking at him. Marty silently wondered if Nelly might understand what he was going through.

"You don't have to commit to anything right now. All I ask is that you consider this an option. Maybe even speak with some of the other vets who have been paired with their service dog, and those who haven't. Get an idea for what it's all about." Soft eyes met his and Marty knew that whatever he decided, Nelly was the one dog trainer he'd work with.

Without knowing her story, he knew that she understood his difficulty. Maybe it was because she was married to Sam Marley, a guy Marty knew had a very difficult time with the adjustment home. And from what he'd heard, Sam didn't even truly begin to heal until Rogue and Nelly came into his life.

While Nelly was already taken, Marty still felt a draw to her. Not a romantic one, but more like that of a kindred spirit. Someone who understood him better than his VA doctors. In that very moment, when Nelly who wasn't even a military veteran, showed him hope in her eyes, he knew that she could be trusted.

"Nelly." Marty stopped and cleared his throat. Then he looked around the room and his eyes settled on a picture of Nelly and a man in uniform. He stood up and walked over to the picture. Leaning in his eyes focused on the two in the picture. He didn't recognize the man. At first, he thought maybe it was Sam in uniform, but it wasn't.

Standing next to him, Nelly sighed. "That's my brother, Henry."

"He's Army. Is he still in?" Marty leaned in closer trying to see the service medals on his Class A uniform but couldn't make them all out. However, one was familiar. He knew it well since he had been stationed in Iraq and earned it along with all US service members who served in Iraq or Syria. The blue, tan, and orange stripes were what set it apart and caught his attention. His Inherent Resolve Campaign Medal had two bronze campaign stars and one Arrowhead device. He earned the latter thanks to the need to parachute into a hostile situation on his second tour in Iraq.

A sniffle sounded next to him and Marty turned to see Nelly wiping away one lone tear. "I'm sorry. I had no idea."

Nelly held up a hand. "Don't worry. I'm fine. Henry served in Iraq, like so many of the residents at the ranch. And he did come home, but he was never the same after his tour. He's the reason I only train dogs for disabled veterans. If my brother had a dog, I know he'd still be here with us today."

There wasn't much Marty could say, so he kept quiet. He never quite knew what to say when talking about a person who had died. Especially one who probably had committed suicide. He guessed that was why she didn't say how he died, only that he died after coming home not quite the same.

But, hearing that Nelly was confident her brother would still be alive if he had a service dog when he came home brought all sorts of questions up. Questions he wanted to ask, but didn't know if he should. He sucked in a breath, but expelled it instead of asking what was on his mind.

"Go ahead. It's alright. I hate that my brother is gone, but if something surrounding his death can help even one person to stay alive, then who am I to keep quiet?" Nelly sucked her lips in and then released them before licking them.

Marty scratched the side of his head and then made up his mind – he was going to ask his questions. "Thank you. If I ask something that is out of line, or you just don't feel confident talking about it, let me know. I won't take offense."

She turned to look at Marty who looked her directly in the eyes. "Thank you. But I think it's important to talk about these situations. In case you hadn't guessed it, he committed suicide after coming home."

Marty nodded and looked down. "I figured as much." He paused and got his thoughts in order before blurting out something insensitive. "I think what I'm most curious to know is what he suffered from. Was it PTSD? Or something else?"

Evidence of the emotion roiling through Nelly was all over her face. Marty noticed another tear rolling down one cheek.

Nelly wiped it away and sniffled. "He was in the same roadside bomb attack that injured Sam. Turns out they were buddies." Nelly chuckled. "You know, Sam and I butted heads just about every second until we discovered that he and my big brother were close friends back in Iraq. After that, everything changed for us." A small smile soon overtook her sadness, and it was evident that she was deeply in love with Sam.

Marty wondered if the love the two of them shared isn't what helped them both heal.

A noise brought them both out of the little bubble they had shared for a few moments. When Marty turned around, he saw Sam entering with Eloise.

Sam looked between his wife and Marty. Then he noticed they were standing in front of the picture of his wife and her dead brother. "Did we interrupt something?"

Praying that Sam didn't think there was anything inappropriate going on between him and Nelly, he held up both hands. "No, not at all. Nelly was just telling me about you and her brother being close friends back in Iraq. What a small world."

A gasp escaped Eloise and her eyes widened. "Really? You two already knew each other before you came here?"

Marty walked to Eloise's side and shook his head. "That's the strange part, they didn't."

Sam walked up to his wife and kissed her forehead. "Hey, beautiful. I missed you."

Nelly leaned into Sam's shoulder. "I always miss you when we're apart."

"Oh." Eloise sighed and put a hand on her chest. "And here I thought Sam was this gruff, grinchy sorta guy."

Marty chuckled and then put a hand over his mouth when Sam turned to look at them.

"I was. Until the love of a good woman melted my heart." Sam wrapped his good arm around Nelly's waist.

"I think he meant that the love of a good man melted my heart." Nelly turned loving eyes up to her husband.

Without a word, Marty and Eloise left the two lovebirds alone. Once outside, they both chuckled nervously.

"Well," Marty put his gloves on. "That was awkward."

"But sweet," Eloise added.

"So, should we head out to the tree farm now?" Marty asked.

"Did you get a chance to speak with Nelly about a service dog?" Eloise zipped up her jacket and then donned her wool beret.

Marty waved his hand out in front of him back and forth. "Kinda, but I still have some questions. They can wait. I think the newlyweds need more time together." He shook his head and chuckled all the way to the truck.

"You know, I think I'm starting to like Christmas music." Eloise began to sing with the song on the radio – *Santa Claus Is Coming To Town* along with Randy Travis.

Marty sang out loud and very off key. It was so off, that Eloise looked at him funny.

"Is that your real singing voice? Or are you just making fun of me?" She turned a little bit in her seat so she could get a better view of him behind the wheel.

He cleared his voice and kept his eyes straight ahead on the road. One of his hands gripped the steering wheel a bit harder than needed and he felt a twinge in his hand. He relaxed his grip just enough to loosen the tight handhold. "Well, I can't breathe too deeply right now, so it was the best I could do, all things considered."

Out of the corner of Marty's eye, he caught the signs of her blush before she turned to look out the passenger side window.

"Sorry about that. I keep forgetting."

Now Marty felt bad. "No worries. I'm feeling a lot better, but there are still things I can't do as well. And besides, I have a rotten singing voice, so I do tend to sing even more off key, just to make people laugh. But you have a nice voice. I wish you'd keep singing along with the radio, I liked it."

"Really?" Eloise turned back toward the driver. "You want me to keep singing? For reals?"

Marty was surprised that Eloise didn't realize she had a nice voice. It wasn't going to win her a recording contract on one of those singing contest shows, but she did sound very nice. At least to his untrained ears she did. "Of course I do. Come on, I'll try to sing as best as I can if you'll join me?"

When Luke Bryan's version of *Run, Run, Rudolph* came on, both jumped in and sang along. They continued singing to the country Christmas songs on the radio as they drove out to the tree farm. When they drove into the parking lot, Elvis Presley's *Here Comes Santa Claus* was playing and out of the front window Marty and Eloise watched their own Santa Claus walking into the lot wearing his fancy Santa suit with shiny black boots and all.

Eloise pointed the man out. "Do you think the radio and our Santa coordinated this entrance?"

Marty chuckled lightly and put a hand on his chest to rub out the ache that began. "I wouldn't put it past Santa and the radio to work together. I swear, this must be the most Christmassy town I've ever heard of."

"I think you might be right. I've never seen a better Santa than Chris." Eloise put her hand on the door handle and started to get out.

Marty said, "hold up." He jumped out of the truck and almost ran around the front to get her door for her. "Here, let me help you. The snow is very sloshy here in the parking lot."

"I can open my own door." Eloise pursed her lips and glared at him.

"I never said you couldn't. But my momma raised me to be a gentleman. And a gentleman opens doors for ladies, even those who can do it themselves." He returned her glare.

Two middle-aged women walked past them at that moment. One stopped and smiled as she put her gloved hand over her heart. "I see chivalry isn't dead."

Her friend turned around and saw Marty and Eloise still standing at her truck door. "I just love it when a man opens my door for me. I wish more still practiced the art of respect for a woman."

Eloise looked at the two women and Marty saw her cheeks turn pink. He loved it when she was embarrassed, it made her look so soft. Unlike when she was in full-on ADA Coordinator mode. Then, she was more like a prison warden.

Marty tilted his head and grinned from ear to ear. If he had been wearing a cowboy hat, he would have removed it and put it over his heart and bowed in their direction. He realized it was high-time for him to get one. Not that he was a real cowboy, but he liked the Stetson hats he'd seen around the ranch and figured it would help with keeping his head warm. His knit beanie worked just fine, but he stood out in the sea of cowboys.

"Sorry." Eloise grumbled. "I'm not used to nice men."

That stopped Marty dead in his tracks. "What do you mean? Aren't the men in Texas nice? I thought the South was known for its nice men."

Eloise sighed. "I'm sure they are. And sorry, I'm just having a tough time. Don't mind me. I get in these melodramatic moods once in a while. It will pass."

Marty put a hand on Eloise's shoulder. "Hey, talk to me. We're friends, right? Let me help you."

"Sorry, it's nothing. Don't mind me. An old memory, that's all. I've met plenty of nice men." Eloise backed up and turned to head into the tree farm. "It's time we get to work."

"Wait up. I think this is more important. Did someone hurt you?" Marty prayed Eloise hadn't been injured in any way by a man. That was one thing that always got his anger up, a man hurting a woman. It was uncalled for. Men were created to care for women, not hurt them. And he knew that women were independent and could care for themselves, but it was a man's job to protect.

She ran a hand down her face and looked at Marty. "I wasn't born with my bum foot. I was in a car accident and trapped for hours before I was rescued. Before I was even out of the hospital, my fiancé broke up with me. He couldn't handle having a wife who wasn't perfect. So yeah, I was hurt by a man. But not like you thought."

Eloise turned around and with her head held high, she walked into the Christmas Tree farm ready to help families find their perfect tree.

Chapter 19

Eloise shook her head. What had she been thinking when she made that blasted comment about men? She didn't need Marty, or anyone, feeling sorry for her. Yes, her fiancé couldn't handle her handicap, and that sucked. But not all men were mean like that.

It's just. Well, she was feeling jealous of what Nelly and Sam had. Before her accident she thought she had that with Marco. But obviously she had been wrong. Her mother told her it was better she find out before they were married, than after the wedding. Men like Marco were selfish, vain, and just plain arrogant. She wouldn't have been happy with him in the long run. And she knew it, too.

She had moved on from Marco a long time ago. But every once in a while, she felt herself going down that path of depression. Eloise had been through enough counseling to know that she had actually lucked out with that guy breaking things off. And after that, she'd become super self-reliant. Some might even say she was too self-reliant. But she didn't mind.

But, the opening the truck door for her and helping her out of the truck? That was a bit much. Once in a while, when her arms were full, she did like it when someone opened the door for her. That was nice, since her arms were full. But opening the door just because she was a woman? That was over the top. And she thought men did it as a way to try and push women down a rung on the social ladder.

Didn't matter that her dad had once explained to her why men still preferred to hold open doors for women, and that it had nothing to do with women being the "weaker sex" as so many stated. Instead, it was an outward expression of an inward emotion, respect. When a man opens doors for a woman without being asked, or even thinking about, it means he respects her. It's not his way of saying she's the weaker sex.

Marty caught up to Eloise and interrupted her train of thought. "I'm sorry your ex did that to you. That was evil, plain and simple evil. There are a lot of men, and women, who do that sort of thing regularly. Society has become all about oneself. And it's important to take care of yourself, sure. But it's more important to put other people's needs first." He shrugged. "Well, that's what my parents taught me growing up."

"Thank you. I do appreciate you. But, I don't need a man to open my car door. I think that's just a bit...well...unnecessary. At least, when we are both in the car, or truck, I think it's fine if I open my door myself." Eloise paused and looked closely at Marty. She noted his turned down lips and sad eyes. "But," she held up a finger. "I do love it when a man opens a door for me when we are both walking toward it. Like store doors, house doors, etcetera."

Marty nodded. "I think I can live with that. And maybe you're right, asking you to stay in the truck while I run around the side may not always be the best thing. But you can't deny that when it's raining, and we only have one umbrella..." He let his words trail off as he shrugged his shoulders, then began walking away.

Eloise heard the chuckle as she quickly followed Marty into the tree farm. "I see your point."

It was hours before they had another chance to chit-chat or joke around. The tree farm was packed with people looking to buy their perfect family Christmas tree. Not to mention all of the people who were perusing the handicraft market, the carnival area, and those who were just taking in the Christmas ambiance.

The place screamed Christmas paradise.

And Eloise knew that it was contagious. She couldn't help but smile as she looked around and saw all of the happy people in one place. Even though it was loud, she was having a great time. After school, the families came in droves with their kids, all of whom had either Christmas candied apples with little Santa hats on top, Christmas tree shaped and colored cotton candy, or any of the assortment of cake pops and hot Christmas drinks that Lottie sold from her Frenchtown Roasting coffee cart.

When one woman walked by with a hot cup that was topped off with a mile high whipped cream and peppermint topping, Eloise knew it was time for her to take a break. "Hey, Marty. I think we need a hot coffee break. What do you think?"

Marty looked up from where he was writing in his book and looked in the direction Eloise was faced. "Ah, yes. I think it's time for a hot peppermint cocoa. That looks fantastic. I've seen several people drinking those today."

"Yummy." Eloise waited patiently for Marty to finish the paperwork so the family who had just chosen a ten-foot tall Grand Noble Fir tree could go and pay for it before the dad and his teenaged daughter began chopping it down. Well, she was as patient as anyone could be who was on the trail of the best hot cocoa around.

"Is that really necessary?" Marty pointed down at Eloise's foot.

"What?" She looked down and noticed that her foot was tapping, and her arms had been crossed over her chest. "Oh, sorry." She shrugged and un-crossed her arms. The moment Marty had finished his paperwork, Eloise pulled on his sleeve to get him moving toward the hot cocoa cart.

Once they had their hot drinks, Marty led them to a bench next to a warmer. "Let's sit for a little bit."

"Good idea." Eloise took a sip of her hot cocoa and just about died and went to heaven. "Just the perfect amount of chocolate and peppermint."

Marty took a sip and closed his eyes. "I don't think I've had anything that made me feel the magic of Christmas this year until now." He closed his eyes again and took another, longer, deeper sip of the silky-smooth hot beverage. It warmed him from the top of his head to the tips of his toes.

"You know, I have to agree with you. I haven't enjoyed Christmas this much since I was a kid, and it's only the first week of December." Eloise's voice trailed and she looked down at her lap.

Marty took his hot cocoa away from his lips and frowned. "What's wrong?"

"Jerod called earlier; we're going to meet up tomorrow night to review my report. I should have it done by then. And once that happens, I'll be off, back home. Texas is great, I love my state, but I've never seen anything like this before. I wish I could stay longer and enjoy more of this festive season." Eloise rubbed her nose and then took a sip of her hot chocolate.

"Did you ask Jerod if you could stay longer?"

Eloise shook her head. "Didn't have a chance. I'll ask after he's read my report." She sighed. "He might not like it and I don't want to stick around if he's unhappy."

All of a sudden, Marty sat up straight and stared at her. He put his hand on the bench between them. "Are you saying that you're going to deliver a bad report?"

"Huh? What?" Eloise fidgeted with her mug. She should have checked herself before speaking. Of all people, she knew better than to speak before thinking. It wasn't that her report was bad, necessarily. But it did have some ideas for improvement.

His nostrils flared and it was very evident that Marty was doing everything he could to keep his anger in check. "Are you going to blame my injury on the ranch or Jerod?"

Her eyes widened and her hat flew off with how hard she shook her head. "No, of course not. That was an accident. After seeing everything the storm did, I'm actually surprised there weren't more injuries."

She held up a hand as Marty opened his mouth. "Hold up. I'm not saying that I think Jerod or anyone else did anything to put you in danger on purpose. I do believe the house and barn are in good shape. That storm was a very bad one. I've heard stories from people in town about more destruction. What happened at the Crooked Arrow wasn't anything out of the ordinary. It just happened to happen to veterans who were already injured."

"So, what are you saying?" The man sat back in his seat, visibly relaxing a little bit.

Eloise was glad that he wasn't wound up as tightly as he had been just a moment earlier. "I'd rather not speak to you, or anyone else, about this until after Jerod has had a chance to read the report. It's his ranch, after all."

When a sour look overtook Marty's normally happy features, Eloise knew it was time to change the subject, and get back to work. "Well,

I think I need to get back moving again before my toes freeze to the inside of my boots." Her chuckle sounded off to her.

Marty didn't smile or chuckle. Instead, he stood up and threw his empty cocoa mug into the trash can that was closest to their bench. Without a word, he headed back to the tree section and by the time they reached the grove of Douglas Firs, he had a half smile plastered on his face.

Eloise wanted to tell him everything would be fine, but she wasn't sure. Her findings were nowhere near as bad as she thought they'd be when she first arrived. However, that didn't mean there weren't issues. Okay, maybe not issues, per se, but she did have some suggestions for improvement. In her experience, most small business owners didn't take her suggestions well. But, that was something to worry about later.

Now? She needed to focus on the young family headed her way. A mother holding a toddler who was bundled up almost as badly as that little boy on A Christmas Story appeared in front of her. Thankfully, the dad who held the little gloved hand of their daughter who couldn't have been more than eight or nine, hadn't decided to wrap her in twenty pounds of puffy coat, like the toddler. Poor kid, Eloise thought. Even if the mom put him down, he wouldn't be able to walk. At least, she thought it was a boy. The only indicator was the blue coat. Or was it more of a thick blanket that was wrapped around the kid multiple times?

Instead of thinking about it anymore, she smiled and asked how she could help them find their perfect tree.

The little girl grinned up at Eloise and said, "I'm picking out our tree today. Santa is going to put lots of presents under it for me." Her face lit up and if Eloise wasn't wrong, a little golden halo spread over the angelic girl's head.

Eloise bent over and returned the little girl's smile. "Really? How do you know? And what about your little brother? Will he get lots of presents, too?"

When the little girl squished her face up and shook her head, it took all of Eloise's self-control to keep from laughing.

"Santa only told me that he was going to bring lots of presents." Her face cleared up and she waved her hands all around her. "Everyone knows that if you don't tell Santa what you want, you don't get any gifts." She rolled her eyes as though Eloise was just silly for not knowing this fact.

"That's true. You do need to tell Santa what you want." Eloise stood up and nodded. Her face grave, she turned to look at the baby in the mother's arms. From a distance, the kid looked as though it was big enough to be a toddler, but from close up she could tell it was only a little baby. He was maybe six months old.

"Hudson can't speak yet, so he doesn't get any presents from Santa." The little girl crossed her arms over her puffy pink jacket and nodded.

The mom and dad chuckled.

"Cindy, Hudson will be getting presents, too. Santa knows what little babies need, and want, for Christmas without them needing to tell him." The Mom lightly shook her head and looked at Eloise. "We've told her this many times, but she has it stuck in her little head that only she's going to get Christmas gifts this year."

"Ah, yes. I get it." Eloise had seen it before, when an older kid didn't have any siblings, they got everything. Then, when a kid did come along later on, the older one was jealous. Not wanting to call Cindy out for her only acting out her typical kid behavior, she changed the subject. "Okay, what type of tree did you want to get this year, Cindy?"

Little white gloved hands spread out and her eyes rolled heavenward as though it was totally obvious. "Well, duh, a Christmas Tree."

"Cindy!" The dad spoke up for the first time since Eloise spoke with them. "Be nice. I think the tree lady," he stepped closer and looked at her badge, "Eloise, was asking what type of Christmas tree you wanted."

"Exactly. Did you know that there are more than thirty-five types of trees that can be used for Christmas? And that doesn't even count the variety of cacti that can be used as a Christmas tree." Eloise pulled the pamphlet out of her apron's pocket.

"Cacti?" Cindy scrunched her cute little button nose. "Who would want a cactus for a Christmas tree? You can't put presents under a cactus."

This time, Eloise did laugh. "I might have to agree with you. But lots of people in desert areas put lights and decorations on cactus. When you get home have your mom or dad look up pictures for you on the Internet. I think you might be impressed with what some people do."

"Honey, not everyone is as blessed as we are to live in Montana where there are plenty of trees we can use for Christmas." The dad smiled that smile only a patient father has developed over years of practice.

Eloise knew this because her dad used to give her that smile when she was a kid. Actually, he still did it once in a while. She went on to discuss the trees they had on the farm and discovered that the little girl thought the only tree that could be a true *Christmas Tree* was the Blue Spruce. "You know, I think I agree with you. The Blue Spruce is a very majestic Christmas tree. Come on, I'll show you where they are."

As they began their trek to the five-foot-tall trees, Eloise looked behind her to make sure the family was trailing.

Big mistake.

Chapter 20

Not far from Eloise, Marty was helping a family put a tag on their ten-foot tall Blue Spruce. Before the father even walked away to pay for it, he heard a scream that caused a lightning bolt to pierce his heart. He turned his head to see who had made the noise that he'd heard too many times in his nightmares.

Two rows over he noticed a familiar jacket on the ground and people moving to surround her. "Eloise!" Marty ignored the question coming from the family he had been helping and ran to her side.

"Eloise, what happened? Are you alright?" Marty knelt on the snow-covered ground next to the woman he'd begun to think of as his pretty friend.

"Oh, it hurts." Eloise hissed in a breath and then expelled it. "My foot."

"What happened?" Marty asked again.

A little girl Marty hadn't seen before knelt down on the dirty, trampled snow next to him. "She tripped." Then the girl pointed to a light brown patch of something sticking up out of the snow.

"What is that?" Marty squinted to see what had caused Eloise to fall.

One of the other customers bent down and shoved the snow away. Instead of picking it up, he stood back up so Marty could see it.

"What is that doing out here?" Marty couldn't believe his eyes. Laying in the snow was a snow shovel. Most of it had been fully covered by the snow, but part of the wooden handle had been sticking up and must have been what caused Eloise to trip.

All he could think was that this would cause Eloise to tell the VA that none of the injured veterans could volunteer at the tree farm anymore, it was too much of a hazard. He didn't believe that. The residents of the Crooked Arrow had been volunteering for the past two years at the farm. None of them had been injured. At least not so that the VA was notified.

"Here, let me help you up and we can head inside so you can warm up." Marty leaned over to help Eloise up.

Once she was up, she put some pressure on her bad foot and almost fell again. If Marty hadn't been there, she would have.

Eloise was panting heavily from the pain. "I don't think I can walk."

"Do you think it's broke?" Marty wanted to lean down and take her boot off so he could check it, but then there would be no one to help her stay upright.

"I'll go get some help," The dad of the little girl volunteered.

"I'll stay here, Daddy." The little girl moved closer to Eloise's foot. "Do you want me to take your boot off? I can see if it's broken."

A sort of chuckle-snort escaped Eloise and she grinned at the little girl. "Thank you, Cindy. But I think I should keep my boot on until a doctor sees it."

"I'm going to be a doctor when I grow up." The little girl gave Eloise such a serious look, that Eloise believed this girl would do it.

"That is wonderful. We need more excellent doctors." Eloise winced as she tried to put some more pressure on her bad foot. "A tree farm is nowhere for an injured person to be."

Marty bit his lip. He knew she was in pain and probably embarrassed from tripping over a snow shovel. But he did not like where her words were taking him. "Why don't I carry you to a bench where you can wait in more comfort for a doctor."

He was about to put his arm behind her knees, when Eloise screeched, "No! I can hobble if you help me."

Marty pursed his lips together showing his disapproval, but he said nothing. Instead, he put one arm under her arms and around her back.

Eloise put one arm around his strong shoulders and nodded. When Marty began to slow walk forward, Eloise hopped. She would hop four or five times and then Marty would stop for a quick break. They continued this pattern until he found a bench they could sit on while they waited for an EMT.

An ambulance would park at the farm when it wasn't busy, since most of the town was usually there. And most of the injuries would happen at the tree farm when it was so busy. Which made Marty think that they wouldn't have to wait long. He had seen an EMT earlier in the day, so maybe one was still there.

"How is that?" Marty sat Eloise down carefully on the bench. He stood in front of her waiting for her to get comfortable.

Eloise moved around a little bit before a resigned face looked up at Marty. "I'm as good as I'm going to get."

Marty sighed and rubbed a hand down his face. Then he took the seat next to Eloise. "I'm so sorry you hurt your foot. We have good medical personnel here in Frenchtown. You'll be well taken care of."

The little girl, Cindy, sat next to Eloise. "Do you want to hold my baby brother? Mama says holding a baby helps her to feel better."

Cindy's mom chuckled. "Cindy, honey. I don't think it works when someone has fallen down and hurt themselves."

"Yes, it does. Remember last week when I fell and scratched my knee? You put Hudson in my lap and I stopped crying." Cindy's earnest face caused several of the gawkers to chuckle.

"Out of the mouths of babes," one woman said before moving on.

Another replied, "she's not wrong. Snuggling a baby always helped me to smile when I was younger."

Marty doubted holding a baby, no matter how cute, would help someone who might have a broken ankle.

Before he could think any more about babies and pain, a woman stopped in front of them carrying a red medical box that had battery operated lights and tinsel surrounding the large handle of the box. "Hi, I'm Amanda. I heard you took a tumble. Where does it hurt?"

A half hour later, and one giant ace bandage around Eloise's right ankle, Marty and Amanda helped Eloise to get back to the Christmas store so she could sit in a comfy chair around the fire while Marty left to get the truck. He was going to take her to the urgent care facility in town.

While the EMT was fairly confident it wasn't broken, she did think that Eloise had a very nasty sprain. One that would require her to stay down for at least a week.

Once they were in the truck and on their way back into town, Marty smiled over at Eloise. "Looks like you're going to get your wish, after all."

"What wish was that? The one where I made a complete fool of myself in front of most of the town?" Eloise scoffed. "No, thanks. I think I can do without that wish."

"No, the one where you get to stay in Frenchtown longer. We can't send you home injured like this, now can we?" Marty felt a sigh of contentment come out. While he felt bad that

Eloise was injured, he couldn't be upset that she would have to stay for a little while longer.

When they arrived at the Urgent Care, it was obvious someone had called ahead. Eloise didn't have to wait to be seen and the doctor on duty had already heard about her fall. All that was needed was an X-ray to double check that nothing had been broken. So Marty sat down in a waiting room chair while Eloise was moved around in a wheelchair. He noted the calming, light blue walls and the pictures of cute little animals all over the place. It wasn't something he'd do, but the décor was rather nice, for an urgent care waiting room. There was even a TV in the corner playing those cute family-friendly full-length cartoons.

Instead of watching TV, he turned to his phone. While he wasn't sure if Jerod had been updated regarding Eloise's fall, he figured he should give the man a head's up, just in case. The drive into town had been quick and Eloise was more concerned with trying to focus on anything else but her pain. So Marty didn't have a chance to feel her out with regards to what she was going to do, or say, about the tripping injury.

Marty still wasn't sure what her report was going to say, either. The last thing they needed was a report insisting they close down the ranch. He knew that there were already several success stories of men, and women, who had come to the ranch broken in more ways than one, and had healed up enough to integrate back into society with jobs. And some even found love. Not that finding love was a real selling point for the ranch, but it was a sign that people were recovering and moving on from the ravages of war. That should mean something to the VA, shouldn't it?

There were only two other people in the waiting room, and Marty didn't want to air the ranch's dirty laundry. In this town, there were ears everywhere. One tiny phone call could be shared with the entire town and surrounding ranches and farms before the day was out.

Instead of calling Jerod, he texted the man.

Marty: *J, Eloise tripped over a snow shovel at the tree farm. We're at urgent care now. She's going to be fine, a bad sprain. But I doubt she'll be able to travel for at least a week.*

Jerod: *I'm sorry to hear she's injured. Will you bring her back to the ranch when done?*

Marty: *Yes.*

Jerod: *Text me when you're home and I'll come back to join you. I'll also let Dana and Megan know.*

Marty: *Thanks.*

Even though they didn't have to wait to be seen, it still took close to two hours. After texting Jerod, Marty did watch the cartoon.

"Hey, look at you." Marty stood and walked to where Eloise scowled down at the boot on her foot and lower leg.

"I have to wear this blasted boot and use these crutches. Then come back in a week and see how my ankle is healing." Eloise leaned her armpits down on the crutches and sighed.

"Is it broke?" Marty scratched his head wondering why she was in a boot if she only sprained her ankle.

With a sigh, Eloise shook her head. "No, but it's a very bad sprain. And since it's my bad foot the doctor wants to make sure I don't do anything to make it worse."

"Sooo, I take it this means you're going to let me open doors for you? And wait for me to help you out of the truck?" Marty grinned remembering their joking from earlier in the day.

Steely eyes looked at Marty and he felt a boulder drop in his stomach. "Ah, too early?"

"What do you think?" Without waiting for a reply, Eloise began to make her way to the front door. When she stopped in front of the exit, she sighed. Then she waited for Marty to open the door for her.

Marty couldn't help but feel that their earlier conversation was prophetic, somehow. However, it didn't make him feel good. If he could have prevented her fall, he would have. It was the sort of thing that could have happened to anyone, at any time. It was just plain dumb luck that it happened to the one person who could cause some serious issues if she wanted to.

"Thanks." Eloise grumbled as she hobbled out of the door.

Marty made it to the truck before she could and he stood on the passenger side holding the door open.

When Eloise stood in front of the open door, she scowled. "I suppose I'll need your help getting inside. The truck is a bit too tall for me to manage right now."

"Of course. I'm happy to help." Doing his best to hide his smile, Marty took the crutches from Eloise and laid them against the side of the truck. Then he put his arms around her back and under her knees. He lifted her up in a seated position and slid her easily on to the front passenger seat. His instincts told him to also help with the seatbelt, but he caught the look of anger on her face and backed up.

While she belted herself in, Marty put the crutches in the bed of the truck and then went around to the driver's side. "Do we need to stop by the pharmacy before heading home?"

"No, they gave me a reusable ice pack I can tie to my ankle once I'm home. And I can just use Tylenol for the pain."

The moment the truck pulled into the ranch, the front door opened and out came several of the staff and residents.

Chapter 21

Feeling mortified and still in some pain, Eloise opted to spend the rest of the day in her room. Dana was more than happy to help bring her dinner to her room.

"Poor thing, she's miserable." Dana brought the partially empty tray back into the kitchen and emptied it of its contents. "She's still in some pain, even with the Tylenol, but worse than that is the fact that she's embarrassed. It wasn't her fault, it could have happened to any-one. I even told her that. Things happen on farms and ranches."

Marty shook his head. "That was something that shouldn't have happened. Who leaves a shovel out in the snow? And on a path to Christmas trees? What if a little kid tripped over it?"

Jerod rubbed a hand over his face. "I know. I spoke with Cody about this and he promised that it wasn't left out by any of his staff. And I know none of us would have done it. All we can think is that some kid was trying to surf the snow with it and dropped it before he was caught. Then the big snow storm hit and it was covered up until now."

"Surf the snow?" Marty's brow furrowed and he asked what that meant.

"Think snowboarding but with shovels and other types of boards that can glide across the snow. The local kids saw some Xgames feature in Japan. The island kids there used boogie boards and small sleds to basically ski down a hill. But since the boards didn't have bindings, they crashed a lot. The local kids have tried it using all sorts of equipment. Snow shovels have become a favorite since you can hold the handle and it helps to keep you on the "board" and even gives a bit of steering control."

"But, the tree farm isn't on a hill." Marty blinked and looked out the window. "In fact, most of the ranches around us have better hills than the tree farm."

"Oh, there are hills. They're small and perfect for learning. But they're in the back of the farmland." Jerod rubbed his chin and shook his head. Everyone is going to have to be more careful with equipment and locking up the sheds."

"You know how many were on the farm this past week, with the events moving from the town hall to the tree farm?" Dana asked. "Too many to count, or even try to remember. But you're right, everyone is going to have to be more careful with equipment and locking doors at the tree farm. It's like Grand Central for the rest of the year."

"I'm just glad we aren't getting any new residents for a couple of weeks yet. We might have a couple come right before Christmas, but they haven't decided for sure." Jerod pulled his phone out and checked the calendar. "She can stay through the New Year if she wants."

"That will give her time to really see how we operate. I didn't think one week was going to be enough. Maybe, if the snow clears up enough, we can do a day trip to Glacier when she's feeling better. I bet she'd love to see it at Christmas." Dana sat up taller and then listed off all of the things they could do at the park for Christmas.

Jerod lifted a hand. "Hold up, there. I enjoy Glacier just as much as everyone else does, but we have a lot on our plate already through the end of the month. With so few residents right now, we can't give Cody as many hours as we have in the past. So let's hold off on a trip to Glacier for now."

Dana sank back into her chair. "I know. I guess I just wanted to show Eloise the best we have to offer. You know, butter her up a bit."

Marty chuckled. "I think the best thing is to focus on what you normally do, let her see the usual stuff. Isn't there a sleigh ride? I bet she'd be up for that next week. And I heard about a giving tree. Where is that located now that the town hall is closed?"

Dana's mood visibly improved and she started ticking off all of the local things they do for Christmas. "You're right. We have a lot to offer right here in Frenchtown. There's also the Christmas carol night, the gingerbread contest, and Santa's circle. Just to name a few."

Marty and Jerod exchanged confused glances. "What's Santa's circle?" They both asked in unison.

Dana clapped her hands and giggled. "Oh, you're going to love this." Then she paused and thought for a moment. "Although, Eloise might not. There's a lot of walking involved. It's a progressive dinner in town. Santa sets up different stations at some of the businesses along Main Street and everyone takes turns stopping in. Some will start with dessert, while others will start with the main course. And then others will start with hors d'oeuvres. It's a lot of fun, and new this year to the offered events."

"What started this one?" Jerod asked.

"Well, since almost all of the events have been moved to the tree farm, the town council thought we needed something in town. In past years, most of the Christmas events kept people in the center of town, near the businesses. With all of the people out at the tree farm instead, some of the businesses complained that they wouldn't get the normal traffic and therefore would lose out on sales." Dana snuggled closer to Jerod, who sat next to her on the couch.

"Are you cold?" Jerod stood to put more wood on the fire. When he came back, he brought a throw blanket and put it over Dana when he pulled her closer to him.

"Thanks." Dana tried to stifle a yawn, but failed miserably when the rest of the room's occupants echoed her large yawn. "Sorry, I thought when I found out I was pregnant that I'd not really have any issues with fatigue, or even with my own body temperature. At least, not until later in the pregnancy. But in addition to some morning sickness, I seem to be having issues with other things as well."

"Well, I think that's my cue to get up and leave." Marty stood, and he was followed by Tony who had been quiet during the conversation. The two men left the room and headed into the kitchen. With Buffy close on their heels.

Marty went to the coffee maker, that always had a hot pot of coffee available, no matter the time of day. "Do you think Dana will come back in here and clean up the day's coffee stuff?"

Tony took a seat and furrowed his brow. "I doubt it. We could do that for her. When we're done here, we could wash up all that's left and get things ready for tomorrow."

Marty poured a mug of coffee for Tony and handed it to him. "That's a great idea. I wonder if there are other things we can do to help out? I don't know anything about pregnant women, but I hear they go through a lot before bringing a baby into the world."

Tony took the offered mug of hot coffee and put in sugar and creamer. "You're right about that. I've been here since the two of them first got together and I know firsthand how much Dana does for all of us. Maybe we can talk to the others and figure out a way to help split up the workload?"

After Marty fixed his coffee, he took a seat at the small kitchen table, across from Tony. He looked at the man who had been injured so badly in Iraq that he'd needed a couple skin grafts. And he had permanent hearing loss on his left side, which was why he had a service dog. Marty always tried to look Tony in the face when speaking so the man could understand what he was saying by not only hearing out of one ear, but also through his meager ability to lip read. "I bet we could get more than just those here on the ranch to help. I wonder if her family and friends in town would be willing to make up some dinners that we could freeze and pull out when Dana isn't feeling well?"

A laugh erupted from Tony just as he was about to drink his coffee. He had to wipe some of the spilled drink from the table. "That is probably one of the most important jobs. None of us are good at cooking. Several are wonders on the grill, but in this weather?" He shook his head.

No one wanted to be outside cooking on the grill in the snow and cold. It had barely been in the high twenties all week. One day it was thirty-seven and the sun did melt some of the snow, but even that was still too cold to barbecue in.

The two men sat quietly drinking their coffee and each was in his own little world until Tony lifted his head. "Is Eloise going to shut this place down?"

Marty shook his head and took a bracing sip of coffee. "I hope not. Before today I wouldn't have thought her report would be bad enough to do so, but now?" He shrugged, not knowing what the woman would do.

"Can't you use your charm on her?" Tony grinned before getting up to walk to the pantry.

Marty watched as the Army Captain rifled through the snacks on offer and pulled out a couple of granola bars. "Here." Tony threw one to Marty.

"Thanks." Marty caught the flying snack and started to open it up.

"Well?" Tony waited for Marty's answer.

"Oh, you were serious?" A hard lump went down Marty's throat and he had to cough to clear it all. "I don't think she's into me."

"Oh, please. You know she is. Just use that smile of yours on her and she'll melt at your feet. Then give the ranch a good report." Tony started to chuckle.

Marty laughed and shook his head. "And what would Hope have to say about that?"

Hope was Tony's girlfriend. She was also Dana's cousin and came over to the ranch to help out when she could.

"What would Hope say?" Dana asked when she walked into the kitchen. She made her way to the pantry where she kept the tea bags, then headed to the stove.

Marty jumped up. "Here, let me help you." He took the kettle and added fresh water to it before setting it on the stove to boil.

Dana put her hands on her hips. "I think I can make my own tea."

Tony put up his hands. "We know you can."

"It's just that we want to help where we can," Marty added.

A small smile began to work its way across Dana's face. "Thank you, that's very nice. But what was that about my cousin?"

Jerod walked in and walked over to his wife by the stove. "That's a great idea. We should see if Hope can come and help out a little bit."

"Not you, too." Dana shook her head. "Guys, I'm barely pregnant. Just give me some time to get used to the changes and I'll be fine. You do know that cowgirls can be pregnant and still work the ranch like usual?"

Marty's eyes shot up to the top of his forehead and he exchanged a harried look with Tony.

"I know, I know. And through the ages the women in your family worked the farm and never once took time off until their water broke." Jerod put his arms around his wife and leaned in to kiss her on the forehead. "I know you're strong. Just please, let me help. I can't carry the baby for you, but I can find a way to make your load lighter. Give you more time to plan for the baby."

"Well, that would be nice. Okay, maybe Hope can come over. It would be nice to have someone else around who understands that pregnant women aren't China dolls. We aren't going to crack into a million pieces if we have to work." Dana pushed her husband back as she went to prepare her tea.

"We were just talking about how we can do dishes." Marty and Tony went on to discuss other ways they could help more around the ranch.

"Besides," Marty added, "it feels good to help someone else. Gives me a purpose again."

Jerod nodded. "I hear ya. Okay, we'll figure out who can do what once Dana and Hope put a list together of what we can do to help."

Nothing more was said that night about the pregnancy, but plenty was said about Eloise and her report. A report that Jerod was supposed to have received that night.

Chapter 22

A shaft of light coming through the blinds in her room hit Eloise right in one eye. She blinked that eye, then the other eye slowly began to open. "Ow." She put a hand in front of the offending brightness and turned on her side. "Nope. Not gonna work."

It seems in order to escape the morning rays, she had to turn on her right side. The side with the bum foot that was reinjured only the previous day. Putting any pressure on that bad foot or leg wasn't something she wanted to do.

She turned on her back again and sighed.

Grumbling, she slowly turned on her other side and then sat up. She'd slept without the boot on, and her foot did feel better, but she wasn't in the best mood. "I thought I was going to like Christmas again." She looked up to heaven. "What happened with that?"

When God didn't respond. Or at least not in a voice she could hear, she sighed and slid off the bed and hobbled over to the chair where the boot sat. She sat down and slid her foot in the adjustable boot and sighed, again. "I think I have a better understanding of what the returning veterans go through, but didn't I already learn that lesson? Huh?"

Eloise looked up at the ceiling again. "Lord, what is the lesson here?"

A knock sounded at her door and she jumped. "Okay, okay. I got it."

The knock sounded again. "Eloise? Who are you talking to?"

Eloise put a hand on her chest and let out the breath she had been holding. "Dana, come on in."

The woman smiled and looked as though she'd been up for hours. Her hair was perfectly pulled back into a long ponytail, and she had put on just a little bit of eyeliner, and some lip gloss. She was also dressed for the day in blue jeans, a light blue sweater set, and brown cowgirl boots. "I thought you'd sleep in later. Are you in pain?" Worry creased her forehead.

"No, well, yes. I'm aching, but not truly in pain." Eloise scrunched her nose. "The sun woke me." She turned to look at the offending window and frowned. "Wait, if the sun is up, then it must be later than I thought."

"It's almost nine. But with your injury, I thought your body would sleep all morning." Dana came over and opened the blinds just enough to peer outside. "Looks like it's going to be a nice day. We might even see some snow melting today."

Eloise chuckled. "As long as it doesn't decide to freeze over, I'm fine with that."

"Here, let me help you. Do you know what you want to wear today?" Dana closed the blinds again. This time ensuring that not even a sliver of sunlight made its way through.

Eloise shrugged. "Something warm and comfortable. I think I have a set of sweatpants and a matching hoodie in my drawer."

Dana rummaged through the bottom drawer and stood up. "Oh, this is cute." In her hands was a pair of pink sweats with *Houston* in large, bold, white letters down the side of one pant leg. The white hoodie had *Houston* in matching pink words across the chest. "I bet it will be warm and cozy. Perfect for today."

"Thanks, I think I can handle it from here." It wasn't as though Eloise didn't know what it was like to not be able to use a leg. After her crash it took months before she was able to put any pressure on her right leg. Her current injury wasn't anywhere near as bad as that first one.

"I'll be in the kitchen fixing your breakfast. Would you like some eggs today?" Dana put her hand on the doorknob but didn't open it until after Eloise answered.

"Thank you, that would be nice. And plenty of coffee and Tylenol." Eloise tilted her head to the side and gave Dana a half smile. She was starting to wake up and her chest began to fill with gratitude for this wonderful hostess.

Here this woman was pregnant and she was more concerned with Eloise than herself. A bad sprain can't compare to being pregnant, but Dana was still more interested in helping others. Eloise figured Dana was a huge part of why this ranch was so successful. She'd have to reread her report and make sure she noted how thoughtful and caring the owner's wife was.

It took some effort, but by the time Eloise made it to the kitchen, she had two drops of sweat running down her face. "Is it hot in here? Or just me?"

"Hm?" Dana turned around and gave the woman a big grin. "Have a seat. And I think you just put forth a huge amount of effort to get here so quickly. I bet you cool down after a few minutes."

Not sure if that was true, Eloise took a seat and fanned her face with a hand as she waited for Dana to bring her a mug of coffee. "I'm totally bringing back a suitcase full of this coffee when I go home." She smelled the scent of hickory, fruit, and some herb she couldn't put her finger on. "It's just divine."

"Thank you. I happened to be the one who roasted this particular batch of beans the other day. I'm glad you like it." Dana's face lit with what Eloise could only assume was pregnancy hormones.

Dana was always pretty, but the past few days since she discovered she was pregnant, the woman beamed happiness. No, Eloise thought to herself, it was more than happiness. Dana embodied joy. And not just the joy of the season as so many others had. It was as though joy just naturally bubbled up from this woman. Maybe there was something to the old adage about love and babies?

Not that Eloise wanted that. Not anymore at least. She'd had her fill of romance and had her heart broken. It wasn't something she wanted to experience again.

Still, she couldn't help wondering what caused the woman in front of her to glow and exude joy. Especially when Eloise knew that Dana was tired.

And cold, it seemed.

Even after sitting at the table for a few minutes, Eloise was still very hot. It wasn't like the oven and all of the burners were on in this kitchen. Dana was only using one burner and from her angle, Eloise could tell that the oven was off. She waved a hand in front of her face and wondered if she shouldn't grab a Diet Coke instead of the hot coffee.

"How are you feeling this morning? Any better? Do you need something for the pain?" Dana asked over her shoulder before she poured the scrambled eggs onto a plate.

Eloise took the offered plate that also had two slices of bagel already spread with butter. On the table in front of her was a tray that held several jam and jelly options. She'd heard the guys talking about huckleberry jam, so she decided to give that one a try. "I'm much better today. I'm sure by the time the doctor sees me I won't need this boot any longer."

Dana's eyes went down to the foot that Eloise had pointed at. She arched a brow. "I think the doctor said you'd need it for a few weeks. Don't push yourself. One of the things we like to remind everyone around here is that bodies heal on their own schedule. It's best not to push it."

Not wanting to argue, Eloise nodded before taking a large bite of the eggs. She closed her eyes and savored the tangy flavor of the gouda cheese that had been cooked into the eggs. Then she bit into the plain bagel with a good smearing of huckleberry jam. "Oh, that's good." She said around a mouthful of bagel and jam.

The jam looked like raspberry, but the tartness combined with the sweetness on Eloise's tongue reminded her this wasn't raspberry jam. It was more of a cross between a blueberry and blackberry jam. And it was just one more thing to love about Montana.

"I wonder if I can get this jam back home. It's really good." Eloise took another bite of her bagel, forgetting all about her cooling eggs.

Dana turned around from the sink where she had been doing dishes and grinned. "Well, Montana and Idaho are pretty much the only states to have wild huckleberries in any sort of large quantity. The bush doesn't grow outside of the Pacific Northwest. At least, not very well."

A glob of jam was on the edge of Eloise's lips. "I guess I'm just going to have to bring another suitcase home with all of the wonderful items I can't get back in Texas."

"Or," Marty's eyes zeroed in on Eloise's lips. His eyes darkened as he licked his lips. When he spoke, it was with a deep, husky base, "you could just stay here."

Eloise's heart beat a million times a minute and for one second, she thought she'd pass out from the intensity of his gaze. When he kept his eyes on her lips, she licked them and tasted the sweet/tart of the jam that had been left on her mouth. She inhaled and broke their connection when she realized that he was only staring at the jam on her lips, and not really at her. She picked up her napkin and wiped at her lips so hard, there was no way she had any food left on them.

Marty cleared his throat. "Is there any coffee left?" He turned from staring at the woman, to looking at the coffee pot.

Eloise eyed Dana and wasn't sure, but she thought the woman might have smirked before she turned back to the sink.

"Sure, there's still a lot of hot coffee. Help yourself." A soft chuckle came from Dana.

Eloise decided to ignore the laugh since her cheeks had to already be ten shades of red by then. She didn't need to be any more embarrassed than she already was.

"So," Eloise decided to change the subject and get everyone thinking about something else. Something besides her inability to eat properly.

"What have you been working on today, Marty?"

He plopped down at the table and clunked his mug on top. "Nothing, really. Even though I'm feeling so much better, Jerod still won't let me do much more than brush the horses. And I've already brushed them down for today."

"I have to head into town, but there's a few things I need done around the house, if you're up for it?" When Dana turned around, all signs of joking and teasing were gone. Instead, she bit her lower lip and waited.

"Um, sure. What can I do to help?" Marty sat up straight and instantly sported a smile.

Eloise knew that some men didn't do well with sitting around. She also knew that Marty was one such man. She'd already seen his need to work. While she admired that trait, she also knew that in order to heal properly, the man needed to take it easy. So the fact that he was at the ranch, and not at the tree farm, had her wondering what was going on. She kept quiet and waited to see.

"Well, I need the rest of the Christmas decorations brought into the living room. If they're too heavy, then get someone else to do the lifting." Dana arched a brow. "I mean it."

Marty lifted his hands in surrender. "I know, I know."

"Good. Then just take the items out of the boxes and start decorating the house. I don't really care, except for the tree ornaments. Leave those to the side. Tonight, after dinner, we'll all have a good old-fashioned tree decoration party." Dana set the tea towel she'd used to dry her hands with to the side and grabbed a travel coffee mug from the shelf above the coffee maker.

"I can help, too," Eloise offered.

Dana turned around with the travel mug in one hand and the coffee carafe in the other. "I don't want you to overdo it, either. No lifting at all for you."

With a grin, Eloise looked between Marty and Dana. "I never said anything about lifting. I was thinking I could supervise." She took a long sip of her coffee and felt a deep sense of satisfaction once she'd finished the mug.

Marty chuckled. "I see how it is. You don't trust my decorating skills, do you?" He narrowed his eyes and watched Eloise.

She set her mug on the table and leaned in conspiratorially. "Actually, I think your idea of decorating is putting a Santa on one table, then a cowboy hat with some lights on the wall." She sat back and crossed her arms over her chest, just daring him to say otherwise.

He spluttered, "How, when. Who told you?"

Dana laughed. "You mean to tell me that's how you have decorated in the past?"

Marty leaned back in his chair. "Well, not exactly, but close enough. Back in Iraq I had an Air Force blue cammo hat with a string of battery-operated lights that was nailed to the wall next to my bunk. My roommate had a stuffed Santa that his girlfriend sent him. But that wasn't on the table, it sat on his bed."

The room erupted into laughter.

When Dana calmed her laughing down, she said, "Alright, Eloise is in charge of Christmas decorations. Marty, you just follow her lead."

"Wait a minute." Marty shook his head. "Miss Christmas over here hasn't done anything more than I have for the past five years, or so." He crossed his arms over his chest and raised a brow when he returned Eloise's stare.

"That's only because I haven't had any reason to decorate. No one to come over and see my condo. I'm kinda excited to see what you have and get some cute decorations going here. Or at least, some more. I know you have some already up, but for a group of people who work at a Christmas Tree Farm, I would have expected more." With a tilt of her head, Eloise waited for Marty's comeback.

Instead, it was Dana who responded, "Well, it's been kinda hectic here the past two weeks.

Normally, we do have more decorations up. At least the main tree is up and decorated. I only have the tree in the formal living room to decorate tonight."

"And the large family room still needs some festive décor," Eloise added.

Marty had to add his two cents, too. "What about the large dining room? I only saw some garland in there."

"Okay, okay. We are a bit behind. But I trust that you two can get it all finished." Dana pointed at each of them. "Just don't overdo it. You don't want to be bedridden and miss out on all of the fun, do you?"

"No, Ma'am." The serious response from Marty had Eloise thinking she needed to be very careful. So she echoed his response.

"What do you say I help you get settled into the family room? Then I'll go and see what boxes I can easily carry in?" Marty stood up from the table and took his empty coffee mug to the sink.

"I could use a refill of my coffee, then I think I'll be ready to direct your decorating efforts." Eloise couldn't help but grin and shake her head just a little bit. She was going to enjoy bossing Marty around.

Chapter 23

Covered in dust and who knew what else, Marty grumbled as he looked through the boxes in the storeroom. "There better not be mouse droppings in here."

"Nope, just rats." A booming voice from behind Marty called out.

Marty jumped and turned around to find Dixon grinning.

"Hey, man. What are you doing here? Weren't you supposed to be at the tree farm today?" Marty pulled the small box he was going through to the front of the storeroom and then rubbed his chest.

Dixon pointed at Marty. "That's exactly why I'm here. Jerod heard what Dana assigned you and he brought me back so I could supervise."

"Oh, no. Not you, too." Marty moaned and leaned his head back.

"What do you mean?"" Dixon walked past Marty and began hauling boxes that were marked "Christmas" toward the open door.

"Eloise is in the family room. She's going to be supervising my decorating efforts." He scoffed and rolled his eyes.

Dixon grinned. Normally, he was a man of few words, but this Christmas he seemed to be coming out of his shell. Not that Marty knew him well, but people talk. And the word on the ranch was that Dixon was quiet. "Sounds like I wasn't needed here after all. Should I give you two some privacy?" He waggled his brows.

Marty chuckled and punched Dixon's shoulder. "No man. It's not like that. And besides, she can barely move around. It's not like I'm going to turn on some Christmas music and ask her to dance."

"Romantic, huh? I see how it is." Dixon moved out of the way of Marty's fist before he could punch him a second time. "Come on, fess up. What's going on with you two?"

"Nothing. She's headed back to Texas just as soon as the doctor clears her. I'm here for a while yet. And when I leave, I'll most likely move back home with my folks until I find a job." Marty's parents lived on an island in the Outer Banks of South Carolina.

Dixon stood up from the box he was looking inside of. "You mean you don't plan on staying in the area?"

Marty turned around and tilted his head when he thought about what Dixon said. "Why would I stay here? I have no idea whatsoever I'm going to do when I graduate from the ranch. I don't even have a place to stay, other than my parents' house."

Dixon took a moment to get his thoughts in order. Marty had seen how the man liked to think before he spoke.

"You know, most of us plan on leaving and going elsewhere when we first arrive. But over time, things change. Montana is like nowhere else on Earth. The people are real, salt of the Earth types. And they have been great at welcoming every one of us to the area. In fact, there are owners and hiring managers who have specifically asked Jerod which of us is ready to move on to a new job."

"I've heard about how almost all of those who graduated from here have stayed in the area because they had great job offers. But I'm not an engineer or a cow expert. What could I do?" Marty noticed a box labeled 'Christmas' and leaned down to peek inside.

"I don't know, man. But don't make any long-term plans yet. Focus on today, and let tomorrow work itself out." Dixon picked up one of the boxes Marty had pointed out and took it to the door of the storeroom. He placed it just outside the room for when they headed back to the family room.

"Is that what you're doing? Living in the moment?" Marty hadn't heard if Dixon was ready to move on or not. Nor had he heard what plans Dixon might have for a job when he did leave. In fact, Marty didn't even know what Dixon wanted to do when he left the ranch.

With a nod, Dixon bent over and picked up another box. "Yup. I don't even know what I'm going to do when I leave here, or even when I'm leaving. I've made a lot of progress in my healing lately, but I'm not planning to leave any time soon. I still have some work to do on my head before I can leave and get a civilian job."

"Have you thought about going to work for one of the alphabets?" Marty's original plan had been to serve two terms in the Air Force and then move on to the FBI, or another agency, but things changed.

Dixon chuckled. "Na, man. I don't think I'm cut out for the CIA, or even Homeland. I think that when the time comes, I want something quiet."

"Maybe with animals?" One of the things that Marty did know for sure about Dixon was that he was good with farm animals. "Have you thought about going to veterinarian school? The VA will pay for your degree."

"Yeah, I've thought about it. But I don't know if I want to go to Vet school. That's a lot of schooling. And the VA will only pay for my bachelor's degree, not the Doctorate that's needed to be a Vet." Dixon knelt on the dirty ground and began looking through one of the smaller boxes he'd seen in the corner.

Marty stood up from the box he'd just rifled through and looked at Dixon. After thinking about what he knew of the man, which wasn't much, he decided he liked the quietness that surrounded his new friend. "Have you thought about being a chef? Or maybe something in computers?"

Dixon didn't hold back. His laugh was hearty, deep, and loud. "Seriously? Me? A chef? I can barely barbecue a hamburger. Forget about cooking anything decent."

Marty held a hand up and grinned. "I just threw out some ideas. I know you used to drive a truck for the Army. I highly doubt you want to be a truck driver now. And both of those jobs would keep you relatively in the background. Well, as long as you didn't become a celebrity chef." He grinned from ear to ear at the thought of Dixon becoming a celebrity of any sort.

Dixon shivered. "Bite your tongue. I never want to be in the public eye." He paused to think about his options. "Although, computers do sound interesting. Maybe I could design video games?"

Marty paused and looked at the man. He wondered if Dixon had mad skills and was holding back. "Have you ever done any coding before?"

"Nah." Dixon waved a hand in front of his face. "But I've played a lot of video games in my time. How hard could it be?"

Marty shook his head. "Okay, okay. I see you really haven't thought about your future yet." He paused for a minute and thought about what his VA counselor had once asked him. "What did you want to do when your time in the Army was up?"

A distant look crossed Dixon's face as he leaned against the wall in the storeroom. "For a time, I thought I'd become career Army. I was a truck driver, but I was thinking about seeing how to go about changing my MOS to something different when my contract was up."

"Really? Like what?" Now, Marty was curious about the man. What did Dixon secretly want to do?

"I was thinking about becoming a medic. The roadside bomb that took my leg wasn't the first time I'd been hit. It was just the one that took me out of the Army. I'd seen lots of bad things in my time and even helped save a couple of lives." Dixon shrugged and pushed off from the wall.

"Why don't you become a nurse? There are lots of men who become RN's. It's a great career. And I doubt anyone would have an issue with your leg." More and more companies wanted to hire injured veterans. And having a prosthetic no longer held the stigma it once did. Not with all of the servicemembers coming home injured over the past thirty years.

"I don't think I want all of that schooling. And I really don't know if it's what I want anymore." Dixon shook his head and picked up another box that Marty had just finished going through. "I think we have enough boxes to get started, don't you?"

Marty knew the man wanted to change the subject, and he couldn't blame him. When a man had a plan for his life and it was all of a sudden taken away so violently, it was tough to find a new path. He knew that from his own experience. Nothing ever prepared you for such devastation as war. But the aftermath of everything might even be worse.

While serving on the battlefield, living day to day was the only way to go. Shoot, living minute to minute sometimes was all one could manage. But when you had plans for what should come next, and they're ripped from your body, literally and figuratively, it's tough to get centered again and know which way was up and which was down. Marty was still trying to figure that part out. Let alone what steps to take next.

It didn't matter that Dixon had been there for two years already. Two years, two weeks, it didn't matter. All that mattered was getting through the here and now. Marty knew that he wouldn't be making any future plans. Not yet. He still had to find a way to get through his past. "Sure, man. Let's get going with what we have."

"I can't believe they still have boxes and boxes of Christmas stuff in here." Dixon's laugh was a bit forced, but they had been discussing something pretty heavy.

Marty knew that he shouldn't have taken the conversation so far, but he really didn't know what he was going to do. Except for moving back in with his parents. It really was his only choice. Sure, he had a monthly stipend from the VA, but it wasn't enough in this day and age to live off of. He'd need something more to afford a decent place in a safe area. Even rent in Frenchtown, Montana wasn't cheap.

Chapter 24

"It's about time. I was just about to send out a search party for you." Eloise stood on wobbly legs and grinned at Marty.

Marty led the way into the room carrying what looked to be a small box. Eloise arched a brow expecting that box to be light. Behind him, came someone she didn't expect to see.

"Don't worry, he's not lifting anything heavy." Dixon walked through the door with a shy smile and headed to one corner of the room where he put down the two boxes he had carried in. "I'll go get the rest if you two want to discuss where everything will go. I'm only the muscle, not the designer."

Eloise couldn't help but smile. She clapped her hands together. "Thank you, Dixon. I really appreciate your help. As I'm sure Marty does, too." She looked at the man in question, willing him to agree.

"Ah, yes. Thanks, man. I do appreciate the help. I think that if Dana or Jerod had seen me carrying anything, they would have tanned my hide like I was some little kid who got caught doing something naughty." The grin on Marty's face had Eloise wondering if he was speaking from experience.

"That's why the bossman brought me back here. Think of me as your own personal pack mule." Dixon's grin faded when he realized what he called himself.

Eloise had to suck in her lips to keep from laughing. She loved that he just called himself a donkey. "I'd say you're more like the moving man than an animal." She winked, to let him know she was only teasing him.

Dixon rubbed the back of his neck and turned his head down. "I'll be back with the rest of the boxes."

"Sometimes, I wonder if that guy is intending to joke around, of if he really is that naïve." Marty watched Dixon leave the area before he turned to the few boxes that they had so far. "I found some really great decorations. Some of these must have been left here by the previous owners. They might even be antiques."

That caught Eloise's attention and she turned her eyes from the empty doorway and back onto Marty. "Really? What sort of décor did you find?"

"Check this out." Marty leaned over one box and pulled out an antique Santa that looked to be in almost perfect shape. "It was in a plastic bag, I only took it out while in the storeroom." He pointed to the bag in the bottom of the box.

"Wow, that's...wow." Eloise hobbled over to where Marty stood and took the Santa in her hands. It was less than two feet tall, but the furry red suit the jolly elf wore was the sort she'd seen on an old Normal Rockwell painting. This Santa had a shining gold buckle on his black leather belt. The white fur on the suit was still in fantastic shape. She wondered if the statue had ever been taken out of the plastic covering. There was even a tiny table next to Santa with milk and cookies.

"Do you think Dana intended for us to use this?" Marty was only just now thinking about the possibility that Dana might not have wanted this out on display.

Eloise looked up and screwed up her lips. "Honestly, I don't know. If this were mine, and it were an antique, I doubt I'd want it out around a bunch of military guys. No offense,

but some of the guys here are a bit rambunc-
tious."

"Don't I know it." Unsure what to do, Marty
rubbed the back of his neck. "Why don't we put
it back in the bag, and the box, and ask Dana
when she gets home?"

"Are there other items you think could be antiques?" Eloise would love to have the Santa out
on display, but not in an area where it could get
hurt. Maybe she could ask Dana about putting
it in the curio cabinet in the dining room.

For the next two hours Eloise and Marty
worked closely together on sorting the Christmas decorations. He would pull items out and
she would tell him where they might look
best. They were in complete agreement on the
placement of everything except for the wagon
wheel that had Christmas lights and decorations on it.

Eloise wanted to put it in a back corner, but
Marty thought it should actually go in the entryway.

"This is a ranch, after all, Eloise. This is exactly the type of decoration that should be seen
when a visitor comes over." The offending item
was in Marty's hands and he was about to leave
the room they were in so he could put it up in
the entry.

"Wait. I don't think that's something Dana would want everyone to see." She fidgeted with her hands and refused to look Marty in the eyes. They had worked so well together up until this one thing. Why couldn't he see how ugly the wheel was?

He put it on the ground and let out an exasperated sigh. "You're from Texas. Surely, you've seen plenty of these in houses every Christmas. Shoot, I wouldn't be surprised if you've even seen undecorated ones up year-round in more houses than you can remember."

That was the problem. People who weren't from the mid-West always thought that tacky décor was the hallmark of a country home, or a ranch. "Maybe it was back in the sixties, but not today. Most people who do have these sorts of things have them out in the barn or a man-cave. I don't know anyone who puts these up for Christmas where guests can see. I have only seen one up, and that was in a barn. Actually, it was in a tack room. My guess is that some guy was given it as a gift and didn't want to offend the giver, so he put it up out of sight."

"Oh, come on." He lifted one arm and motioned toward the front of the house. "It would be perfect. Maybe we can even start a new trend. What do you think? Wanna step out on a ledge and try something daring?" He waggled his brows.

"What are you two arguing about?" Dixon walked into the room and took one look at the gaudy wagon wheel and busted out laughing. "Oh, that's priceless. Please tell me you're going to put it up in the barn?"

"See?" Eloise pointed to Dixon but glared at Marty. "Even Dixon knows it's atrocious."

"Atrocious? Are you kidding me? That is probably one of the best Christmas decorations I've ever seen." Dixon chuckled and nodded at Marty. "Right?"

"That's what I said. But Miss Christmas decoration here," Marty pointed at Eloise, "said that it's ugly and we shouldn't put it up."

"No, no. Please tell me she didn't." Dixon shook his head and pursed his lips.

"What's all this commotion?" Dana walked into the room and looked around at everyone. "Oh, that's where the wagon wheel wreath is. I've been looking for that. Thanks." She grinned and took it from Marty.

"See." Dixon pointed at Dana and grinned.

"Wait, you like that thing?" Eloise couldn't believe what she was hearing. How could anyone like it? It looked as though it was a real wagon wheel that had been used over a hundred years ago and should have been either in a museum, or on a bonfire.

Dana picked it up and held it close to her body. The thing was almost as tall as she was.

Eloise couldn't understand how the woman was able to pick it up and hold it for so long.

Dana looked around at the faces looking at her. "This is a family heirloom. My parents gave it to me when I married Jerod. We added a couple of small decorations to it. But each new couple who gets it adds something to it. My parents added lights, but I changed them out a few years ago and now they are the colorful LED ones It's really beautiful when plugged in."

Eloise plopped down on the chair and put her face in her hands. "A family heirloom? Did one of your grandparents use it to get here, or something?"

"My great-great-grandfather rode a wagon from New York to here. This was one of the wheels. Everyone who made it got a piece of the wagon. I think ours is the last surviving piece. My family has taken great care of this wheel since it's a symbol of the sacrifice my family made well over a hundred years ago to get here and stake a claim in our land." Dana's chest puffed up and she looked as though she couldn't be prouder of her family heritage.

Feeling like a fool, again, Eloise looked up and apologized. "I'm sorry for saying it was ugly. Knowing the history behind that wheel makes it one of the nicest decorations I've ever seen. Where do you display it?"

"We put it in the family room on the wall next to the TV. It's something we look at all the time during Christmas. Then it goes back in storage to keep it safe the rest of the year." With a sigh, Dana turned her eyes on the wheel. "I wish we could keep it up year-round as a reminder of my family history."

Seeing the wistful expression on Dana's face, and hearing her story, Eloise knew exactly what she was going to get Dana and Jerod as a thank you for hosting her so long and taking such great care of her. She only wished she could be there to see their faces when they opened the gift. However, the knowledge that they would appreciate it for years to come was enough for her. Now, if only she could drive herself in town to find the right craftsman to make it.

"Here," Dixon took the large wheel from Dana. "Let me help you put it up."

Everyone went to the family room and Eloise watched as Marty and Dixon worked together to get the wheel on the wall securely.

"Great job, guys." Eloise hobbled back and took a look at the wheel and the rest of the room. "You know, it actually does look great in here." She grinned and clapped Marty on the shoulders. "Nice job."

"Thanks, now how about you help me make that yule log?" Marty's white teeth shone through his smile.

Eloise took in a deep breath and prayed she wouldn't ruin his big dessert. "Do you think we should watch that cooking show episode again? You know, just to make sure we get it right?"

"No worries." With his phone in his hand, Marty pulled up a clip on YouTube. "Here is the scene right here. We can watch it if we need to, but I have the recipe printed out in my room. I'll go get it." He left to get the printed recipe, leaving the other three in the family room.

"Right, y'all work on that and I'll go rest until everyone gets back. I think there's a lasagna in the freezer and some French bread in the bread box. I can also toss a salad to go with dinner." Dana looked at her watch. "I'll go put the lasagna in now, it will take over an hour. Then I'll rest for a short time. Please wake me if I sleep for more than thirty minutes."

When Dana left the room, Eloise turned her gaze to Dixon. "We're not gonna wake her, right?"

Dixon shook his head. In a low voice, he responded, "I know she was all excited when she saw the wagon wheel, but did you see her eyes? She's utterly exhausted now."

Eloise looked out the door to make sure that Dana wasn't hovering nearby. "Agreed. We should let her sleep. If Jerod wakes her, that's fine. But I don't want to. She could use all the sleep she can get right now."

Marty sauntered back into the room with a piece of paper in his hand. "Alright, who's up for some baking?" He waggled his eyebrows.

"Uh, not me." The sheer look of terror that crossed Dixon's face was almost enough to make Eloise laugh.

She had to cough to cover up her inability to hide her chuckle. "You mean you can hug a cow, but you can't handle baking a cake?"

"Hey, now." Dixon raised his finger and pointed at her. "A yule log isn't just a cake, it's a creation. I may not know much about baking, but I know enough to stay clear when someone attempts to make one of those." He shuddered. "And a cow just lays there or stands. She doesn't make things difficult. But call me when it's ready for some taste testing."

Marty scratched his eyebrow and looked at Eloise. "I guess it's just you and me?"

For some reason, that statement sent a shiver down Eloise's back. She wasn't sure if it was sheer terror, or something else.

Something much more enticing.

Chapter 25

Marty should have known they'd end up dirtier than those chefs on the show. Even though the contestants weren't actual chefs, but celebrities for some other reason, they always seemed so clean. He had even worn an apron. An apron of all things!

"You know, I think you got more on your skin than you did your clothes." Eloise pointed to his face and arms. Arms that had at one time been uncovered.

Now? They were covered with flour, cocoa powder, and he wasn't sure, but was that cream sticking to the hairs on his arms? Marty lifted his arm and sniffed. "Nope, that's the mascarpone cheese." He grinned. "I wouldn't say too much if I were you, miss flour power." He pointed to her face and her overall being of messiness.

She looked down at herself and frowned. "I think that was your fault, thank you very much." The look on her face was anything but grateful. Especially when Eloise crossed her arms over her chest.

He put his arms up in self-defense. "Alright, alright. I admit it, this might not have been the best thing to make."

"You think?" Eloise arched a brow and then glared at him. "We should have started with sugar cookies, or something easy like that."

Dana walked into the kitchen and whistled. "Wow. I don't think I've ever seen this place so messy."

"Don't worry, Dana. We'll clean it up before we're done." Eloise bit her lower lip. She had hoped the woman would have slept the night away. However, since she went to bed so early, she probably got up for a snack.

Dana chuckled. "No worries. I'm just glad you're having fun."

Marty tilted his head to the side. "How do you know we're having fun?"

A glint entered Dana's eyes, but it left when she cleared her throat. "Because, you aren't fighting, just flirting." And with that little comment, she turned and left the kitchen.

"We aren't...she didn't..." Eloise's face felt hot and she refused to look at Marty.

Marty was curious. He wondered if Eloise felt something more than just friendship. He had been feeling something himself, but hadn't been sure. That was until just now. He thought back to all of the time they'd bantered, not fought. And the time when they were apart and he realized he missed her company.

Then, when she hurt herself by tripping over that shovel at the tree farm? He almost had a heart attack thinking she was severely injured. Could it be that he found her more than just pretty? Was there a real attraction between them? Or was that just the hopeful comments of a pregnant woman?

He wasn't sure what to say or do, so he scratched his head. "Gross. I shouldn't have done that."

"What?" Eloise's high-pitched voice sounded indignant. "What's gross? That you might have been flirting with me?"

Marty looked up to see flaming eyes glaring at him. The woman had her messy hands on her hips, and he wanted to flee as quickly as he could. Give him an angry terrorist and he knew exactly what to do. But an angry woman? He was clueless.

The only thing Marty knew to do was surrender. If he'd had a white flag he would have waved it. Well, he might have run, but with the mess they made all over the kitchen, he knew he'd slip and fall on that floor. "Wait, that's not what I said." He held his hand out for Eloise's inspection. "I was talking about my hand."

Eloise blinked a few times and looked from his hand to his head. "Oh, I see." She pointed to his head. "Yeah, that's gross."

Marty's shoulders relaxed just a little bit when he realized that he'd diffused a hostile situation with a woman, possibly for the first time ever. He looked around the room. "What do you say we clean up before we finish the decorating portion of the yule log?"

A tiny smile tried to edge its way onto Eloise's face, but she sucked her lips in to stop it. She sniffed. Then looked down at herself and nodded. "I say we clean up the kitchen, and ourselves. Then maybe tomorrow we can ask Dana for help with the decorating part? I really don't want to get the chocolate icing all over the place. That might prove to be more difficult to clean out of the crevices than cake batter."

"Or specialty cheese." Marty grinned. "Agreed."

It took them longer to clean up the space than it did to turn it into a battlefield. Marty was just finishing up with the mopping when he turned to see Eloise. "Watch out."

But he was too late. Eloise's boot didn't do well on a wet linoleum kitchen floor. Her foot slid out from underneath her and she was heading for the ground. Marty knew it would be a hard hit if he didn't get to her in time.

Without even thinking about his own injuries, he dropped the mop and put his arms out to grab the woman. But he had miscalculated.

With a bang and a boom, he felt the air whoosh out of his chest as he hit the floor with Eloise in his arms. At least he broke her fall. But his head didn't hit the ground. At least not directly. Her hand was behind his head when it hit.

Eloise winced and Marty recognized her pain instantly for he also felt it. Not just in his chest, but also in his low back. He didn't know how, but somehow the mop handle was on the ground beneath him.

"Sorry," Eloise whispered.

But Marty couldn't think about any of the pain, or her words. All he could do was focus on her lips. The way they moved when she breathed. How pink they were. And how badly he wanted to kiss those lips of hers.

"I'm not," his whispered reply was barely more than an exhalation of breath.

Marty began to move closer to her lips, as hers began to move closer to his. It was instinct. He'd been trained for years to work on instinct. Sometimes, an airman's instinct was more accurate than the best intel. Rocky was proof of that. He'd led them around bombs that their best intel never even heard about. Down paths that should have been more dangerous but turned out to be the safer paths.

Now? His instincts were screaming at him to go in for the kiss.

And he had no desire to disobey.

The moment his lips touched hers, an electric shock went through his system. Then it was followed by a warmth he'd never felt before. Something he knew he'd want to feel again and again.

Her lips were softer than he ever thought possible, but also strong when she returned his kiss.

It was forever, yet not nearly long enough, when she pulled back. Her sweet breath flowed over his lips and cheek. She leaned in and kissed his cheek before she rolled off of him.

The moment her body moved away from his, he felt bereft. An important part of him was now gone and he wanted it back. He turned to look at her but instead of seeing a glow of happiness, the type he figured he was sporting, he saw pain.

"Oh, no. Did I hurt you?" Immediately, Marty went into airman mode, and he jumped up. "Here let me help you get to a chair. What hurts?" His eyes looked her up and down. Her boot was still on properly. Her clothes were mussed and there was a splash of water on one side of her shirt, but nothing else looked out of place. There certainly wasn't any blood on the woman. And none of her appendages were hanging wrong. Actually, he thought they were all perfect.

Everything about her was perfect. Her lips were swollen, as though he'd kissed her for hours upon hours. Something he wanted to do, but knew he shouldn't do. While their kiss probably only lasted for thirty seconds, maybe forty-five, he knew that he had to take things slowly. It was his job to ensure they didn't go too far. A full-on make-out session like what he'd done once or twice in high school would send him off the rails. Especially after how he responded to her from just that first, sweet kiss.

Marty led her to a chair and leaned down in front of her, ignoring the real physical pain he felt in his chest and back. "How can I help you?"

Eloise shook her head and that was when he noticed the sheen of water in her eyes.

"Oh no. Please tell me I didn't hurt you." Marty felt awful. He knew he'd taken the brunt of the fall, but maybe her hand that had gone behind his head to cushion his fall was hurt? He took her hand in his and felt it for any damage. The skin was smooth and clean. Nothing looked amiss with her hand. Then just to be safe, he took her other hand. It was fine, too. "What's wrong?" He leaned in closer, trying to give her his emotional support.

Eloise just shook her head again. Then her shoulders jumped and if Marty wasn't wrong, she hiccupped. "Sorry."

"Don't be. Do you need water?" Marty had never subscribed to any of the old wives' tales for stopping hiccups. In his experience, the best way to get rid of them was to lean back a little bit and open his airways. Then take a bunch of long, deep breaths. That always seemed to help get rid of them faster than anything else. Although, when he was a young boy, he liked the spoonful of sugar method best.

She nodded, then hiccupped again.

Marty stood and went and grabbed a glass. Then he filled it with ice and water from the refrigerator door. With the water filter in the fridge, the local water was quite good. Marty had always drank bottled water, even when he was home. But here in Frenchtown, the well water on the ranch had a good taste to it. It wasn't bogged down with all the chemicals most city water had. This one was full of nutrients from the land after running through rocks and who knew what else underground.

"Here." He handed Eloise the glass and she took a few sips.

"Thanks." Once she finished the glass, she set it aside and looked around the room. "I'm sorry."

"For what? Falling? It's not like you knew you'd slip on the floor. I should have done a better job getting the water off the linoleum so no one would do just what you did." One of his hands rubbed his lower back and the other rubbed his chest. Marty prayed that he hadn't set back his healing from the attack by the mad cow.

"Does your chest hurt?" Eloise bit her lower lip and winced. "We shouldn't have made that yule log together."

He pulled a chair closer to her and sat down. Marty knew his pain was causing Eloise pain. It wasn't her fault. The cake making was his idea, after all. "Don't even worry about it. I'm fine. I'm more worried about you. You look like you're in pain. What hurts?"

The softest sound came from her, and Marty had to strain his ears to hear her. "Did you just say your heart hurts?" He sat back and looked at her. No one had said she had any heart issues. He thought he'd heard of people pulling muscles that were close to their heart and that could cause pain that made a person think their heart was in danger.

"Yes." This time, she snuffled and wiped her nose.

Marty realized she was in some serious pain. "Oh, Eloise. We need to call for help." He stood up and was about to go and call for Dana or Jerod. Or anyone who might be able to help. He might even need to call an ambulance.

Her hand reached up and grabbed his wrist. "Sit down. We need to talk."

A different sensation filled his body this time, one he didn't want to experience ever again.

Dread.

Chapter 26

Eloise had really and truly loved that kiss. It sent her heart all a flutter and her entire being felt so light and wonderful. But then she remembered where she was, and who she was kissing. It was wrong, and she knew it.

While Marty wasn't her client, he was the subject of her inspection. If anyone found out she'd kissed him, she would lose all respect from her peers. The government would probably never hire her again, nor would any other company.

But she wanted to kiss him again, oh so much. She needed to know if the emotions that surged through her were an anomaly, or something she truly felt. And then, when she thought more about it, pain shot through her heart. The pain of love and loss, and rejection.

Eloise Sullivan wasn't going to allow anyone, no matter how sweet and fun they were, to break her heart again.

"Oh, my stars and stripes. Where to start?" Eloise muttered to herself.

"How about with what just happened." A sharpness entered Marty's voice; one Eloise hadn't heard before.

She honestly tried to look him in the eye, but as her gaze began to move up to his face, she stopped at his chin. She couldn't get herself to look at his lips. Those wonderful, soft lips that made her feel so special only moments before. And now? She could tell that they were no longer soft. The way his bearded chin moved and tightened told her he was upset.

Upset with her.

Did he know what she was going to say? Or was he upset that she kissed him? Wait, she didn't kiss him, did she? He kissed her first and she just responded, right? She thought back to the kiss and felt herself melt at the most delicious memory she'd ever had. It would probably go down as her number one kiss for the rest of her life. There was no way anyone would be able to match that kiss. At least, no one other than Marty. And she wasn't going to be kissing him again. That she knew for certain.

Eloise licked her lips before saying anything. "I'm sorry. I shouldn't have kissed you. It was wrong."

This time, she was able to look past his chin, and past his lips when she heard him exhale. The expression on his face was enough to give her a heart attack. She caused him pain, and there was nothing she could do to take it away. Would telling him more make it hurt worse? Or hurt less? She wasn't sure, but she had to do something.

Lines were etched around his eyes, his beautiful brown eyes that held hints of green and gold. And before now, he'd always had a certain sparkle when he looked her in the eyes. Now? It was nothing more than a flinty glare that sent shivers up and down her spine. She could see how he did what he did in the Middle East.

She knew dealing with terrorists wasn't an easy task. It was the sort of thing that either broke a person, or made them stronger than Teflon. What she saw looking back at her was Teflon. No, scratch that. What she saw was titanium. The man in front of her was dangerously strong. She wouldn't hurt him with what she had to say. Would she?

Hearts were hearts. They did what they wanted, no matter who held them.

Knowing that Marty was strong and probably already knew where she was headed, if his look of indifference was any indicator, she decided to just be out with it. Eloise always held that ripping the bandaid off was much easier than slowly peeling it back. "What we just did went against my code of ethics. We can't kiss. Not again. I'm sorry. I never should have let that happen."

There, she'd said it. And she kept her gaze on him, sorta. Her eyes had moved off to the side of him, over his shoulder. But she could still see his face and it hardened even more than before.

"I see." He cleared his throat. "Is there anything else? Did you hurt yourself in any way?"

She shook her head. For some reason, her throat was dry and it didn't want to work. Since her water was all gone, she needed to get more. But when she stood up and grabbed the glass, Marty took it from her.

"More water?" His tone wasn't as harsh as it had been, but it wasn't his normal jovial sound, either.

Still unable to speak, she nodded her head. The moment she got the water she was headed to her room to cry. Marty was tough, Eloise knew this. But his stilted walk and Teflon demeanor told her he was hurting. She also noticed he kept rubbing his chest. Either his heart hurt and he didn't know how to handle it, or his bruised ribs were causing problems again. Most likely it was the latter since she landed on him.

The next morning she felt better, but not much. And when she walked into the kitchen, she noticed the silence that greeted her. The room wasn't empty, it was full. Full of people glaring at her.

Eloise looked down to see if something was wrong, but she was put together fine. Then she wracked her brain to think if she'd said anything to anyone about something that might make them all mad. She hadn't. She hadn't even filed her report yet, so that couldn't be the issue. "Good morning."

All she got in response was a snort. Eloise wasn't certain, but she thought it came from Tony. While he wasn't as quiet as Dixon usually was, he still wasn't all that talkative. And she'd never received a snort from him, or anyone else at the ranch.

Whatever was going on was something she didn't understand. After she poured herself a mug of coffee, she turned around and noticed that everyone was glaring at her. With a deep sigh, she put her mug down on the counter. "What?"

No one answered her. They all turned their heads away from her and looked down at their plates. Those who had already finished their breakfast picked up their empty dishes and put them in the sink. They all said something to Marty, then left.

The only ones left with her were Marty, Jerod, and Dana.

"Okay, what did I do?" Eloise motioned to all of the people who had just left the room in some sort of bad mood.

She looked from one sad face to another. When she stopped on Jerod's face, he looked up at her.

"Did you file your report this week?" Jerod's mouth was in a tight line and he glared at her.

"No, I'm not quite done with it yet. I have a few more tweaks to make before it's ready. Why?" She really had no clue what brought that question on.

"Because, I got a call from the VA. It seems that you did turn in a report to them. One that has caused them to rethink sending patients here to us." Jerod crossed his thickly muscled arms over his chest.

"What? I did no such thing." Eloise wracked her brain to see if maybe she'd accidentally sent something, but she hadn't. Then it hit her. "Oh, no. No. That's not right. I didn't send in an official report." She put a hand over her face.

Dana stood up and walked to Eloise. "What? What did you say?"

Eloise began to pant and took shallow breaths. "No, this isn't right." She felt herself begin to hyperventilate and had no clue what she should do.

A hand jutted out in front of her with a brown paper bag. The type she used as a kid when she brought her lunch to school.

"Here, breathe into this. It'll help." The softness of Dana's voice hurt Eloise's heart.

They thought she'd reported them for something bad. Shoot, even the VA did if they were rethinking sending vets to the ranch. But she'd fix it. She had to. How silly she'd been. As she breathed in and out into the bag, she wondered about some of her previous reports. She never maliciously filed anything bad. Sure, there were some places that needed a lot of work, but then there were those that just needed a bit of help to get back on track. How many of them had she closed with her scathing reports?

Would she cause the Crooked Arrow to close? This place was good. No, it was better than that, it was great. An actual lifeline for the vets who came here. So far, they haven't had a single failure. Not one of their patients had been sent back to the VA or just plain turned out for not healing.

In fact, they've been very patient with those who needed extra care. Tony and Dixon had been there for two years. Although Tony's case was different. He needed more surgeries to get better. His tenure at the ranch wasn't out of the ordinary. But Dixon suffered from extreme PTSD and a fear of crowds. From what she'd learned about him, he was finally starting to turn around. Even though his healing was taking a very long time, Jerod didn't seem to care about the time, or the expense of still having him there.

Once she finally got her breathing under control, Eloise took the bag away from her mouth. "I'm so sorry. I'll fix this. It was just a miscommunication when I was injured. I never said anything was wrong with this place. In fact, I'm going to recommend that the VA use your ranch as a model for more. I've never seen something like this place. The way people have healed and moved on to become productive members of society is something to be studied and recreated all over the country."

Dana rubbed Eloise's back. "Thank you."

Jerod uncrossed his arms. "There is more to it than just this place. I don't know if you've seen how we all pray and attend church. As well as give of our own time. But when you put other's needs above your own, something happens inside. And when you let God inside of your heart, even more happens."

"But, you have all of these programs for the vets. The cow cuddling, horse riding, volunteering at the tree farm." Eloise waved her hands all around her. "And the pace of life here in general is very different from the city."

Everyone agreed with her.

"Yes, and we have a great counselor on staff. But the best counselor and the most important program, is God." Jerod sat back in his chair. "We don't force anyone in to church. We don't force anyone to pray or read the Bible. But we do put a Bible in each person's room. They are free to read it whenever they want. I pray before each and every meal. Dana and I do a couple's Bible study each evening in the family room, with the TV off. People see and hear what we do. When God is invited into a home, it's hard for anyone to ignore him."

Eloise winced. She knew what he was saying. She'd grown up in church and had at one time said she was a Christian. Since coming here she'd felt God's presence in a way she hadn't for many, many years. She had always said that she and God lost touch after her accident, but that wasn't true.

In fact, last night she thought back to when she stopped attending regularly and reading her Bible on a daily basis. It was when she and her fiancé had taken their relationship to the next level. A level that was supposed to be reserved for husband and wife. They had both said it was only natural they shared a bed since they were engaged and would be married soon. Most Christians did it nowadays, so why shouldn't they? Marco had said they were only getting a head start on the combining of two into one. That was a good thing, wasn't it?

After that first time together, she felt guilty. Of course, she did. But she did have a ring on her finger. All that was left was the legal part of it right? They had already professed their love for one another and told their family and friends and committed to getting married. The only part left was the legal stuff. God knew they were a couple. They knew they were a couple. Everyone knew.

But when Marco broke off their engagement, a part of her soul went with him. They really had gotten a head start on combining their lives together. So when he broke their connection for good, it broke her, too. That was when she realized that sex wasn't something to be shared until it was much more difficult for a husband to leave his wife than it was for two people who weren't legally tied together yet, to break up.

Until that point, she'd gone to church on occasion, read her Bible when someone asked a question, and joined in on the family premeal prayers. But after that, she had turned her back on God. Although, she told anyone who'd listen that God had turned his back on her.

However, what she'd seen and experienced in this home since she first arrived showed her a different side of it all. Being a Christian wasn't just attending church or doing those outward things that she'd always thought was necessary. It was in the heart.

The hearts of everyone here were so open. When she first arrived, sure there was some pushback, but she knew now that it was because of how she'd interacted in the beginning. She was distrustful and probably a bit rude to them all. A chip on her shoulder was something that had been used to describe her in the past.

But she didn't want to be known for rudeness. She looked at Dana and wished she could be like that sweet woman. Dana had been nothing but nice to her since the beginning. Even this morning when she came in, and everyone else was frosty to her, something they totally had a right to do. Dana had been sweet and showed compassion.

The realization of everything that had happened in just a few short weeks hit her hard.

So hard she had to sit down and really think. And this new bit of information was even more difficult to swallow than those horse pills she had to take when she left the hospital.

"What did the VA say?" Eloise asked, hoping it had nothing to do with her in the end.

Jerod stood up and walked over to refill his mug of coffee. "They said that our ranch was full of accidents and nowhere a recovering veteran should be. They were going to reevaluate our license and for the time being, no more veterans would be offered a slot here. And any grants I had applied for would be on hold."

This was the death nail of a non-profit who operated with the government's blessing. If they took away their license, then this ranch would never see another dime from any grant, no matter who it was that put up the money. She hung her head and wanted to cry. No matter that she had cried herself dry the night before. "I'm so sorry. I'll make sure they understand that's not the case and I'll be sure to share my extremely positive report with them today."

Finally, after being quiet the entire time, Marty walked over and asked, "then why did they think you wanted to shut us down?"

Eloise looked up into the questioning face of Marty. Gone was his angry stare. In place of the anger was confusion and a need to understand.

Which was something she understood herself. "I'm so sorry. Before I left Texas I did think I'd be shutting this place down. I couldn't understand how a real operating ranch could help an injured veteran recover from not only physical injuries, but also PTSD. It made no sense to me. Especially after you had been rammed by a cow, of all things."

"And a place that used cow cuddling as part of its therapy program must be lacking somewhere?" Marty arched a brow.

Eloise winced. "I'm so sorry. I should have come with an open mind, instead I showed up here with preconceived notions of how a therapy ranch should operate, even though I hadn't seen a real one before."

"I thought you said you'd seen one in Texas not too long ago?" Dana asked.

Eloise nodded. "The ranch I inspected was very different from this one. It was more of a day spa set on a ranch than anything else. They had individual counseling sessions in addition to group sessions, like you do here. And they had horseback riding as well as wagon rides. They had two cows and enough chickens to supply them with all the eggs they'd need in addition to being able to cook up a few chickens each month. They even raise a few turkeys for holiday dinners." She chuckled.

"And those concrete walkways with the bumby things and handrails you spoke about?" Jerod asked.

"Yup. Not a real working ranch. The ranch was the backdrop, that's all. Nothing like here where you do more than work the ranch and offer counseling sessions. You also provide an opportunity for the veteran to feel not only wanted but needed again. Most people join the Military to serve. And your requirement for volunteer hours around the tree farm or town provide a way of serving the local community. Something they probably miss from their time in service." It was all starting to come together for Eloise now.

She'd done her research and had interacted with enough veterans to know how they felt about serving. Especially the injured ones. They never got a sense of closure on their time in service. And being told they weren't human enough to keep serving always seemed to add to their poor mental health. Sure, there were those who no longer wanted to help or serve, and that was completely understandable. But for those who still had that innate desire to do for others, it had to be tough not being able to anymore. And even tougher to be told they were no longer good enough to help anyone else.

Especially since the Crooked Arrow Ranch had proved that anyone can help someone else. They did it every day.

Eloise stood up and looked all three of them in the eyes. "I'm going to head back to my room and call the man who hired me for this inspection. I'll explain to him what really happened at the tree farm, and how I think this place is the best situation for anyone who wants to be on a ranch. I do think that in order for it to work, the veteran needs to want to be here. But that's not what we're discussing. I don't see any reason to shut this place down. In fact, I'd like to see your programs expanded. I love the idea of the Alpaca and sheep. That's a wonderful way for an injured veteran to interact with animals while still providing a service that we need, wool for clothing."

"Don't forget, we are also going to start working with another ranch not too far away that is helping women of all ages who have been rescued from human trafficking. They are going to learn how to make items with our wool and then sell them," Dana added.

"I love that concept. And I think that the government will to, when they hear the truth." Eloise left with a mug of coffee shoved into her hands by Dana at the last minute. She smiled at

the sweetest woman around and then headed
back to make that difficult call.

Chapter 27

Marty waited to hear the noise of a door down the hall closing before saying anything. He listened to the soft sound of one shoe hitting the ground followed by the pounding noise of a boot touching the ground. After he heard the snick of a door closing, he turned to Jerod and Dana. "Do you think it really was a misunderstanding?"

Dana nodded. "I do. I know when she first arrived, she was a handful and had her own ideas. But since she's been here, I've seen a huge transformation. I think that God is working in her. And I also believe that He's going to use her for some good here."

Jerod scratched the beard growing out on his chin. "What do you think she's going to do for us?"

"I don't know – exactly." Dana twisted the towel in her hands. "All I know is that God's given me peace when I think about Eloise. And something in my soul says that she's going to usher in something big here." Dana's eyes briefly ran to Marty, but then she turned her attention back to her husband. "Trust her to do the right thing. That's all I can say."

"I don't trust her, not anymore." Marty couldn't understand why he had kissed her the day before only to have her shut him down so quickly and effectively. Was she really trying to shut the ranch down but didn't want the news to get out until after she'd left? She couldn't leave yet. She still had her follow up with the doctor before he would clear her for flying home.

"Do you trust God?" Jerod asked.

Now that was a loaded question if Marty had ever heard one. It wasn't easy to maintain a close relationship with God when one served for so long in the Middle East. And he was usually out in the desert longer than he was back at the base. They had a Chaplain, but it wasn't the same as the church he attended back home. Sure, he prayed, and even read his Bible. But he wasn't as good at it as he knew he should be. And he rarely attended services when he was at the base in Iraq. He usually spent his Sundays on base sleeping when he wasn't out in the pit.

He never got enough sleep when he was out on patrol. It wasn't easy sleeping in the open desert. And they always had to take turns with security duty. So even if he could sleep, it was always interrupted when he was woken up to take his turn at guard duty.

"I do trust God, but that doesn't mean I have to trust Eloise." Now he sounded as though he was a petulant child who didn't get the ice cream he wanted. Only in this case, he didn't get the girl he wanted.

But did he really want the girl? Not if she was working behind their backs to shut down the ranch. Even though Marty had been there for such a short amount of time, he knew that the place was special. And not just because there were other Army and Air Force there. No, he felt a sense of peace he hadn't experienced since the first time he ever set foot in the Middle East.

"True." Jerod crossed his arms over his chest and leaned against the kitchen wall next to the fridge. The image of the big man next to the fridge put his size into perspective.

Marty realized in that instance how big Jerod really was. While the fridge was taller and wider, Jerod wasn't much smaller than the machine. He stayed quiet while Jerod just looked at him. A sense of unease crept up his spine and he thought about what Jerod said. Marty knew that if he trusted God, then there was no reason to worry about what Eloise might, or might not, be doing. If God wanted this ranch to succeed, it would. It may not be easy, and there might be some setbacks. But if God was behind this, then it would work for His glory in the end.

At least, that's what he remembered from his church days.

"Fine." Marty threw his hands up and shook his head. "What should I be doing?"

"First," Dana interjected, "get rid of your attitude. If this was just miscommunication, give Eloise a chance to fix the problem. Maybe even help her, if you can."

Marty thought about what Dana just said, but didn't have any clue how to help Eloise. "What can I do? I don't know the people she's working with."

"True." A pensive look crossed Dana's face. She took a few more seconds to think and then her eyes brightened. "How about you write out your experiences here so far, and what you think of this ranch. You should be seen as being objective since you haven't been here very long."

Marty slapped his hands. "Fantastic idea. I'll do just that." He left the kitchen and decided to head to his room to write out his thoughts. But before he was even halfway there, he realized he left something very important behind and turned back around.

When he was outside of the kitchen door, he stopped when he heard Jerod consoling Dana. "Shh, it's alright. Everything will be fine."

"But how do you know? We have a baby on the way. Now's not the time to lose our grants." It sounded as though Dana was sniffling.

Marty hoped she wasn't crying. He hated it when women cried. He never knew what to do. In fact, he wasn't sure if he should just turn around and head to his room, or make some noise and go into the kitchen for what he left behind.

"God is in this entire situation. I know it. I can feel it deep down inside." Jerod's soft words of encouragement for his wife also hit Marty's heart.

If God really was in this, then why was he worried? Marty wished he trusted God as well as Jerod did. He looked around the hallway and noticed all of the Christmas decorations and remembered he was supposed to be helping out at the tree farm. He really wanted to help, but today he was assigned a job here at the ranch. And he was going to do it, too.

Forgetting all about his mug of coffee, Marty turned and headed back to his room. But before he could make it there, he almost bumped into someone else who was practically running toward the kitchen. "Oomph."

She was the last one he wanted to see at that moment. Marty's assignment was to write out his thoughts, and he needed to do that. But the excitement on Eloise's face had him wondering what was going on with her. Plus, he still wasn't sure how he felt about her and the whole fiasco.

"Marty! Good. I'm so glad I found you. I just got off the phone with my contact at the VA. Let's find Jerod and Dana before I tell you." Eloise grabbed his hand and led him back down the hallway toward the kitchen.

When they entered the room, Dana was in Jerod's arms and she was wiping tears away from her cheeks.

Eloise stopped quickly and Marty almost rammed into her back. When the woman let his hand go, he stepped around her. "Is everything alright?"

"Sorry, pregnancy hormones. The tiniest thing sets me off these days." Dana shrugged and moved to make a fresh pot of coffee.

Not believing the story, Marty screwed his lips and glared at Eloise. She had been the one to cause the pain he had heard, and seen, coming from Dana.

"I'm so sorry for the confusion. I don't know why Reginald from the VA acted that way. He had no right to do that. And my contact even told me so. Before I even reached Steve, there was already a bunch of higher-ups meeting to discuss Reginald's behavior. Steve promised me that everything was going to work out fine. In fact, he had already had a discussion with the regional VA Manager and the head of the US Government Grant Office." Eloise beamed as though what she just said made any sense to anyone other than her.

Maybe it did and maybe Marty was the only one confused. But Jerod looked just as confused as he did. Only Dana brightened and walked to Eloise. She picked up the other woman's hands. "Really? What do you think that means?"

Eloise licked her lips and looked around the room.

Nelly and Sam had joined them.

"Hey, no one answered when we knocked so we figured everyone was out back in the barn, or something. What's going on?" Sam looked around at all of the faces in the room.

Even Rogue and Razzle looked at everyone. Then Razzle walked over and sat down next to Marty.

"Hey, boy. Good to see you again." Marty smiled and leaned down to pat the dog's head.

It seemed that every time the dog came to him, Marty couldn't help but smile and feel a little bit of his heaviness, grief, or whatever negative feelings he was experiencing, leave. "You really are a gift from God, aren't you?"

Razzle licked his hand since Marty's face was out of his reach.

Everyone, Jerod included, laughed when they watched the man and what was sure to be *his* dog. Or was it dog and *his* human? The jury was still out on how it all worked.

"Okay, can someone tell me what's going on?" Nelly looked around and her brows furrowed. "I got a very weird email from the VA, one that I'm not sure is accurate and I can't get anyone to call me back."

Dread filled Marty and he stood up. He ran a hand down his face and then looked to Jerod. That man's face had turned white as a ghost. "Please tell me that the VA hasn't threatened to take away your grants?"

"No, they told me that the Crooked Arrow Ranch no longer qualified for my trained dogs. What's going on?" The dog trainer crossed her arms over her chest and waited for an answer.

"Oh, boy." Dana gulped and reached out to Jerod.

"Why don't y'all take a seat and I'll get us some coffee. Eloise, can you explain what's going on?"

Jerod led his wife to the nearest chair. Then he leaned down and spoke only to her, "would you like some green tea? Or maybe the chamomile blend that Lottie made for you?"

"How about the peppermint blend? I think I want the added comfort." Dana kissed her husband's cheek and sat back while he went to make the drinks.

Marty had never seen Dana sit while someone else made coffee and tea for a room full of people. She'd always been the consummate hostess. Her need to sit and not do anything left him feeling as though she wasn't doing well. Not well at all. And it was most likely all his fault.

If only he hadn't jumped in front of that mad cow. But then he remembered what would have happened if he hadn't, and decided he did make the right choice. Was there something else he could have done to save the ranch?

"Please, don't worry about any of this. It's getting cleared up now. In fact, I think both this ranch and yours," Eloise nodded in Nelly's direction, "are going to get more funding, and more veterans. Probably not until the new year, though."

"Wait, what?" He must have heard wrong. Marty was sure Eloise was saying that everyone was going to be fine, and more money was going to be made available to both ranches. But how was that possible when one of the big wigs at the VA said the ranch would most likely be closed down?

Both of her hands flew around her face erratically and Eloise giggled. "Sorry, I'm just so excited. I can't believe what I just heard."

The rest of the room was silent as though they were waiting on pins and needles.

It was Marty who pressed her forward. "Well? What is going on?"

"Sorry, sorry." Eloise shook her head and sighed. Then she sat down and took a long drink of the coffee Jerod had placed at the table in front of her. "It seems that when I was injured, one of the guys at the VA who isn't too happy about ranches like yours," she motioned toward Jerod. "Well, he decided now was his chance to put an end to them all. So he told the man in charge of these outside medical programs that it was too dangerous. He even went so far as to say that Marty was gored by a bull."

Nelly snorted. "Really? Gored by a bull? And the VA uppity up guy believed it?"

Sam shook his head. "You'd be surprised at what those suits will believe. Especially when it comes to money."

Eloise pointed to Sam with her left hand while the pointer finger on her right touched the tip of her nose. "Exactly. It's all about money. It seems this disgruntled guy, had a plan." She shook her head and looked off into the distance. Then she drank more coffee.

<h1 style="text-align:center">Chapter 28</h1>

The woman was wired. Whether it was from too much caffeine already, or something else, he couldn't say. But caffeine was most likely to blame. The ranch did tend to offer it up like candy to a little kid.

"Don't you think you might want to hold off on any more coffee? Maybe try some chamomile tea?" Marty asked once he noticed how her hands shook.

She looked down at the empty cup in front of her. "Oh, yeah. Probably right."

Jerod stood up. "We have a large selection of caffeine-free tea. What would you like?" The kettle he used for Dana's tea still sat on the stove top.

"Um, whatever Dana had is fine with me. Thanks." Eloise smiled at Jerod and then sat on her hands. She squirmed in her seat like a little girl sitting in church on a warm summer day just itching to get back outside and play.

But she wasn't a little girl.

This wasn't church.

And it most certainly wasn't the sort of day anyone wanted to be outside and playing. Plus, her foot was still in the boot, and she had a couple more days of rest before she could look into getting it off.

"Well? Don't stop. Keep going," Sam urged. He could be a bit surly, but after working at his ranch a few times and helping with the dogs, it didn't appear that Eloise was the least bit intimidated by the man.

"Right, sorry." Eloise winced. "Where was I? Oh, right. The disgruntled VA guy, Reginald. My contact, Steve, knows Reginald. And it seems that the guy has a cousin who wants to run a mountain camp for returning veterans. But he was denied funding."

Sam furrowed his brow. "But mountain camps are also good, just like the ranches. Different settings work for different people. So why would he be denied funding?"

"Good question." Jerod asked. "I have an old Army buddy who went to one when he came home and it helped him. I highly recommend finding the style, or setting, that an injured vet feels comfortable in and going there if the hospital setting doesn't work."

"Pft." Marty almost laughed. "I doubt the hospital setting works for very many returning veterans."

Nelly stood and put her arms out. "Hey, you guys can discuss settings and styles until the cows come home, but not until *after* we hear what Eloise has learned today."

Everyone around the table grumbled. Even both dogs woofed a light sound that to Marty's ears sounded like agreement. He looked down at the dog who had taken up residence next to his chair. He put a hand on the dog's head and Razzle leaned in to his touch. A sense of belonging filled Marty's chest and he knew he needed to talk to Nelly again when this was all over.

"Right, so Reginald's cousin has scammed the VA and a few other places out of grant money. Every couple of years he starts a new," Eloise used air quotes, "non-profit but never does what he says he's going to do with the money. Instead, he seems to live the high life."

"Whoa." Marty sat back in his chair and thought about all of the people who could have been helped if that previous grant money had gone to legitimate non-profits. "Are you saying that Reginald tried to close this place, and

Nelly's too, down so that he could funnel the money to his cousin?"

Eloise's eyes widened and she nodded. "That's what Steve thinks has been happening. It seems Reginald took a few things I said early on and twisted them around to fit his narrative." She smiled at Jerod when he put a mug of hot tea in front of her.

Nelly put up a hand. "So, does this mean that I'm good to keep matching up dogs with the Crooked Arrow residents?" She nodded toward Razzle and Marty.

Everyone around the table smiled when they saw how Razzle looked up at Marty with what one could only read as love. The dog was as close to Marty as he could get without being in his lap. And he only had eyes for the injured TACP airman.

Eloise licked the peppermint tea from her lips before speaking. "I can't really say for sure. But I think everyone should work as usual. My guess is that within a day or two it will be worked out. But I can say," she turned to look at Jerod. "That Steve and his boss are very excited about the ranch working with the ladies who have been rescued from human trafficking. They know that those women aren't under their purview since they aren't veterans, but they still like the idea. Steve has also spoken with someone he knows over at Homeland Security and they are going to put together a list of other grant opportunities for both ranches."

"Wait, what's the deal with those rescued ladies? I know there's been talk about helping them, but I thought it was just talk so far. That we needed more women here to be the go-betweens with them." Marty knew that Jerod wanted to help the ladies at the White Rose Ranch, but he'd thought it was only *talk* so far.

"Declan is really working with them since he's the area alpaca and sheep expert. But Marnie was also interested once she heard about them. Nothing is certain yet. It's just something we're looking into. And you're right." Jerod rubbed his chin and winced. "They aren't too thrilled about working closely with a bunch of alpha men. I think when we have more women here, then we can look closer at helping them."

"What about the women in town? Surely there are ladies in town, or on other ranches, that would like to help them?" Eloise hadn't been in Frenchtown long, but Marty knew she'd met a few ladies and liked them.

One was the town's new librarian, Cheyenne Thompson. She'd been over here once last week talking to Eloise about different ideas she had to made the library more accessible to those who needed it. Specifically, using audiobooks for those who have poor eyesight. But a lot of the older ranchers and farmers don't have Internet access at home. They have to come into the library to download a book on a device and then take it home where they could use it.

Jerod took a seat next to his wife and held her hand.

After Nelly finished her coffee, she smiled at Sam. "You know, I could probably take some of my dogs over there to meet the ladies. While they aren't emotional support dogs, they might help some of the ladies feel better. You've seen how the dogs take to people who need them."

"I am working on getting a license to train emotional support dogs. It will take a while, but maybe that's another way we can help out." The old burly Sam was someone Marty had never seen, just heard tales about. But the Sam he knew and saw daily was an inspiration to him.

It was good for Marty to see residents who have graduated from the program and went on to do good things with their lives. And training dogs to be whatever a person needed was a very good job. While it wasn't Marty's calling, he did have a huge amount of respect for both Nelly and Sam. They were the perfect couple.

All of a sudden, Eloise sat back in her chair with her shoulders rolled forward and a sad look on her face. Gone was the excitement and antsy women who had just shared some of the best news anyone at the ranch could have hoped for.

"What's wrong?" Marty hoped they weren't getting ahead of themselves with how happy they all had become. It would be worse than before if Eloise had oversold the good news.

"Nothing." Eloise shrugged.

"Is there something else? Did we misunderstand that everything will be alright?" Marty asked in a voice so low he doubted anyone around them could hear it.

Everyone else around them were all talking and had ignored Marty and Eloise's quiet discussion.

"No, it's nothing like that." Eloise assured him.

"That's good. Then what's wrong?" He pressed her for more information.

She sighed. "It's just that I realized I won't be around to see all of the new projects come to fruition. The next year here is going to be amazing. I'm very happy for you all, but I wish Texas wasn't so far away."

Maybe it was a good thing Eloise had told him the kiss was a mistake. Marty realized in that moment that he wanted more than anything for her to be there with him, and the rest of the team, to see what was going to happen. Something inside of him knew that big things were coming for the area. But more than that, he wanted to be holding her hand when they played out.

Marty's emotions had gone round and round that morning. Actually, since last night, he'd felt so many different things. Now, confusion marred the happy moment. Everything was going to be just fine with the ranch. The other two ranches he knew about would be doing well, too. Which would only bode well for other ranches and farms in the area. God was working wonders here, and he was happy about it.

But he was also sad that Eloise wouldn't be around to see it all. She helped to bring some of it about, if what she said the VA guy wanted to do was accurate. And he knew she was correct. Marty had learned today not to distrust Eloise, but to trust her.

Even her decision the previous night to stop his kiss was the right call. When Eloise left, Marty wasn't going to be happy. Not at all.

Chapter 29

Eloise didn't know how she got through the rest of the week without crying again. But she did. Instead of being sad, she was so busy she didn't have time to think about Marty and the fact that she would be leaving next week and would probably never see him again.

"So, I can travel next week?" Eloise wanted to make sure she understood the doctor and what he was saying.

"If you continue to heal the way you are, then yes. But if you have any swelling, or extreme pain, then no. I'll need to see you again. And when you get home, please set up an appointment to see your regular doctor, in person, as soon as possible. I want him to examine your foot to make sure you're healing up nicely." The doctor shook her hand and bid her good day.

When she left the doctor's office, Dana was outside waiting for her. A pang of sadness hit her heart that it wasn't Marty. Since she'd arrived he'd been her constant companion. Well, until a few days ago. After that fiasco with the VA he tended to keep clear of her.

Not that Eloise could blame him. A part of her was glad that he wasn't always close by sending her heart into overdrive. Whenever she saw him, she could feel the pace of her heart picking up and her stomach did somersaults like she was a teenager having her first crush.

Another part of her wished he could be by her side every minute of every day. But she knew that was foolish. It was going to be hard enough to say goodbye as it was.

"So? Good news or bad?" Dana asked once they were inside the truck.

"Good news. I can go home next week. I have to follow up with my doctor, but the boot comes off and I just have to be careful." Eloise pulled her gloves off and put her hands in front of the heater vent to warm them up. The inside of the truck cab was chilly.

"Then why the sad face?" Dana changed the radio station to the country Christmas hits of the past four decades.

When the smooth baritone of Clint Black came on the radio, Eloise relaxed just a little bit more. She took her time with her response. If she'd answered right away, she would have said Marty. But he wasn't the only reason she was sad.

Being in Frenchtown for the past few weeks had done a number on her. She'd been more sociable and friendlier than she could even remember. In fact, she thought she might have found her tribe. One of her teachers in college had spoken about certain people that just made you feel at home. People who liked you just as you were, flaws and all. Those were what he had called a tribe. The good folks of the Crooked Arrow, and even those she knew in Frenchtown like Nelly, Sam, and Lottie, had become her tribe. She didn't even understand how that happened so quickly.

So, once she had taken a moment to consider her words she said, "I think I'm going to miss this place when I'm gone."

Out of the corner of her eye, Eloise saw how Dana had to bite her lip to keep from grinning.

"Oh yeah? Then why don't you stay?" The woman said as she turned out of town and onto the highway that would take them home.

"Because my condo and my life are all back in Texas. Not to mention my family." Eloise knew that mentioning her family last was very telling. While she wasn't on bad terms with her family, she did love them, they had just grown apart. Mostly because Eloise had sequestered herself in her small condo ever since the accident.

"Did you know they have these things called smart phones? You can call up family and friends to talk for as long as you like. You can also do video calls on them." This time, Dana did let herself grin.

"Ha, ha. I know. But, I've never lived so far away from my family before. I'm not sure how I'll like it. And what about my job?" Even Eloise knew that was a lame excuse. She worked from home and traveled to job sites when needed. There was nothing that said she couldn't move to a different state.

"That's what airplanes are for." Dana turned the volume on the radio down. "You know, you could stay with us until you find a place. I bet there are a ton of places you could find. A lot of the ranches have smaller houses on their property that they rent out. Some even have Wi-Fi included."

Eloise laughed when she remembered how few ranchers and farmers were connected to the web at home. "I think I'd prefer to live in town, if I were to move here. But still, I don't know. That's a huge decision."

"Yes, it is. And it's one that really should be prayed about before deciding. Either way."

Dana had always been friendly toward Eloise, and never once did she doubt the woman's motives behind her inspection.

Eloise appreciated the generous friendship Dana had offered her from the very beginning. But could she really pick up her entire life and move it to the middle of nowhere? She had friends back home and family.

Well, okay, the friends weren't really there anymore. And that was all Eloise's fault. She knew that. And her family lived on the outskirts of town. In all honesty, it wasn't like she saw them all that much anymore. Usually, her schedule kept her quite busy with little time to spend at her parents' house. And they rarely came into town, preferring the peace and quiet of the small piece of property they had.

Then she thought about Marty. He'd been so distant the past few days. She liked him, she really did. And that kiss, her heart still beat a million times a minute when she thought of it. Her hand moved up to her chest involuntarily and rubbed at the pain she felt. Eloise knew he had every right to be upset with her, she had been part of the problem, but it was finally working itself out. And it looked as though the ranch, along with Nelly's business, would be in much better shape than before.

Plus, that woman's ranch, The White Rose, was in line for more funding, too. While nothing was finalized, the government didn't work that quickly, everyone was in agreement that this area was a good investment.

Before they arrived home, Eloise's phone rang. Without looking at the caller ID she answered it, "Hello."

"Eloise Sullivan?" A voice she didn't recognize was on the other end and she pulled the phone back to see the number. It was from DC but not a number she knew.

"Yes, who's calling?" Eloise sat straighter in her seat and glanced over to Dana. The woman had turned the radio down even further when she first answered her phone.

"This is Dorothy Shilling with the US Department of Agriculture. I was hoping to speak with you about some funding opportunities for the Frenchtown, Montana area."

This woman probably was looking to find Jerod, or someone else who had applied for agriculture grants in the area. "Okay. What can I do for you?" Eloise knew that her voice sounded unsure, because she really was unsure what this was about.

However, since the woman was supposedly calling from a US Government office, she'd listen and see what was happening.

"I understand there are several organizations in the area who have applied for a variety of grants. One to help returning veterans and another to help women who have been rescued from human trafficking. Is this correct?" The sound of paper shuffling behind Dorothy's words could be heard on the phone.

"Yes, I believe so. But I must say I don't know much about the White Rose Ranch." Which was true, Eloise had been there once and that was it. And that was only two days ago when she met with the woman who ran the ranch, or what there is of it so far.

"I'd like to set up a meeting with you, the ranch heads, and myself for next week, if that's possible?" Dorothy asked.

Eloise looked at Dana, and wondered if she should put the call on speaker. Dana would be better to speak with than Eloise. "I am sure they would all be interested in talking with you, but I won't be here. I'm heading home to Texas early next week."

"You don't live in the area?" More sounds of paper rustling came over the line. "Why was I given your name as the local contact?"

"Honestly, I don't know. I'm an ADA Coordinator and the US Government hires me to conduct inspections for organizations that received federal funding. My time here is up and

I was planning on heading home." This conversation was starting to confuse Eloise. She wondered who it was that gave her Eloise's contact information.

"I see. Is there a local grant coordinator? I'm coming into town next week for a few days to speak with various people and I'll need a point of contact if things work out."

"This town is too small, but maybe there is one somewhere else in the state? I can check and get back with you, if that's alright?" Eloise wanted to help everyone here, she just wasn't sure how. Yet.

"It's quitting time for me, and I'm spending the weekend with family. Will you still be there on Monday? I was planning to fly out Monday morning, so I should be there early afternoon. Even if you aren't the area coordinator, maybe you can introduce me to the locals?" Dorothy's request wasn't out of the ordinary.

It was fairly common for someone who was knowledgeable about an area to introduce someone from DC when they came to town. Eloise had done several introductions in Houston in the past. She'd even driven down to Dallas and assisted others in that area.

While Eloise didn't have her return ticket yet, she could stay for a few extra days, she supposed. "Sure, I'll see what I can do to help facilitate some introductions. Do you have a place to stay in town yet?"

"Yes, I'm booked at a local B&B. Is this your cell?"

They spoke a few more minutes and Dorothy agreed to send Eloise her itinerary so they could meet up on Monday. Which meant that Eloise was going to have to get back on the phone and find out who in the area could meet with Dorothy next week and help her with her project.

After she hung up the phone, Dana asked her what that was all about.

"It's strange, but not uncommon. Would it be alright if I stayed a few more days?" Eloise went on to explain who it was and why she needed to stay.

"Of course, you can stay as long as you like. Off the top of my head, I don't know of anyone else who could do what you can. I'll have to speak with Jerod and Megan. They would know if we have an area grant coordinator, or someone like that." Dana turned off the highway and headed down a short road that took them to the ranch.

When they parked out front, Jerod walked out to greet them, followed by Marty and Megan.

Chapter 30

"Hey there, how'd the doctor appointment go? Did you get the all clear?" Jerod grinned after kissing his wife's cheek.

"I did, but it seems I am going to stay a little bit longer, if that's alright?" Eloise closed the truck door behind her, hoping that her request would be acceptable to everyone, not just Dana.

"I hope you know that you're welcome to stay as long as you like. But why do you need to stay longer?" Jerod didn't seem upset, just curious. He still smiled and put his arm around his wife's waist when he escorted them all back inside the house.

"Why don't we all head to the kitchen and I'll make coffee and tea? Eloise has some interesting news to share with you." Dana took off her outerwear and then moved toward the kitchen.

"I'll be heading to my office, call me if you need anything." Megan turned in the opposite direction of the kitchen.

"Megan, I think you might need to hear this as well. I received an interesting call from the Department of Agriculture on our way back." Not wanting to cause any issues with Marty, but still hoping he wasn't mad at her, Eloise looked at him and smiled. "And you might be interested as well."

Marty put a hand on his chest. "Me? Why?"

Eloise shrugged. "I'm not really sure, but I think it might be an all-hands-on deck thing next week."

While Marty was curious, he knew he wasn't part of the management team at the ranch. And since the inquiry behind his accident was supposed to be closed, he had no idea what was going on. When he looked at Eloise, his stomach rolled and an image of their kiss replayed in his head, and heart. He wasn't sure why she wanted to stay longer, but if she wasn't interested in him, then maybe she just didn't realize how awkward this was for him.

He had worked hard the past few days to stay as far away from her as possible. Every time he saw her, he wanted to reach out and touch her, hold her hand, push a stray hair out of her face.

Anything to feel that sense of connection they shared when they kissed.

Which was why he was so confused. He knew when a woman was into him, and she enjoyed that kiss just as much as he did. Marty had also noticed how when she looks at him, her cheeks turn pink, and her eyes dilated. All signs of interest on her part.

Since she was heading back to Texas, he had understood her need to not let things go any further. He did. But still...

While Marty thought about Eloise, they had all quietly entered the kitchen and took their seats. He noticed that Eloise offered to help Dana with the coffee and tea. Even though Dana drank a cup of coffee in the morning, she'd begun drinking caffeine free tea the rest of the day. He had no clue why a pregnant woman couldn't have coffee, especially since she did have one cup in the mornings, but he knew absolutely nothing about being a mom in the making. So he had said nothing when he saw Dana put a tea bag into a mug of hot water.

He did notice how Dana eyed the coffee everyone was drinking. And he felt bad for her. Was it tough for her to see everyone else drinking her favorite drink while she had to have a substitute? If so, then he figured she was already going to be a great mom.

And when he saw Jerod take a mug of hot water and put a tea bag in it, he couldn't help but grin. The big cowboy always had a mug of coffee in his hands. If he felt the need to sacrifice his favorite drink alongside his wife, then Jerod was on his way to being a great dad.

Marty needed to shake himself out of his thoughts when he started to wonder if he'd be able to do such a thing if his wife was pregnant. That was not something he was ready to consider. Not even close.

And with that thought, he sat as far away from Eloise at the table as he could. Sadly, it put him across the table from her and he couldn't help but look at her.

He did have the decency to turn away anytime she looked his way. The last thing he needed was for her to think he was some sort of stalker. He wasn't. When she left, he'd leave her be and do his very best to forget all about her.

It might take time, but he'd do it. It's not like they had fallen in love with each other, or anything crazy like that. But when his heart pounded out its denial of his thoughts, he figured he better pay attention to what was being said.

And not fantasize about the beautiful blond-haired, blue-eyed woman who had captured his imagination.

He cleared his throat and looked down at his mug. When he tuned back into the conversation, his heart stopped beating. She was going to be in town all next week?

"Eloise, we don't have an area grant coordinator. In fact, I don't think there is one closer than Seattle." Megan winced and looked at Jerod, who nodded.

"Please, would you consider staying and helping us with whatever this woman is hoping to accomplish? If she's with the Agricultural Department, then we need someone who knows how the government works." Jerod chuckled. "We've actually been thinking about hiring a company who can act as an intermediary for us and the government. You know better than I do how difficult they are to work with."

Eloise bit her lower lip and nodded. "That's true. They have some strange requirements. And all of the hoops one has to go through." She shook her head.

Megan reached out and squeezed Eloise's hand. "Thank you. You don't know how much we appreciate your help."

"Feel free to send us an invoice for whatever work you do next week. We'll find the money to pay you." Jerod's hand squeezed the mug so hard, his knuckles turned white.

"I won't be billing you for anything. You've been so gracious and hospitable by letting me stay here. I've saved a lot of money by not having to rent a car or a hotel room. I'll gladly help in any way I can. Just know, that I'm an ADA Coordinator, my specialty is helping the disabled. I'm not sure what I can do to help with Agriculture." Eloise's pretty nose scrunched up.

Marty chuckled. "I am willing to bet that you'll know more than you realize."

All heads turned his way and he realized he'd said it out loud. He hadn't intended to speak.

"I don't know if she's going to have questions about you, or for you, but can you be on hand to help out as well?" Jerod asked.

Marty knew he was still on limited duty. But the tree farm needed more help. He'd spent the previous day there helping and knew that they were understaffed. "What about the tree farm"

Megan shook her head. "Don't worry about them. School is out after today and several of the local students will be helping until Christmas. Daniel told me last night that with those kids, most of you guys won't be needed."

"So, does that mean that I'll get my guys back for the next few weeks?" Jerod grinned, but it was obvious to everyone that he didn't mean it.

"Well, there is still a need for more help, but I don't think Daniel needs as much as he did.

So, if Dixon and Tony still want to help, Daniel won't say no." Megan was seriously dating the tree farm foreman.

Marty had heard they were talking about marriage, too. But he wasn't sure about any of that. His counselor's love life wasn't any of his business. "Of course, I'll help wherever you need me. But I'm not sure what I can do to help. Will you be around?"

Jerod nodded. "Of course. I'll be as involved as I can. But it might be nice for this DC woman to see one of our residents. She might have questions for you and what it's like to be here."

After Marty set his empty mug on the table, he nodded. "I'll be happy to help."

TRIPPING OVER CHRISTMAS

$\mathscr{C}hapter\ 31$

Eloise wasn't sure what to expect when Dorothy arrived on their doorstep Monday afternoon, but it wasn't a woman her age. Maybe it was the name? Not too many people in her generation had that name anymore. And she had sounded so formal on the phone. But Dorothy was from Washington, DC. Business casual wasn't something she ever saw when she had been there. Not that she traveled there often for work, but it did happen on occasion.

"Dorothy?" Eloise asked, with Dana by her side. The two had waited close to the front door for the woman to arrive. And when they heard a car pull up, not a truck, they assumed it was her.

"Hi, Eloise?" The woman asked. She was in a tan pantsuit with a cream blouse underneath.

She had on a long, dark brown wool coat that matched her outfit perfectly. The only thing out of place were the black snow boots. But those made sense considering where they were.

If Eloise had to guess, she'd bet the woman wore high heels on the plane and didn't change her shoes until she got in the car at the airport.

Dana welcomed her in and ushered them into the formal living room, where Jerod and Marty were already sitting with a tea and coffee tray waiting. Eloise was surprised at what a great hostess Dana had proven to be. Jerod's wife could easily entertain royalty with how well she handled every situation.

Once the introductions were over, Dana asked, "would you like coffee or tea?"

"Coffee, please. It's been a long day." Dorothy sat back and breathed in the coffee aroma once she had been served.

"I know you all have a lot of questions, as do I. But I wanted to have an initial meeting to let you know in person that there are quite a few people in DC who have been looking at your ranch, and a few other places in the area." Nothing on Dorothy's face looked as though she might be worried.

However, Eloise didn't like what the woman had just said. It was never a good thing when the powers that be in DC looked closely at anyone outside the beltway. Eloise had seen several places go out of business when that happened. In fact, she'd never seen anything good come of special attention from the government. When they wanted to know something, they usually contracted with people like Eloise. The only time they looked closely themselves, was when there was trouble.

As Eloise was about to say something, Jerod cleared his throat. "Does this mean that I should be worried?"

Dorothy looked at Jerod, then her eyes widened. "Oh, no. It's nothing like that. This is actually a good thing." She smiled. "I wanted to come here personally to speak with you all because it's not too often good things like this happen."

"I'm confused." Megan stood up and paced to the window. "I am usually the one who applies for the grants, and I've never spoken to you or anyone from your office. What's really going on?"

Leave it to Megan to get right to the point. Eloise grinned. She hadn't spent a lot of time with the counselor, but the woman had left a good impression with Eloise.

Dorothy took another sip of her coffee, then set it down on the side table next to her. "I realize this might not seem like a good thing, but I have good news to share. Multiple agencies want to assign grant money to this area." She looked at Eloise and smiled. "This lady sent in a report that caught a lot of attention. And with the holidays only days away, I think people wanted to do some good before the year ended."

"So, you want to give us money? What for? Please tell me it isn't one of those rotten programs that certain wealthy people have started. The sort where they pay farmers and ranchers to sit on their hands while the food supply either moves offshore, or under their thumb?" Jerod's eyes darkened and he fisted his hands on his thighs.

Eloise had heard of these programs. A lot of farmers sold out in the past few years and at first, no one worried. But now that so much of the nations' food supply is coming from foreign lands, even she was worried about what might happen. But she stayed quiet.

Dorothy's face blanched. "No, this isn't like that. In fact, my office doesn't support that behavior. No, I'm here to ensure that you and other ranches like yours, flourishes." She picked her mug back up and took another sip, then set it on her hand in her lap. "You see, we just went through a very thorough audit and it seems my office has a lot of grant money that has to either be awarded before the end of the year, or it goes back to the US Treasury coffers."

Everyone in the room sat straighter.

"I've heard that sometimes this sort of money comes with strings." It was Marty's turn to look as though he was unsure about the possible goose that's going to lay the golden egg.

If what Dorothy was saying was true, then it was possible that millions of dollars could be directed to Montana this month. Eloise knew that would change a lot of lives. It would also mean that other people who needed help, would be coming to Montana for years to come.

"I'm exhausted, but I want to ensure you that this is very good for you, and for the White Rose Ranch." Dorothy turned in her seat to look Eloise straight in the eye. "Were you able to contact them? Are they willing to meet with me tomorrow?"

"Yes, the woman who runs the ranch, and her right-hand lady, are coming over for lunch tomorrow. We can all spend the afternoon here discussing anything you want." Eloise had set up the dining room to also double as a meeting room.

Dana had brought in a whiteboard and all of the supplies they might need, including borrowing a projector from the library.

Dorothy stood up and straightened her pant legs. "Thank you so much for the coffee. It's actually quite good. Better than anything the government pays for, that's for sure." She chuckled.

"I work part-time at the local coffee shop where we roast our own beans. I get such a good discount that it costs the same to buy their coffee as it would to buy the cheap stuff in the grocery store." Dana beamed. She was quite proud of her coffee roasting expertise.

No one, including Eloise, ever thought she wasted one penny on coffee from the Frenchtown Roasting Company.

"Good to know. I'll see you tomorrow." She picked up her purse. "Eloise, can you walk me out?"

Eloise nodded and followed the woman outside.

Once they were standing next to Dorothy's car, Eloise asked. "Is everything really as good as you made it out to be?"

For just one moment, fear began to take root in Eloise's stomach. But once Dorothy smiled, she began to hope. Hope that DC might actually be doing some good for the people in Montana. And for those who needed it most, instead of a politician's pet project.

Dorothy nodded. "What is your situation? Would you be willing to relocate here? Or maybe work here temporarily until we find someone else?"

The question came from nowhere and had Eloise's head spinning. "What?"

"Sorry, I'm getting ahead of myself here. But we are going to need someone who understands how to work with the government and be a go-between. Someone who isn't deeply invested in the ranches here. All told, we have almost one hundred million dollars to spend. And after what I've seen, I think we should award it to this area. We can set up a special fund, if you'll manage it, and then we can dole out the money quarterly to any non-profit in this area who is working with wounded veterans, or women that have been rescued from the slave trade." Dorothy's nostrils flared at the last words.

Normally, a grant didn't cover such a broad area. But since Dorothy was from the Agricultural Department, it might work. Eloise thought for only a moment. "I think something can be arranged. But I need to know the scope of work you're expecting here. Most of the food grown or raised on this ranch doesn't necessarily go into the general food supply. Some will, but most will stay local."

"And that's what this grant is for. It can help ranches like this one to expand and ensure that we become food independent once more." Dorothy stopped before saying much more, but Eloise understood where she was going with that one statement.

The food supply had become a political hot topic. And something that certain politicians used for their own benefit. Eloise wasn't on one side of the aisle or the other, but she did live in Texas and believed that her food should be from America, not South Africa, or South America. Those nations needed to feed themselves, not send their food to the highest bidder.

And after the recent world-wide pandemic, it became very evident that America had sent too much offshore. At least, in Eloise's mind.

"I think I understand what you're saying. And I agree. I don't know what plans Jerod has for expansion, but I do know he has a lot of ideas for things to do. Most of which is centered around helping more veterans recover." Even though Eloise had taken the whole tour of the ranch from Jerod, and he spoke about ideas, she knew money was an issue for him, so he hadn't planned out too much.

"Sounds like we are both on the same page. If you can find yourself a place to stay in town, then I think you'll be the perfect person to act as the Grant Manager here in Montana. And the best part is that it's going to be for the entire state, not just Frenchtown. So there will be some travel, but it will be good for everyone here." This time, Dorothy didn't wait for a response. She opened her car door and got in. She waved when she drove off.

The moment Eloise went back inside, Marty was there with a giant smile. "Well, what did she say?"

Eloise rubbed her face and shook her head. "I'm not really sure what's going on here, but it looks like every program that Jerod has even thought about will be funded for years to come, including a large expansion for the ranch."

"What?" Jerod boomed as he rounded the corner. "Did she say how much money was involved?"

Eloise guided everyone back to the living room and once they were seated, she repeated the conversation.

"So, you're moving here?" The incredulity in Marty's voice shook Eloise to the core.

Did he want her to go away and stay away? Why didn't he sound happier about her moving here?

Eloise sucked her lips in and thought about how to respond. "We still have a lot to discuss. I'm not going to sell my condo unless I have an actual contract from the government. But, it does look as though they are going to fast track the program. It's a bit political, but if we can get the money moved to an account here, then it will be very difficult for the government to take it all back, should any politician decide they don't like what's happening here."

They spent the next three hours going over and over the situation. But by nine o'clock, Eloise was too tired to keep talking. "I've really got to get some sleep. The rest of this week is going to be busy. And we have a lot of people coming over tomorrow for lunch and an afternoon of discussions. I suggest you spend the morning going over your questions and writing them down. I really don't know any more than what I've said already." She wanted to add *a million times*, but held that bit of sarcasm back.

She could understand the questions and unbelief. Eloise barely believed it herself. If she hadn't spent the past five years working with governmental agencies, she wouldn't believe it one bit. This was a true miracle. Eloise knew without a shadow of a doubt that God had been working to make this happen.

"Hey, wait up." Just as Eloise left the living room, Marty caught her.

She was so tired, she didn't want to spend one more second talking. All she wanted was her pillow. Plus, she was weak. For the past few days she'd seen Marty too much to be able to

keep her distance. And now that Dorothy wanted her to move to Frenchtown, well...She knew
she wouldn't be able to keep her distance from
Marty much longer.

"I'm tired. Can we talk tomorrow?" Her eye-
lids drooped and her shoulders sagged.

Marty took her hand in his. "I'll walk you to
your room, if you don't mind?"

At least he asked. She figured it couldn't hurt,
so she nodded. Not even realizing that he still
held her hand. All she knew was that she felt
warmth radiate throughout her entire being.

"I wanted to thank you. I know this is a lot
and you were planning on heading home this
week. I hope you can get home in time for
Christmas with your family." He squeezed her
hand and that was when she realized that they'd
been holding hands while they walked.

The memory of him holding her when he
kissed her the other night woke her up enough
to turn her head and look at him. Marty was
staring at the floor as they walked. She could
see he wasn't smiling, something he had been
doing a lot of since they met. And she hoped
he wasn't upset with her still. "Are you still mad
at me?"

"What?" His head shot up and looked directly
into her eyes.

She noticed the gold flecks glistening with the hallway light shining on his face.

"No, not at all. I'm truly grateful for everything you've done. I just wanted to say how sorry I am for the way I acted last week. I should have known you wouldn't have sent in a bad report." He sighed. "I think I'm just...I don't know. Still having some trouble coming to grips with things. I have a long way to go before I'm better. And I know this place is exactly what I need right now. The thought of it being taken away scared me, and I don't scare easily."

Her heart went out to the man who was opening up to her in a way he hadn't yet. The sad part was that she liked it. And she liked him. But he was right, Marty had a ways to go before he would be ready for a relationship. "Thank you for sharing with me. I truly appreciate it. And I'm so happy this all seems to be going in the right direction. I'm going to message my contact in DC and see what he knows. It just sounds too good to be true, you know?"

Marty chuckled and nodded. "I have to agree. If I had any connections with the government I'd be calling them, too."

They stopped in front of her door, and she yawned. Not one of those cute ones the heroine of a rom com did, either. Hers was loud and long. And when she was done, Marty caught the bug, too.

Eloise chuckled. "I'm sorry about that. I really am tired."

"Me too. And thank you again." Marty lifted her hand to his lips and kissed the back of it as though he was some sort of Regency era gentleman, and she was one of those titled ladies she loved to read about in Regency romances.

Chapter 32

When Marty woke up the next day, he was excited. Actually, it was more than excitement that swarmed his entire body. He was ecstatic. Eloise let him walk her to her door, and she didn't get upset when he kissed her hand. It was a start.

The best part was that she was moving here. That would give him time to get to know her better. They could take their time and be real friends before hopefully beginning to date. Because make no bones about it, Marty Winters wanted to date Eloise Sullivan. He just had to be patient.

"Good morning," he greeted the small group when he entered the kitchen. "Where are Tony and Dixon?"

Jerod lifted his mug in greeting. "They are taking care of the animals and then heading to the tree farm. We all agreed that for today, at least, they should be at the tree farm."

"Is it because the women from the White Rose Ranch don't like men?" Marty winced when he said those words. It wasn't that they didn't like all men, it was that they didn't trust them. Not yet. And he totally understood where they were coming from. "Sorry, I think I need coffee before I say anything else."

"Foot in mouth disease before coffee?" Jerod chuckled. "That's what most of us had back in Iraq. The doctor even confirmed it when he handed out mugs of coffee one day."

"That was your unit?" Marty laughed and shook his head. "I heard about that. It happened between tours for me, and when I got back to Iraq I heard about the unit who all had coffee prescribed to them for saying a bunch of stuff they shouldn't have."

Jerod rubbed his neck and squirmed in his seat. "Okay, how about we change the subject?"

"No way. I want to hear more about this." Dakota, who had been quiet since Marty entered the room grinned. "Have you seen the meme with the guy who had a real foot coming out of his mouth? It's so gross, it's awesome."

Everyone else joined her in her chuckling, except for Jerod. His face was beginning to turn pink. Marty wondered if he was the main cause of that rumor. Could he have been the one who mouthed off to his commanding officer when the coffee was all gone? It was brave to do that, but also stupid. Probably why the doctor made such a big deal about the prescription and the medical diagnosis of foot in mouth disease.

"Yeah, yeah. Laugh it up. But let's get serious. We have a busy day today." Jerod stood up and made a show of heading over to the coffee maker and pouring himself another cup of coffee.

His projection had been accurate, too. They had a very busy day. But it was also quite productive. Especially when Marty realized that Eloise smiled at him and even opted to sit next to him at lunch.

"So, how do you think it's all going?" Marty leaned close to Eloise and whispered.

She leaned closer to him, close enough that their heads almost touched. "I think it's going very well, so far. But we won't really know until Dorothy gives me the paperwork."

"When will that be?" He wasn't sure, but he thought he saw some papers hanging out of the briefcase Dorothy had with her. He prayed those were the ones they needed, and she'd give them to Eloise later that day.

"Probably not until right before she leaves. I think she wants to hear what everyone wants today, and then tomorrow start the tours. She even wants to see what Nelly has going. She'd like to see Nelly expand. Although, that would mean she'd need to hire more trainers. She can't personally train more than what she's doing now." That was one of the areas Eloise had looked into last week, when she was at Nelly's ranch helping with the dogs.

Marty knew exactly what she was referring to. Nelly had told them both that she could only train five or six dogs at any given time. She did have their training staggered so that she had a new dog ready to go every few weeks. But once she placed the dogs she had, it would take a lot more time before she had any new ones ready. All of her dogs were close to being trained. And it took on average three to four months to train a dog, then there was another two weeks of custom, individual training once the dog chose his or her human partner.

The next day, they all went to Nelly's ranch to see the dogs in training.

Nelly's grin was a mile long. "Thank you for coming out here. I'm so excited to show you our dogs. And I know they are excited to see you, as well." She waved to them to follow her.

The ladies from The White Rose Ranch were also in attendance. Serena, the woman who ran the ranch, had shown interest in service dogs only the day before when Nelly was talking about the benefits of a service dog, not only for veterans, but for anyone who was suffering from PTSD, or a slew of other medical issues.

Marty knew without being told that the ladies at Serena's ranch were suffering from PTSD. How could they not after their ordeal. They might even have other issues. His heart went out to them and he wished he could help them all. If it were up to him, he'd be out there pounding the pavement looking for any and all women and children who'd been abducted.

"Marty?" Nelly waved him over. "Can you help me out here?"

"Sure, what do you need?" His face heated when he realized he hadn't been paying too much attention to Nelly as she spoke about the ranch and what she was trying to do.

Eloise walked next to him and whispered, "have fun."

When he saw her hide a laugh behind her hand, he knew he was in trouble.

Marty couldn't hold back his grin when he saw Razzle bounding toward him. He knelt down and opened his arms. But the dog didn't run into him like he expected, instead, he stopped exactly where Nelly pointed.

Nelly pointed to the spot next to her and in German said, "Setzen."

Marty knew it meant to sit. Then she ordered him to stay and he did. Even though Marty wanted the dog to come to him, he knew better than to try and get in the middle of the demonstration.

"This is Razzle and he's chosen Marty to be his human, but they've not been officially paired. I'm hoping that will happen soon, but for this week, the two of them can show you how a service dog can help a human." Nelly then motioned for Razzle to stand up when she gave the command to stand.

"Marty, do you want to call him?" Nelly nodded, and Marty took it as a sign that he needed to participate.

"Sure thing." Marty cleared his throat. He really didn't like being the center of attention, but this wasn't about him, it was about the future of this ranch. The future of the service dogs that could very well come through here and be paired up with vets who need them, or the ladies at the White Rose.

Nerves made it tough for him to speak. At least until he looked at Eloise and saw her nodding at him. She was smiling and looked at him as though he could do this. Then she even mouthed the words. In that moment, he kept his focus on her for a few seconds as he got his breathing in order. The last thing he needed was a panic attack right in front of the woman holding the purse strings. He needed to be strong and show how he could call the dog to him.

When he looked down at Razzle, he noticed the dog had tilted his head and his eyes were focused on him. Everything else around him slowly disappeared as he looked at his dog, his partner. Marty pointed next to him and in German commanded, "Hier".

Razzled jumped and practically dived toward him, then he turned and took his spot next to Marty. He reached down and patted the dog's head. "Braver Hund." It was important to let the dog know he did good, especially since he was still in training. Although, if Nelly was right, Razzle was ready for Marty.

The only question was, was Marty ready for Razzle?

"Nice job. Thank you. Why don't you take Razzle inside the barn for a treat and take his vest off. He can play the rest of the day." Nelly grinned and shook Marty's hand.

One of the things that Marty had noticed about Nelly was how much she touched the vets. It wasn't in a weird way, she would shake their hands, touch their elbows, and for those she was closer to, would touch their shoulders or back. He realized in that moment - she was connecting with them on a personal level. Not a romantic one, she was married to Sam, after all. But she was connecting human to human.

So many people back at the hospital didn't touch the patients unless they had to. He never connected with anyone there. But since coming to Montana, he'd connected with quite a few people. Everyone at the Crooked Arrow, which included Eloise, had become family to him. Both Nelly and Sam had become friends, something he didn't really have much of these days.

Life here was good. Maybe that fact alone would keep him here. And just maybe, it would also keep Eloise here. With him.

She followed him inside the barn and they spoke for only a short time before Eloise had to get back outside and rejoin the team. Marty decided he'd go too, but he needed a few minutes with Razzle before he left.

When he did exit the barn, Razzle was right by his side. Marty didn't even have to order the dog, he just followed him, like Rogue did with Sam.

Marty didn't get any more time alone with Eloise until after dinner that night. The two of them went out back to watch the stars and talk about the day.

"I can't believe what's happening. My contact, Steve, told me Dorothy was for real." Eloise wrapped her arm around Marty's as they walked out toward the barn.

The night was cold, but clear. The stars could be seen for miles and miles. Marty had seen stars like this when he was in Iraq, but for some reason they didn't feel as comforting as these did. Maybe it was because here - he was home. But back in Iraq he was in the middle of a war zone.

Or maybe, it was the company.

Chapter 33

Eloise couldn't believe she'd grabbed Marty's arm like she had. If anyone said anything, she'd claim it was just to keep her upright. The snow had been melting that day and she didn't need to fall again now that it was freezing up overnight, again.

Since taking off her boot, she'd felt much better, and she was surprised that she didn't even need to use her cane as much. She still needed it, especially when there was ice around. But for tonight, she would use Marty as her assistive device.

Besides, he was much warmer than a wooden cane.

"You know, when I was growing up, we used to go out back and have campouts. We were far enough from the city at that time to see a lot of the stars. But it was nothing compared to these." She knew they were the same stars, but here without the ambient lighting that surrounded her parents' house back home, she could see so many more. In fact, it looked like something from a movie, not real life.

"I think these are magical stars." Marty grinned. He loved being around Eloise, she brought out a side of him he'd not seen since he was a kid. And it wasn't the stupid, immature side of him, it was the playful side of him. With Eloise, he could be himself and have fun. He didn't have to worry what she'd think about his prosthetic foot, or feel the need to joke about it being a bionic foot, just to make someone feel better. No, he knew he could say whatever he felt.

"Do you think you'll be here long?" Eloise had been wanting to talk to him about his future plans, but she hadn't found time all day.

He nodded. "I think so. And not just because I have work to do on the ranch, but because I'm thinking about staying here permanently."

"At the ranch?" Eloise didn't think that was possible, but maybe with the extra grant money there would be a job Marty could do?

"No, I don't think that's what I'm feeling called to do. I don't know what it is, but I want to explore my options here." A look of peace crossed his face when he said that.

Eloise knew he meant it, and she hoped he'd find whatever it was he was looking for. "What about your family?"

"Oh, I'll go home and visit, but I'm not going to move back in with my parents. I really don't need to. I just need a room where Razzle and I can call ours and I'll be just fine." Marty's head lowered and he sighed. "I just included Razzle in my plans, didn't I?" He looked back up to watch the sky slowly moving above them.

Eloise chuckled. "Yes, you did. Does that mean you've made up your mind?"

"I think it does." He turned his eyes from the sky to Eloise. He looked into her eyes and wasn't sure what he saw there, so he asked. "Have you made up your mind about me?"

She nodded. "Yes, I have."

They both moved in closer, but Marty took his time. He wanted to make sure she could back off if she really didn't want this. He looked down at her lips and watched her tongue dart out. Then he felt himself licking his lips in anticipation of when they would kiss.

"Oh, just kiss the girl already." A gruff voice called out from behind them.

Marty moaned and leaned his forehead against Eloise. She was breathing heavily and closed her eyes.

"Sam, did you really have to say anything?" Marty lifted his head from Eloise and turned to glare at the intruder.

Sam lifted his hands. "Hey, you weren't going to kiss her. If she had to wait on you, it would have been the next century before you moved in for the kiss."

"For your information, I was in the middle of moving in. I just wanted to take it slow so Eloise could back off if she wanted." Marty looked up and an exasperated sigh escaped his lips.

The man was chuckling and holding his belly. Almost like a Santa Claus laugh, except he wasn't in a red suit, and he didn't have a bowl full of jelly type of belly. He did however, have a glint in his eyes. "Well, see that you stop this lolly gagging and get down to it. A good woman won't wait around for long." He winked and turned around.

Mortification, or was it frustration, made its way to Marty's face. He felt his face heat, and in this cold, that was saying something. Sam had totally ruined the mood. "Well, that was awkward."

Out of the corner of his eye, Marty saw Eloise nod in agreement.

Eloise put her gloved hands to her face. "To say the least." She turned around and looked at the back door to the ranch house. "I think I'm going to head back inside. I'll see you tomorrow."

"I'll join you." Marty took her arm, knowing that she didn't have her cane with her, and led her back to the house.

Halfway there, something caught his prosthetic foot. He wouldn't have known since he had no feeling in the foot. Contrary to popular belief, there are no nerve endings in a prosthetic appendage. He didn't have a bionic foot, even though he liked to joke that he did.

No, the only reason he knew that something caught his foot was because he totally lost his balance and was heading straight down. A cry came out from next to him and he realized that he was bringing Eloise down with him.

Thanks to his quick thinking, he was able to turn them both so that he fell on the ground, and Eloise was on top of him. "Oomph." All the air rushed out of his lungs and Marty grasped to get air back in them.

It wasn't that Eloise was heavy, it was just that he fell flat on his back at the same time that she fell right on his chest. And the pain was back. He closed his eyes and focused on breathing. It wasn't nearly as bad as when he had been run down by a cow. But he hadn't fully healed, yet either.

Thankfully, it was bearable, and it only took him a few seconds to get his breathing back on track. "Are you alright?" When he opened his eyes, Eloise's beautiful blue eyes were wide and staring right into his own.

"Me? Are you alright? How's your chest? Did I hurt you?" She tried to move off of him, but Marty had wrapped his arms around her and was holding her tight to his chest.

"Just give me a minute. I'll be fine. I'm more worried about you. Did you reinjure your ankle, or anything else?" Marty couldn't take his eyes away from the woman who had captured his breath, and his heart.

The quick, frantic breaths had slowed down and Eloise continued to look directly into his eyes. Then, when she had her breathing under control, her eyes slowly moved to Marty's lips. Once again, she licked her own. When her eyes continued to stay focused on his lips, Marty wondered if she was silently asking for him to kiss her.

Marty was raised to be polite and respectful. When a woman asked for something, a gentleman gave it to her, if it was in his power to do so. And right then, all he wanted was to kiss the girl. He took in a deep breath and put his hand behind her head and brought her closer to him.

Taking his time, he wanted to give her the chance to stop him. After their one and only kiss, she had said it was a mistake. He didn't want that happening again. His heart couldn't take another rejection. He almost stopped what he was doing but the moment her breath hitched, he knew she was ready for this.

He went in for the kiss and the moment his lips touched hers, it was as though fireworks went off in the distance. His mind went blank and all he could do was kiss her more. Marty didn't even think, he moved on instinct and deepened the kiss.

Eloise didn't seem to mind as she gave him exactly what he wanted. No, what he needed. Her head moved even closer, if that was even possible. She tilted her head so that he could kiss her even deeper. It was perfection. Her lips were sweet as honey and her body on top of his was light as air.

Gone was his trouble breathing as joy filled him all the way down to the tips of his toes and back up to the tips of his ears. When sense began to come back to him, he slowed the kiss down and pulled back. He looked into her eyes and saw his own reflection in them. Marty couldn't help but smile and when Eloise returned his smile, he pulled her head down onto his shoulder.

They laid there in the snow for who knew how long. It was only when Marty's backside had gone numb from the cold of the snow did he even think to get up. "Are you alright? I didn't hurt you, did I?"

He felt, more than heard, her sigh. "I'm good. Are you?"

"Yes, but I think I need to get up and warm my backside now." He chuckled and then felt a tinge of pain shoot through his chest. The bruised ribs had mostly healed, but he still did have some trouble if he laughed too hard. So this pain told him that he had set back his healing. But he'd not complain. Not after getting a kiss like that.

Eloise inched off of Marty and stood up. She held a hand out to him. "Can I help you up?"

He didn't want her to fall again, so he grinned and got up on his own, doing his best to hide the pain in his chest. "What do you think happened?"

"Ah, you don't know what that was?" Her cheeks turned pink and she looked at the ground.

Marty walked closer and took her in his arms. "Oh, I know what that was. It was the best kiss I've ever had. Maybe I should rephrase. What do you think caused me to trip and bring us both down to the ground like that?"

She pulled out of his arms and looked around, the area between her eyes were pinched and she put a hand over her mouth. "Look." She pointed to something green on the ground.

Marty bent down to pick it up. When he stood upright, he began laughing.

"You tripped over Christmas?" Eloise watched him laughing for a few seconds before joining him. "I guess we both have a bit of an issue when it comes to walking?" She arched her brow and grinned.

"How did a Christmas garland end up on the ground?" He looked around and then his gaze stopped on a part of the back of the house that he hadn't even noticed. "Look, there's a gap in the garland that was put up on the eaves."

Eloise moved her eyes to see what he was pointing at and then shook her head. "I guess the winds have been pretty bad, and with the snow melting, and then more snow coming down, and then freezing up after another melt..." She let the comment fade and then took the garland from his hands.

"Sorry about that. I hope your foot will be alright." He winced when he thought about the accident she had just over a week before. He knew her foot hadn't fully healed since her tripping incident.

The both of them were a mess. Although, he'd have to say she was a hot mess.

"I'm fine. Really. I think you took the brunt of the fall. Are you sure you're alright? My landing right on your chest didn't hurt you even more, did it?" She worried at her lower lip.

Marty's eyes went to her sweet, soft lips and he had to work hard to keep himself from kissing her again. She was worried about him, and he wasn't sure what she just asked. "Hm? What?"

She chuckled. "Alright, let's get inside and warm up. And unless you're injured, I suggest we keep this to ourselves."

That he heard. "Agreed." Marty took her hand and wrapped it around his arm. As he walked her back inside, he kept his eyes on the ground so that he didn't have another mishap.

Although, he thought to himself, having her fall on him for another kiss might not be a bad idea.

Chapter 34

E loise couldn't believe it was already Christmas Eve. Everything had gone well with Dorothy, and she was true to her word. When she returned to DC the paperwork went through quicker than anything Eloise had ever seen the government do. Quite a bit of money had been specially earmarked for the Montana region. In January they would create a plan and decide which programs to fund, specifically. But in essence, they were going to help the Crooked Arrow expand so they could take in more veterans, and more animals.

The ladies at the White Rose Ranch were going to get more funding to help them learn trades. Trades that could help them to support themselves when they felt they were ready to leave the ranch. Thankfully, the ranch was large enough that they would be able to take in more women without any problems. And hire more counselors, too. They just needed people to help them learn how to support themselves.

Jerod had assured Dorothy that there were plenty of people in the area who wanted to help. From what Eloise had seen, she knew he was correct.

"So, you have your ticket to go home?" Marty didn't look too happy. It was a party and they should all be thrilled with how everything was moving forward.

Eloise rubbed at the lines between his eyes. "Hey, I'll be back. I just need to pack up my place in Houston and get my condo up for sale. Then, when the weather breaks, I'll drive back up here."

Marty pulled her into his arms. "I know, but I was hoping to spend New Year's Eve with you, that's all." He leaned down and kissed the tip of her nose. Since that night when he tripped over Christmas, they had been glued to each other's side. When Marty had to volunteer at the tree farm, she went with him. And when Eloise had to go into town for something related to the government grants, he went with her.

They even went apartment hunting together. Thankfully, a young couple who had recent-ly bought a ranch in Wyoming had vacated a small apartment over one of the stores in town. It was perfect for Eloise. But, it meant that she'd not be able to spend as much time with Marty as she would like. However, she reasoned with herself that they both had a lot of work to do in the new year.

Marty was going to be focusing on his training with Razzle as well as his counseling sessions with Megan. And Eloise was going to have to work hard at setting up the new office she'd need for running the grant programs in the state.

"I can't believe that other branches of the government will be coming out here in the spring to see if we can help with running other programs. I might have to hire some help if there are any more grants thrown our way." Eloise sighed when Marty wrapped his arms around her.

"Well, I might be looking for a job by then. If you're okay with training an old airman who has zero experience in an office, or doing government paperwork, I'd love to apply." The idea of Marty working with Eloise sent shivers down her spine, the good kind.

"You know, I just might take you up on that offer. I'm sure there is plenty you can do to help me out." She pulled back. "Actually, you'd be great at doing site inspections. And with you living here on the Crooked Arrow Ranch, you'll be learning a lot more about ranch life than I will. I think you might be more experienced than you realize."

"Okay, okay, enough shop talk you two. It's Christmas Eve, let's focus on what's happening here, now." Dana grinned and handed each of them a mug of hot cocoa.

"Thanks." Marty grinned and accepted the cup of hot cocoa. "I'm really looking forward to hearing Jerod read the Christmas Story."

"Me, too." Eloise took her mug of cocoa and sat down on the end of the sofa.

Marty sat next to her and they both turned their attention to Jerod.

He'd dressed up in his good blue jeans, a red cowboy shirt, and a green bolo tie. Then he pulled the Bible out from the table next to him and opened it to the first chapter of Luke.

"I'm going to start with verse twenty-seven." Jerod cleared his throat and then began, "And in the sixth month the angel Gabriel was sent from God unto a city of Galilee, named Nazareth, to a virgin espoused to a man whose name was Joseph, of the house of David; and the virgin's name was Mary."

Jerod continued to read the story about how Jesus was born to Mary, a virgin chosen by God to birth the savior of the world.

When Jerod was finished, everyone who had been invited, which was all of the past and present residents of the Crooked Arrow Ranch, and their significant others, as well as Cody and his wife, Sadie, as well as Cody's grandfather, all went into the formal dining room. Dana and a few of the ladies had set up a buffet dinner that also included an unbelievable assortment of desserts.

Marty and Eloise had made their yule log cake again, but had opted to use a few easier ingredients, like a can of thick chocolate frosting to put over the outside, instead of the ganache they used last time. It really helped to make the recipe easier to make. That, along with using a boxed mix for the sponge cake, cut off at least an hour of the time they spent before. The one thing they did keep in was the filling made from scratch using mascarpone cheese.

After Eloise took a bite of the Buche De Noel, she sighed. "I'm really glad we decided to keep the filling the same. But you know what?"

"What?" Marty asked, then took a bite of his cake and sighed in agreement.

"I think we might want to see if we can find a way to make the ganache frosting next time. While this can of frosting is good, it's a bit too sweet. The ganache seemed to be smoother." She licked her fork, then changed her mind.

"On second thought. I think I like the frosting as it is."

Marty chuckled and kissed her temple. "I'll gladly bake it any way you want it as long as we are still together next year."

The look Eloise gave Marty told him she was most definitely planning on staying with him. Maybe even forever.

**The End
Merry Christmas to one and all!
Keep reading for more...**

Character Sheet

Character Sheet

Eloise Sullivan - ADA Coordinator from Houston, Tx.

Marty Winters - Air Force Tech Sgt - E6. served 9 years, on his way to becoming an E-7. His MOS was a Tactical Air Control Party (TACP) He was imbedded with an Army Ranger unit in the Middle East. Still not able to say where.

Razzle - Newest addition to Nelly's service dogs.

Marco - Eloise's ex fiancé.

Christopher Lambton -Santa, retired general store owner

Jessica Lambton - Mrs. Claus. Retired general store co-owner. Their son took it over when they retired.

Hope Lowry - Dana's cousin and dating Tony Sullivan

Leena - newer barista at the Frenchtown Roasting Company.

Anise Banning - Coffee shop barista.

Charlotte Hamilton (Keith) (Lottie Summers)- Owns Frenchtown Roasting Company. Pregnant and due middle of Feb.

Cove Hamilton - Rodeo star. Bull Rider. Married to Lottie

Quinn Keith - Lottie's 11-year-old daughter

Marnie Gallagher - USAF disabled vet, was a cryptologic language analyst - Russian. She was an E-5, Staff Sergeant. She served just over 5 years before her injury.

Declan Walden - Local Rancher. He raises alpacas and sheep for their wool. He's coming over to the ranch to help train them on wool production.

Skeeter Murphy - Wounded warrior, worked the ranch with Jerod. He's 25. Now he's next door with the Henderson's as their foreman.

Jerod Stevens - Cowboy, rancher, former special ops soldier. Owns the Crooked Arrow Ranch

Dana (Baker) Stevens - Barista at Frenchtown Roasting Company. Married to Jerod

Sam Marley - Wounded warrior, graduated and now Is Married to Nelly, the dog trainer.

Mike Blakenship - Wounded warrior, used to work at the Crooked Arrow, he's graduated the program and has a job at a local dairy farm where he is thriving.

Megan Anderson - Councilor at the Crooked Arrow Ranch. Dating Daniel

Jackson - Horse that Sam loves, and now finds Marty appealing. Especially when he brings in apples.

Rocky - K-9 dog from Marty's old Army unit. Belgian Malinois. Cousin to the German Shepherd.

Cheyenne Thompson - New Librarian. She's short, like 5'2" but tall in personality. Blonde hair and light blue eyes, like an Aquamarine.

Dixon Carter - Patient at the ranch and he was a truck driver. Making progress, but slowly. He's taking to the cows and the cuddling program. Tyco seems to be taking a liking to him

Zipper - barn cat who occasionally gets the mice. He's a mouser.

Tyco - Bernese Mountain Service dog

Chef Dane Black - Celebrity chef, runs his own show.

Reginald - VA guy who wanted to have grant money moved from ranches to his cousin's retreats.

Steve - Eloise's contact at the VA

Dorothy Shilling - US Grant coordinator for US Department of Agriculture

The White Rose Ranch - Local ranch that works to help women who've been rescued from human trafficking.

Selena - Runs the White Rose Ranch

Anthony (Tony) Sullivan - wounded warrior, grew up on a Texas ranch. No relation to Eloise.

Buffy – Tony's Service dog - chocolate Labrador (Female)

Author Notes

WOW, I had no clue where that story was going to go, did you? Well, I had some clue, LOL but sometimes stories take on a life of itself. And now it seems I have a whole bunch of stories and places to add in the future. This should be fun!

I want to say that I'm so very grateful for my writing pace to have picked up lately and pray that it continues so I can get back to writing more books each year.

But first, I want to thank Susie B. for letting me use her two dog names, Razzle and Tyco! She's one of my newsletter subscribers and we were messaging back and forth right before I started this book. She told me about her adorable dogs that had crossed over the rainbow, and I wanted to use her dogs' names.

She said yes. So, I hope you enjoyed seeing Razzle on the pages of this book! Keep an eye out for when Tyco makes his starring debut!

I wanted to give a shout out to my sprint partner, Audrey! Thank you so much for helping me to stay on target with this book. I couldn't have done it without you!

Now, the yule log. Yummy!!! Have you ever had one? I've included the recipe below. I hope you give it a try. If you do, please let me know what you think of it. And for those who are lactose intolerant, I'm working on a new version of this. I have had to switch to dairy free this year myself. So I'm still researching possible ways to make it just as delicious without dairy. Those on my newsletter will get the recipe if I do find a way to make it taste good.

I hope you're enjoying my love letters to the veterans who have served the wonderful United States of America! These past two books have combined my favorites, Military and Christmas!

Keep an eye out for what's coming later this year and in early 2024. I'm working on some new stuff!

Yule Log Recipe

Ingredients:

<u>Cake:</u>

1 sponge cake boxed mix (Angel food cake mix is the same)
½ cup unsweetened cocoa powder

<u>Filling:</u>

1 2/3 C powdered sugar
½ C unsalted butter – at room temperature
2 Tablespoons vanilla
1 ½ Tablespoons unsweetened cocoa powder
1 pinch of salt
1/3 cup mascarpone cheese

<u>Ganache Frosting:</u>

(you can substitute this with your favorite can of chocolate frosting, that's what Eloise preferred)
1 cup of boiling hot heavy whipping cream
8 oz dark chocolate chips

Directions:
Use instructions on boxed sponge cake. Mix in the ½ cup of cocoa powder before adding the wet ingredients.

Preheat oven to what the box says.

Using a 13x18 rimmed sheet, put a large piece of parchment paper in it. Then coat with oil or Pam.

Pour the cake batter into the rimmed sheet. Tap the sheet several times to remove the air bubbles.

Place in oven 8-10 minutes. After 8 minutes use the toothpick method to check if the cake is done. You don't want the toothpick to come out full of cake mix, but you don't want it fully clean, either. You need it to be mostly cooked so that it will be easy to roll up.

While it's cooking, take out a clean kitchen towel. Using either a sifter or a strainer, sift powdered sugar onto the towel. Be sure to cover an area that is larger than the cake will be.

Once the cake is done, take it out of the oven and pull the parchment paper back from the pan. Using a long knife, ease away the cake from the edges of the paper.

Then take the cake by the parchment paper edges and turn it over onto the powdered sugar lines kitchen towel. Remove the parchment paper at this time. Sift more powdered sugar onto the back of the cake. Then, roll the kitchen towel up with the cake inside. Roll along the longer edge.

Set aside so it can cool off.

Then begin making the filling. Whip powdered sugar, butter, vanilla, cocoa powder, and salt together in a stand mixer. Use the whisk attachment on high speed.

Take off the stand mixer, then add 1/3 cup of mascarpone cheese. Mix well.

Now is the time to unroll the cooling cake. Using a spoon, put the filling mixture all over the cake. Smooth it down with a cake knife, be sure to get it all the way to the edges. Save a little bit for use later. You'll need it to put the small piece of the log on the edge.

Roll the cake up over the filling. You can use the towel to lift the cake if need be.

Sift more powdered sugar on tope of the roll. Then wrap in plastic wrap and place in the fridge for at least 2 hours. You can also do this the night before you want to serve it. And finish the cake before your event.

After the cake has been in the fridge long enough, pull it out and make an angled cut at least 3 inches from one end. If you want the ganache recipe, then keep going. But you can use canned frosting if you want instead of the ganache.

To make the ganache, heat the cream in a saucepan over medium low heat until it boils. Then pour the hot cream into a bowl that already has the chocolate chips in it. Let it sit for a minute, then begin to whisk until it's all melted and mixed well.

Take the smaller piece of rolled up cake and put it on the edge of the long roll, make it look like a tree branch. Use the filling you set aside to attach the 2 pieces like glue.

Spread the ganache (or canned frosting) over the tops and sides of the log. Just don't put any on the ends that show the swirl of cake and filling.

Next using a fork, draw lines in the chocolate ganache to look like the bark on a tree.

Place in the fridge until it is completely cooled and the frosting has chilled.

Dust with cocoa powder and more of the powdered sugar right before you cut it.

Enjoy!

Contact Me

For those of you who love social media, here are the various ways to follow or contact me:

BookBub: https://www.bookbub.com/authors/jenna-hendricks
TikTok: https://www.tiktok.com/@jennacleanauthor
Instagram: https://www.instagram.com/j.l.hendricks/
Twitter: https://twitter.com/TinkFan25
Facebook: https://www.facebook.com/JLHendricksAuthor
Website: https://jennahendricks.com

Newsletter Sign-up

Do you love clean & wholesome contemporary cowboy romance? Want more? Then check out Finding Love in Montana today!

By signing up for my newsletter, you'll not only receive this book, but a couple more free stories as well! Including the story of how Jerod and Dana got together. They are a favorite couple and I had a lot of requests for their story, so it will be in the second email you get from my new signup newsletter.

If you want to make sure you hear about the latest and greatest, sign up for my newsletter at: Subscribe to Jenna Hendricks newsletter. I will only send out a few e-mails a month. I'll do cover reveals, snippets of new books, special recipes, and giveaways or promos in the newsletter, some of which will only be available

to newsletter subscribers. (https://jennahendr
icks.com/newsletter/)